McAlister's Way

by Richard Marman

Cover art and design, illustrations and graphics by Richard Marman
Brisbane

Published in England

by

ABELA PUBLISHING

Sandhurst, Berkshire, England

Email: Author@RichardMarman.com

Website: www.RichardMarman.com

ISBN 13: 978-1-92583-3-027

Republished in 2018 with Ocean Reeve Publishing

First Edition, 2012

Acknowledgments

I'd like to especially thank my wife Judy and my daughter Sally for their help in following the progress of this manuscript. Thanks to Sheila Yong and Wendy Kleine for their feedback and initial proof reading and Judy Bandidt for the final, goal-keeping edit. Also thank you to Lauren Jones for allowing me to use her charming image on the cover. Thank you to Squadron Leader Mark 'Cowboy' Willcocks for vetting my *Tok Pisin* and Wing Commander John 'Trackless' Millsom for Buick motor car technical support. Finally cheers to John Halsted for being so enthusiastic about this story.

This book is dedicated

to my wife Judy

and my daughters

Sally and Elizabeth

Glossary

AIF	Australian Imperial Force
ANA	Australian National Airways
ASI	airspeed indicator
AH	artificial horizon (aircraft's attitude gauge)
ATC	air traffic control
AVGAS	aviation gasoline (piston-engine plane fuel)
AWA	Amalgamated Wireless (Australasia)
AWOL	absent without leave
AWU	Australian Workers' Union
CMF	Citizens Military Force known as *The Militia* and incorporated into the AIF during WWII
CO	commanding officer
C-of-G	centre of gravity
CSR	Colonial Sugar Refining Company Ltd
DCA	Department of Civil Aviation
GBH	grievous bodily harm
GP	general purpose or general practitioner
HF	high frequency (radio transmitter-receiver)
ICU	intensive care unit
KP	kitchen patrol (military punishment duties)
Knots (Kts)	nautical miles per hour
Max Revs	maximum revolutions (full throttle)
MP	Military Police (red caps)
NCO	non-commissioned officer (corporals, sergeants and warrant officers)

NDB	Non-directional (radio) beacon
OR	Operating Room (theatre)
POWs	prisoners of war
P. W. & I.	Prisoner of war and internment (camp)
RAAF	Royal Australian Air Force
R & R	rest and recreation (leave)
RANVR	Royal Australian Naval Volunteer Reserve
RAR	Royal Australian Regiment
RSL	Returned Servicemen's League
Short Ton	2000 lb (pounds) or 907 kilograms – a weight used mostly in America
TAA	Trans Australian Airlines
VHF	very high frequency (radio transmitter-receiver)
VSI	vertical speed indicator
Sliders	small hamburgers
XXXX bitter	Queensland lager-style beer

Prologue – Grandpa Danny

Parents are funny sometimes, well more than sometimes if they're like mine, but you probably knew that already. They keep you in the dark all the time. My name's Zach McAlister and I turned fifteen back in 2010 when my Mum got sick and everyone tippy-toed around the subject. Dad just said, 'I'll explain later,' but didn't get around to it. They'd been real touchy for ages. Anyway I found out Mum was having a mastectomy. Yeah, I know what that is, I'm not simple, but you don't think about your Mum's boobs, do you? I mean like she's my Mum. My folks were always telling me to grow up, but didn't trust me to cope with serious stuff. I knew I could deal with it. Anyway, Mum went to hospital and I got to go to my Grandpa Danny's place. He lived way out in the country.

Dad put me on a plane at Mascot Airport and Grandpa met me at Merimbula. If you haven't been there, it's a little coastal town in southern New South Wales. I reckon it was as dead as a maggot, but Grandpa kept moaning that too many people have found out about the place and it was 'turning to shit' - his words not mine. I mean what was there to do?

Anyway we bang on out to Grandpa's joint in his ute, it's all rusted and the gears make noises that you don't want to know about. It took about half an hour to get there and it was a bit uncomfortable because Grandpa didn't talk much. Nana died the year before and I think he was still pretty cut up about it. That was the last time I'd seen him (at the funeral I mean). We shook hands and that's about all, like I hadn't seen him for ages before that. He was just a regular old dude, but had a neat scar all down one cheek like a pirate.

The place was old, although it didn't look run down. It was a sandstone wall, tinned roofed building with verandas all around so there was a lot more elbow-room than our inner-city terrace. Stuff was all over the yard, but neatly placed as if Grandpa had some hidden plan to go by. He used to run a dairy herd, but most of the property had been sold off by then. Grandpa kept a few hectares and rode around on horseback. I hoped he didn't expect me to, horses stink. Give me a quaddie any day.

So I'd only been there for like a day and I can't say that we were hitting it off. He wasn't mean or anything and we weren't fighting. We just weren't doing anything.

Nothing.

It sucked, I was bored shitless. I mean the kangaroos, cockies and parrots hanging around were okay, but I soon got used to them. I didn't even mind the odd black snake. I asked Grandpa if he got lonely, but he said he had a couple of mates to play golf and go surfing with. They met every few weeks at the RSL, which was enough company to suit him.

Dad rang and said Mum was doing fine, but didn't go into details.

Anyway Grandpa had to go into town for groceries - he wasn't a bad cook actually and that sure was a plus. But, the thought of thirty minutes silent motoring there and the same back wasn't a great puller. Not that there was anything much to do in town anyway and it was too cold for the beach.

'I'll just chill,' I told him.

Grandpa had actually got around to updating to digital, but daytime TV was gay and all the movie stars in his DVD collection were dead. He even still had a VCR and his internet package was so ancient you could hardly download anything. He actually had a complete collection of *Encyclopaedia Britannica.* I mean they took up a whole bookshelf, but why bother when it all fits on a disk? It's as if he didn't want contact with the outside world. Thank God for Chris Ryan. I had a bunch of his paperbacks to read.

So Grandpa rattled off in his jalopy.

I didn't feel like reading right away, so I looked around the place. Grandpa had a pretty decent three-bay out the back and I thought I'd check it out. Sheds and boys like, you know, they're meant to be, and on a scale of one-to-ten, Grandpa's was a twenty.

There was a mass of power tools, spray guns and just about every gadget you'd need to build a battleship. I opened the fridge in the corner. It was full of beer stubbies but there were a few soft drink cans, so I helped myself to a *Coke*. I nearly tripped over two guitar cases that held a Fender Strat and a Gibson 335. There was a 35 watt Vox valve amp on the floor as well. They'd been used recently and the strings were in good nick. Yeah, things were looking up. There were at least half-a-dozen power points around so I fired up the amp and jammed for a while.

I took a break and poked around some more. Grandpa had some neat stuff, a couple of trail bikes and even a .22 rifle...maybe he'd let me have a go at them. I found some sketch pads full of pencil drawings and water colours – landscapes, portraits and pretty much any other subject you could think of. Some were signed, *Danny*, and dated from back to the 1950s right up to a few years ago. Grandpa had quite a talent and there was a bunch of arty-farty equipment in one corner of the shed. A nearly completed oil painting of Keith Richards rested on an easel.

There was a ton of boxes with papers and crap crammed into them, but one was different. Sure, it contained letters and certificates mostly, but more interestingly, there were heaps of old photos and a strip of six medals. A row of colourful, eye-catching ribbons that each had Grandpa's name engraved on the back along with a number. I think they must give you a number when you're in the military, because they were all the same. The medal on the left was a white ribbon with purple-blue stripes running diagonally and a cross attached. It stood out.

And then there were photos. Some were all dog-eared and ragged at the edges. Others had scratches and were going that brownish colour. Yeah, 'sepia' it's called, I think. Mostly they were of young blokes hanging around tanks and military shit, and lots of choppers. You know, those beat up ones you see in all the war movies. Geez, those guys didn't look much older than me! They were all weighed down with guns and ammo belts and mostly they had a fag drooping from their mouths. They sure looked fit despite the smokes. Sometimes it was a bit hard to pick him out, but in the end I recognised Grandpa in most of the shots. I look at lot like he did then, you know.

I shuffled through the papers. I didn't bother with official looking documents and certificates. Instead I picked up a bundle of letters tied together with a pink ribbon. Can you believe it, a pink ribbon? I opened one and it was from someone called Angela and was pretty mushy so I put it back real quick. There are some places you really don't want to go. One of the letters was scrunched up and looked as if it had beer and coffee stains all over it. The writing had run and it was hard to read.

It was Angela's last letter to Grandpa dated in 1960.

No, she wouldn't wait – she'd waited long enough.

She was so sorry.

Yes, she was seeing someone else.

Dear John...so long.

There was a photo of a pretty blonde girl about eighteen years old among the letters and it wasn't Nan, that's for sure. Makes you wonder, doesn't it? I mean like Grandpa and Nana were inseparable, so why'd he keep letters from an old girlfriend who dumped him about a thousand years ago?

'You seem to have found something interesting to occupy yourself, Zach,' Grandpa said softly behind me.

You'd think I'd have heard the ute coming up the drive, but I didn't.

I spun around looking pretty sheepish. I mean like I had been prying, and I couldn't tell if he was mad or not.

'Yeah, Grandpa,' I said, 'I guess *now* we've got plenty to talk about.'

'OK,' he said, 'but that's hardly the start of it. Are you really interested in the life of an old fart like me?'

He could be so exasperating at times. This is what I really wanted him to do – what I'd been waiting for –you know, to get to know the old boy better.

'Geez, Grandpa,' I said. 'I hardly know anything about you and here's all this great stuff. I mean the axes, the medals and the pictures. Look there's loads more stuff in here.'

'Yeah, I used to be a pretty sharp picker and played in a few bands on and off. I still practise a bit, but it kinda slides if you're not playing with a group. Not your sort of music though.'

He picked up the Gibson and started into some catchy licks, maybe a mixture of country, blues and a bit of rock. He called it rock-a-billy and said it was his favourite music because he'd been brought up listening to it, but I didn't know anything about it.

'Most people like music they hear as teenagers. I was born on the same day as Elvis, you know,' he said and seemed pretty proud of the fact.

'Do you mind if I have a look at this other stuff?' I asked him.

'Fill your boots,' he said putting the guitar back in its case and pulling a couple of stubbies from the fridge. 'Want one?'

I looked doubtful. My dad was a teetotaller and had always been pretty stiff about drinking. In truth I'd tried beer occasionally, but it made me gag, so I shook my head. Grandpa didn't push it like kids would, he handed me another *Coke,* twisted the stubby top off and tossed it into a waste bin. Like the yard, the shed was really quite tidy even with all the stuff hanging about.

I realised how little I knew about my grandfather. I mean my other pop, my mum's dad, was a big mover and shaker in the city who'd made and lost fortunes over the years. I knew all about him because he liked to tell people about his deals, which sounded quite cool in a nerdy sort of way. I guess he was doing pretty well then, which was more than a lot of others after the '08 financial melt-down, because he lived in a posh, harbour-view house overlooking Watson's Bay. He needed to be flush too. Gran was a flashy dresser and liked to be loaded down with bling. Grandpa Danny didn't seem that interested in money.

I dug around in an old metal chest that looked as if had come from the military. **PLT OFF D. MCALISTER 0317367** was stencilled on the top. It was the same number on the back of the medals. There were plenty of souvenirs from all over the world, animal carvings, primitive statues, a massive Seiko watch with four dials, brochures on Japanese super bikes and a whole lot more that Grandpa called his *artefacts*. He explained they were things that had interested him at the time. Apparently he'd been to Africa, South East Asia, South America, Canada, Britain and Europe – freaking everywhere! I found more photos, but these were much older and a touch faded. There were several of a pretty woman holding a baby, others of a soldier in a digger's uniform, some of a happy toddler and a few of a rather sulky looking kid posing stiffly in the front of an old heritage-design Queenslander house.

'That was my mother, your great grandma,' he explained without much warmth. I noticed he called her *mother* not *mum*. That's my dad before he went to New Guinea in '42.'

'Is that you?' I asked and he nodded. 'You don't look very happy for a kid.'

'Sod all to be happy about,' he muttered. 'Well, along about when those snaps were taken anyway, things sparked up later I can tell you.'

Funny him calling a photo a *snap*, it's not a word we use any more.

'Dad says you got up to some pretty dodgy stuff before you settled down. Tell me about it…please.'

'Y'know,' he said, 'I was just about your age when my adventures began…'

We took our drinks and sat in a couple of well-worn lounge chairs on his veranda where he began to tell me about his life. Over the next week we were kept busy with chores around the place and yes, he taught me to ride and I wasn't too bad at it although I preferred the trail bikes. But, after work we'd make a habit of jamming with the guitars before sitting on the porch playing Scrabble and watching the sunset, Grandpa with his beer and me with a *Coke*. We'd chat for an hour or so before dinner. After a few cooking lessons with Grandpa I was ready for *Master Chef*. He kept a mega-veggie patch and had a knack for growing just about anything. I started writing everything he told me in a notebook before I fell asleep each night to make sure I didn't forget anything. Actually it took more than one notebook – a lot more.

Part One – Far North Queensland 1950

Chapter 1 – Capture

When Rockhampton girl Mavis Warren found herself pregnant with George McAlister's baby, he did the *right thing* and they married before too many questions were raised in a time when questions *were* raised and harsh judgements quickly reached. They managed pretty well considering the Great Depression had crippled the world economy in general and Australia's in particular. But George was resourceful and could turn his hand to almost anything. As a seasoned stockman he found regular work at the sale yards and abattoirs. They rented a cheap place, a little rundown maybe, but Mavis tidied it up and kept her vegetable patch in the shade of a mango tree.

The birth was difficult, but on 8 January 1935 Danny McAlister arrived although his first cries were drowned by thunder from a violent, tropical storm that raged for hours. Considering the damage to Mavis, her doctor deemed further pregnancies ill advised and Danny remained an only child. Not that it bothered him as he grew up, because there were plenty of kids in the neighbourhood for playmates. In fact, with only three mouths to feed, George provided better than many men with larger families. So Danny developed into a healthy and happy boy. He enjoyed all the usual sports and was quite good at drawing. Yes, Danny became a normal, well-adjusted young fellow with no worries, hang-ups or axes to grind, but that was all about to change.

Life improved as the world clawed its way back to economic equilibrium just in time for WWII to throw it headlong into bitter confusion. George once again did the *right thing* by enlisting in the CMF and was immediately swept away to war. The last Mavis heard was that George was fighting on the Kodoka Track in New Guinea until a telegram arrived stating he was MIA – missing in action.

She grieved, but had been alone for over two years now and Danny was happy at the local school, so she decided to take a job. With so many men gone to war there were plenty of opportunities and she started work as a typist at the meatworks, staying there until the Japanese surrendered. There was no word of George except a rather sombre letter from Canberra declaring he had been reclassified from MIA to *Missing Presumed Dead*. Not actually *Dead*, just *Presumed Dead*. Although distressing, this proved no great difficulty until Mavis started seeing Stanley Hallet, a foreman at the meatworks. Stanley had ideas of taking George's place and Mavis was faced with an emotional and ethical dilemma. She wasn't much of a church-goer, but still sought the advice of Monsignor Desmond Slaughter about the ecclesiastic legalities of a possible union. Unfortunately the good cleric, although sympathetic, was of little use. It seemed polygamy was okay for Old Testament heavies like Abraham, Jacob, David and Solomon. There was even a little-heard-of fellow called Lamech who had two wives, but that was just to speed up the procreation process back in those early days. The New Testament seemed pretty well down on the whole concept and really polygamy only applied to men anyway. It was just one chap for a woman and that was that. The rub was that no one knew whether George was dead, therefore Mavis was still officially married. She couldn't consider an annulment because obviously the marriage had been consummated – Danny was proof of that – and she felt it would be disloyal to George anyway.

So Mavis was forced to make the choice and opted for a life of mortal sin with Stanley. He was slippery customer and wooed her with post-war scarcities like chocolates, flowers, colonial sherry and even a bottle or two of Maurice O'Shae's Mt Pleasant wine. What woman wouldn't succumb to that?

The trouble was Stanley didn't like Danny and the feeling was mutual. Danny was in the way, needed feeding and consideration while Stan didn't really have time for all that. Worst of all Danny steadfastly believed his father wasn't dead. He had no way of knowing, but he just had a feeling that was so strong he knew George was still alive somewhere. Mavis had to continually intervene between Stanley and her son and there were some almighty rows that could be heard several blocks away. Stan had not yet become violent, but every confrontation drew him a little closer to breaking point. When he was twelve Danny began sneaking out at night and spending more and more time on the streets. He toughened up quickly, mixing with the local bad lads who hung around the Fitzroy River. Most of the kids were older than Danny, but he was big for his age and as puberty approached he shot up and bulked out.

His arch-chum was Charlie, an Aboriginal boy about Danny's age whose father roughed him up whenever he got drunk on flagon sherry, which was pretty much always. So Charlie spent very little time in the shack his mother called home. The gang leader was sixteen-year-old Arty Baines who loved to go bush bashing in stolen cars. He taught all the boys to drive and Danny found he took to it like a natural. They had a fine old time for a couple of years.

Of course it couldn't last. Danny and the gang eventually found themselves hauled up before the law. A couple of constables caught the boys breaking into a truck and Danny was marched home after a few stout clips behind his ears. Mavis was distraught, but it was just the chance Stanley had been waiting for. He assured the police he would deal with the matter, enlisting the help of Monsignor Desmond who arrived on the doorstep the next day.

'Sure 'tis a sad thing, to see a lad so wayward,' the good father crooned, after the initial pleasantries between slurping tea and helping himself to the last Arnott's *Iced Vo Vo* biscuit, 'but I believe we are just in time. 'Tis a sinful life you're leading Mrs McAlister, so it is, and it will lead to sinful ways in your son.'

Monsignor Desmond was not one to pull his punches when it came to matters of piety.

'We can manage,' Mavis said defensively.

'Do you think so?' the prelate challenged. 'Without spiritual guidance, the devil will find serious mischief for your boy and that's a fact. I cannot in all good conscience allow him to fall into the Satan's hands. That I cannot do, to be sure!'

'What do you have in mind?'

'I'd say 'tis best for the lad if we enrol him at *St Ursicinus*. Tis a fine school and Danny can board there during the term.'

And there Stan played his master-stroke as the reasonable mediator.

'Look, luv,' he said, sounding pretty sincere about it, 'Danny's going through a rough patch and needs help. Let's try it for a term and see how he goes. I'm sure he'll enjoy the company of other, good lads and not those hooligans he's been hanging around with.'

Stan realised once the status quo was established, that would pretty well be that and he'd have Mavis all to himself. It sounded very sensible and after a few sniffs into her hanky, Mavis agreed. So a few days after his fourteenth birthday, Danny was packed up and whisked away in Monsignor Desmond's 1942 Buick convertible to the hallowed gates of *St Ursicinus* orphanage and school for boys.

The school was built in the colonial style on a property some miles from town. The chapel, classrooms, administration centre, cold water ablution block and dormitories were surrounded by a ten-foot sandstone wall served by a wrought iron main gate and a smaller postern at the far side of the complex. The cloisters were formed around a gravel quad where Desmond parked his car beside a battered Ford truck used to carry supplies from town. A cricket pitch and rugby field lay outside the walls, but were nothing more than dust bowls in the mid-summer heat. Situated on the Tropic of Capricorn, Rockhampton summers were either blisteringly hot or flooded by torrential downpours from storms or cyclones. *St Ursicinus* made no concessions for climatic extremes and its buildings were either stifling or freezing while its occupants suffered accordingly. Indeed, noticeably more expense and effort had been spent on the chapel than any of the other structures.

Danny was led to a dormitory with twenty beds lined on either side of the room. His belongings were unpacked and scrutinised in stony silence by the school matron, Sister Gertrude, who immediately confiscated his comic books, marbles, shanghai and a bag of biscuits his mother had baked. His clothes were stuffed into a small locker at the foot of his bed. Danny could not determine whether Sister Gertrude was male or female.

'You will make your bed every morning,' the good sister announced, 'and I shall inspect it every morning.'

Without warning she drew a bamboo cane from the folds of her habit and flicked it expertly across the back of his hand. Danny winced and quickly withdrew his wrist.

'And that is what you'll get if I find a single crease in you blankets.'

Danny noticed there were no sheets.

And the beatings had begun.

The Christian Brothers who taught classes were, with a couple of exceptions, equally enthusiastic about caning boys. They caned them for:

- running
- dawdling
- being late
- being early
- sub-standard work (the standard varied from day to day)
- anything else they could think of
- no particular reason and
- especially for questioning *anything*.

Sixty three boys attended *St Ursicinus* ranging in age from about five to fifteen. Some were orphans, others the sons of pastoralists from stations in faraway West Queensland and the Territory while a few, like Danny, were miscreants incarcerated to mend their ways. Charlie was also rounded up and sent to the school to try to curb his pagan hooliganism. Danny regretted seeing Charlie locked up as well, but was delighted to have a friend and ally in that hell ruled so ably in God's name by His servants.

Sister Gertrude oversaw a group of half-caste aboriginal girls fathered by jackaroos. The girls worked in the laundry and kitchen and slept in a dormitory next to the chapel. Some were miserable and desperately homesick, while others surprisingly felt they were better treated and fed than on remote cattle stations or missions. In fact Sister Gertrude's attitude to those girls was vastly unlike her behaviour towards the boys. She was indifferent to the girls and, as long as they did their chores, she let them be. Desmond totally ignored them and seemed to have no interest in females at all. In fact the only thing the Mons showed any affection for at all was his automobile. He loved to go joyriding several times a week, delegating a gang of boys to wash the vehicle inside and out whenever he returned. Needless to say not cleaning the car to his specifications was on the list of caning offences.

Every day after lessons the boys were put to work in the gardens, or scrubbing walls, floors and toilets or any other arduous duties Monsignor Desmond thought up for them. Additionally there was the interminable call to prayer, although Danny couldn't imagine what in hell they had to give thanks for. The food was mainly a foul gruel with stale bread and dripping on good days, but Danny and Charlie made sure they ate whatever they were given to stay as fit as possible. One duty that had unexpected benefits was to wait on the brothers' table. They dined in style and the boys smuggled left-overs back to the dormitory where they shared them out as best they could.

'I've gotta get outa here, man,' Charlie said after a fortnight. 'This place'll kill me for sure. No way this black feller's gonna last long and they told me there ain't no holiday break for me. I gotta stay here forever.'

A week later he made a run for it only to be dragged back in manacles. Two burly coppers dumped him in front of Monsignor who nodded and dismissed them.

'I'll take care of this wretched heathen, ingrate boong,' he hissed as he flexed his cane. 'Don't worry, he won't trouble you again. I shall teach him a lesson he'll never forget.'

The constables were unconcerned about the abuse that was to follow. The fate of one black more or less was all the same to them. They took the Monsignor at his word and drove away while the entire school was summoned to the assembly hall where they stood in front of the dais. Charlie was quaking with tears in his eyes as a couple of the meanest brothers hustled him forward. A few boys were ordered to set a table on the stage and Charlie was held across its surface by one of the brothers while the other wrenched his trousers and pants down to his ankles. Then the monsignor laid into Charlie's buttocks with his cane to the horrified gasps of the boys who received a sharp cut from Sister Gertrude's bamboo switch if they turned their eyes away.

'This is what happens to vile, sinning boys who defy me and thus defy The Almighty!' he snarled.

Thwack!

'The devil has entered his body. He is possessed…'

Thwack!

'He will be exorcised…'

Thwack!

'Our Lord is merciful. Only through suffering will this sinner receive salvation and be saved from eternal damnation…'

Thwack!

'In the name of the Father…'

Thwack!

'The Son…'

Thwack

'And the Holy Ghost…'

Thwack!

Charlie screamed as blood flowed from his wounds, but still Monsignor Desmond continued the beating. Sweat dripped from the cleric's brow and yet he persisted until Charlie's buttocks were ragged flesh and his screams had become mere groans. Desmond was only stopped when some brothers decided Charlie would die if he was punished further. The boy had fainted and felt no more pain anyway. Desmond stepped back panting, his face purple with rage while Charlie was carried to the infirmary. Unfortunately

Gertrude was the institution nurse and it was unlikely she belonged to the Sisters of Mercy Order who ran a school in town. Charlie was laid face down on a cot and pretty much left to pull through by himself.

But he was tough and recovered. Danny sneaked in to see him, bringing water and smuggled food to help Charlie's convalescence. His buttocks bore scars that would never completely heal and he was in constant pain. Yes, Charlie was tough, but not that tough.

A week later he was found hanging from a beam in the sickbay. The discovery was too late as he'd been strangled by a bandage that held his feet only inches from the floor. He was buried without ceremony in a plot behind the school wall. No-one bothered to tell his family. As far as his mother was concerned, he'd simply disappeared.

It was then Danny learnt to hate.

Chapter 2 – Breakout

Danny hated *St Ursicinus* beyond any intensity he could have imagined. He hated the buildings, the work, the lessons, the food, Sister Gertrude, the brothers, but mostly he hated Monsignor Desmond Slaughter. Danny channelled his hatred into sheer determination. He would not let them break him, but knew that to resist on their terms was suicide. He kept his head down, avoided eye contact, studied hard and bore continuous minor punishments thus avoiding major ones. Luckily he was a bright lad and quick at maths, English, science, history and geography. Without a doubt geography was his favourite subject, mostly because he could imagine being in foreign places far, far away from *St Ursicinus*. He developed ways of looking busy and even tried sucking up, but found that impossible. So he strove to simply stay neutral...beige...invisible.

The first term passed with numbing slowness, but no one came to collect him for the holidays. He knew Stanley was behind it, but despised his mother for allowing him to sway her.

'Looks like we'll have the pleasure of your company for the break,' Sister Gertrude sneered with grinning anticipation.

Actually only a handful of boys from the western properties left for the holidays and a few lucky ones didn't return. In a time when folk didn't question their Church, many parents either disbelieved their children if they reported abuse or even suggested they must have deserved it if they received a beating. Life was rough on remote cattle stations and sometimes conditions were no better there, so the boys returned to *St Ursicinus* with resigned dread.

As the dry season progressed and temperatures dropped at night, the boys pulled their inadequate blankets around them and shivered in their beds. It was those nights the boys dreaded most. Often a shadowy figure would prowl through the dormitory and lead a trembling youth from the room. The lad would return before dawn and lie sobbing under the covers trying to forget the horror he'd endured. Danny was obviously considered too old to be desirable and was fortunately left alone, but one of the youngsters called Colin told him what those selected had experienced.

'It's the Mons who's worst,' Colin whispered with tears glistening at the corner of his eyes. 'He takes you to the chapel and tells you to put your hands down there...you know...' Danny nodded. '…And he touches you…and tells you to put it in your mouth…and sometimes he puts it…you know…' Danny nodded again. '…And it hurts, but he cuffs you if you cry…says we're sinners and must be redeemed…. He calls it…redemption.'

'That's not how I'd describe it,' Danny muttered dryly.

'I don't know if I can take any more,' Colin blubbered.

You poor kid, Danny thought, *you can't be more than eleven or twelve.* But w*hat can I do about it? Nothing.*

Danny didn't really know why things happened the way they did, but not many nights passed before Monsignor Desmond again took Colin, whimpering, from the dormitory. Desmond seemed especially excited by boys who were particularly distressed by his attention. Danny heard them go and slipped out of bed, dressed and followed. He knew exactly where they'd be.

Danny eased the chapel door open. Moonlight pierced the stained glass windows where a single candle illuminated the sanctuary. Desmond stood close to the altar where he forced Colin to kneel before him. In quick movements he flung off his surplice and cassock and stood naked. A cat-o'-nine-tails lay on the altar. He raised the whip with one hand while firmly holding Colin with the other. At first Danny thought the boy was in for a flogging, but Desmond began flaying his own back which bore the scars of previous mutilations. Desmond began to chant in a plainsong monotone that Danny couldn't make out. He thought much of it might be Latin, but he also heard *sinner, redemption, atonement, punishment, salvation* and *damnation* repeated often. The monsignor was becoming aroused and drew Colin closer. The boy resisted until Desmond wrenched his hair cruelly.

Danny had seen enough.

'You dirty mongrel,' he snarled between gritted teeth, grabbing the nearest weapon at hand, an alabaster Madonna, from a plinth beside the altar rail. He swung with all his strength and the Madonna shattered to calcite shards and gypsum dust. Desmond was momentarily blinded but swung the whip at Danny, striking him across his shoulder. Danny was in such a rage he barely felt the pain and snatched the only other weapon at hand. He smashed the alter crucifix into the side of Desmond's head, piercing one eye. The Monsignor dropped to his knees clutching his face as blood oozed through his fingers. Colin was frozen with fear and stood gazing wide-eyed at the injured priest.

'Shove off, Colin,' Danny whispered. 'Get back to the dorm. I'll take the rap for this. No-one else will know.'

The boy needed no more encouragement and scurried away without looking back.

Desmond began hauling himself to his feet, gripping the altar for support, but Danny kicked him in the ribs and he dropped to the stone floor, moaning a writhing in pain.

Well this brings my choices down to one, Danny thought and bolted from the chapel. He reached the door just as Sister Gertrude entered. He had no idea why she was up so late. Perhaps she'd heard the noise they'd made. Without thinking, he rugby-tackled her and they crashed against the sandstone wall. She was out cold and Danny didn't stop to see if she'd suffered serious damage. What did he care? He leapt over her body and dashed along the cloisters to Monsignor Desmond's car. The top was down so Danny didn't waste time opening the door. He jumped straight into driver's seat and slumped behind the steering wheel. The key was in the dash; Desmond obviously thought there was no need to remove it. Danny flicked it from *lock* to *on* and planted his foot on the accelerator.

Boom! The car burst into life in a blast of blue smoke and petrol-filled flatulence. Danny crunched the gear lever into first and jolted away. He revved the motor to a roar that filled the quad, shifted into second and charged the gates. They crashed apart as the Buick barged through and wrought-iron ripped across the grill and bonnet. The car dragged the wrecked gates for half a mile before they clattered aside and Danny sped away from *St Ursicinus*. He was laughing uncontrollably with relief and satisfaction.

Just as the Buick slammed through the school gate, Monsignor Desmond lurched, stark naked from the chapel door. He stumbled over Sister Gertrude's prone body and dragged himself up again.

'After him!' he screamed to the empty quad. 'The anti-Christ is afoot! The spore of Satan escapes. In the name of God, give chase. Seize the transgressor, he will be punished…'

Desmond's ranting woke the Christian brothers. No-one questioned why he stood nude in the school quad. Two of them piled into their Ford truck and sped after Danny who now realised he was in deep trouble with no way out. He couldn't go home – that was the first place the police would look and Stanley's reception was likely to be cool at best. He'd probably turn Danny in on the spot whatever his mother said. He glanced in the rear-view mirror and saw headlights behind. It didn't take a genius to work out that some angry friars were on his tail.

The Buick should easily out run the Ford truck, but for how far? Danny had no idea of the car's range or what he'd do when it ran out of petrol. Right now he was heading towards the old Fitzroy Bridge into Rockhampton because it was the only road from *St Ursicinus*. Unfortunately the car's grill and radiator were ruined by the school gate. Water poured onto the road and steam spewed from the bonnet as the engine overheated and faltered, but Danny charged on at full throttle. The pursuing Ford may have been old and battered, but its engine was well maintained and it was closing the gap.

Just as the Buick approached the bridge a cylinder seized with a roar and a belch of oily fumes. Danny lost sight of the road and, choking in the smoke screen, lost control of the car. It swerved and smashed into a small retaining wall at the bridge entrance. Crashing through the barrier, the Buick became airborne then dropped into the river. In a second Danny stood erect and, planting one foot on the door frame, launched himself from the car with all his strength. There was a crack as the Buick hit the surface first. Water sprayed for an instant and the car floated for several minutes before sinking.

Danny splashed into the river a heart-beat after the Buick. Water engulfed him then he burst to the surface, shocked and bruised, but not seriously hurt. He gulped a lungful of air and let the current carry him downstream as he slowly swam towards the city-side bank. The river was past its summer flood and Danny was a strong swimmer, but it was still a fair distance and he was exhausted when he reached the far side. Wharves and jetties lined the riverbank and he clambered up a ladder onto a wooded pontoon and sat gasping for breath.

He saw the Ford's headlights on the Fitzroy Bridge. The truck was stationary although he couldn't make out any figures through the bridge's iron girders.

'Now that's something you don't see every night…'

Danny spun around to see Arty Baines and a couple of Aboriginal lads from his gang who were hanging around the wharves looking for mischief.

'Blimey, Arty, you scared the crap out of me.'

'Spectacular, mate…very impressive.'

'I'm in deep strife, mate.'

'You don't say? Was that the Mons's ruddy car?'

'Yeah, I nicked it.'

'He'll give you a right hiding when he catches you I reckon.'

'Worse than that, I clouted him with an altar cross. I think I knocked out one of his eyes.'

'This just gets better and better.'

'It's all right for you, mate, but I'm for it now. What're you doing here anyway? I thought you were in the slammer.'

'Out with a caution, a clip around the ear and a kick in the pants. Who's on the bridge now?'

'Blowed if I know, probably some of the brothers or that bitch Gertrude if she's recovered. I bowled her over too.'

'You'd better hope they think you drowned, but if it was me I'd be high-tailing it out of town as fast as I could.'

'How?'

'Rattler to Brisbane.'

'Brisbane? What then? I don't know anyone there. I'd starve to death in the streets.'

With no other ideas coming to mind, Arty took Danny back to his shack in an abandoned lot. The other boys melted away realising that GBH administered to a clergyman was going to draw more attention than they needed. Arty's shack was pretty feral, but Danny was so tired he fell asleep on a pile of hessian sacks in the corner. It was mid-morning when he woke. Arty was gone, but turned up a little later with bread, cheese, a pineapple and a couple of old pop bottles filled with water.

'Here get this into you,' Arty said. 'You must be starving.'

Danny gulped down some bread and cheese and drained half a bottle of water.

'You sure have stirred up the town,' Arty said, rather too cheerfully in Danny's opinion.

Arty had a network of snitches and what he was ignorant about in Rocky wasn't worth knowing. An ambulance had arrived at the school and carted Monsignor Desmond and Sister Gertrude off to hospital. The Mons was yelling blue murder and damning Danny to the pits of fiery hell, although it was unclear whether he was more incensed about the loss of the car or his eye. The police were investigating the theft and even thought of using frogmen from a naval unit in Brisbane to help with the search. They were testing some new diving equipment called SCUBA, but by the time they flew to Rocky any trace of a body would have been swept out to sea into the teeth of a host of sharks that patrol the coast. So the chief inspector favoured the version of events that left Danny at the bottom of the Fitzroy River. There was far less paperwork that way. More importantly Rockhampton's Bishop Andrew Tynan was snooping around and apparently asking some probing questions about how *St Ursicinus* was being run.

'The word from some choir boys I know is that His Grace is a very disturbed man,' Arty said. 'He's been up all night and telling everyone things will have to change at the school and he's going to make it happen.'

'That was quick.'

'Yep, when the bishop says jump all the rock-choppers ask, "How high?" It seems some of the kids started talking and now you can't shut 'em up.'

'Yeah great, if they don't brush it all under a carpet. Desmond is a ruddy perving old weirdo and Gertrude's no better.'

'Maybe, but it doesn't solve your immediate problem. If you show up in town, the rozzers will ask *you* some difficult questions. I still think you'd be better off out of here. Maybe Brisbane's no good, but I've got another plan...'

Chapter 3 – Northern Rattler

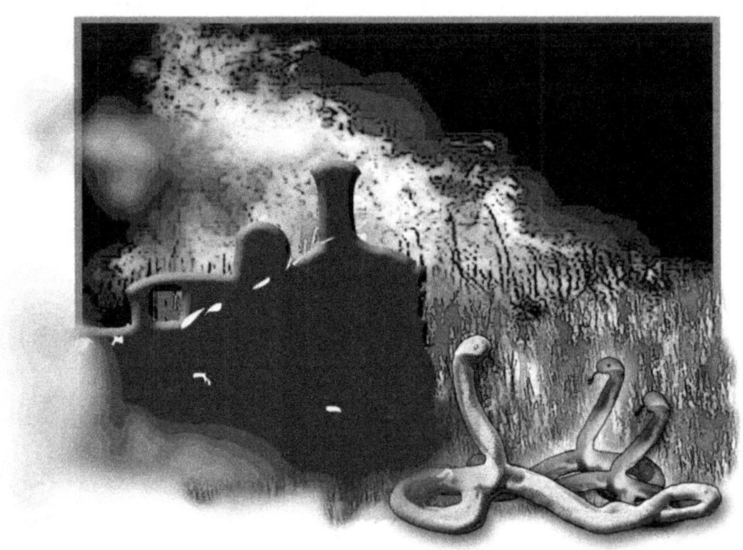

Like all good plans, Arty's was simple: jump a north-bound rattler and get as far away from Rockhampton as possible. There were plenty of trains passing through Rocky so he could ride one up to Mackay. Cane cutting season was well under way and there'd be plenty of work for the next few months. Danny could find a job and wait for things to quieten down. It would give him time to decide what to do next. Arty suggested Danny lie low while he checked for any freight trains leaving in the next few days.

Lying low was a pretty boring business as Arty didn't have anything other than some ancient newspapers to read. But he wasn't gone long and returned in a flap. Things were rumbling around town.

'Those two buggers I was with last night have spilled the beans.'

'What, gone to the cops? That doesn't sound like 'em,' Danny said.

'No, but nicking a couple of port flagons from a grog shop does. The owner saw 'em and tipped off the rozzers who picked 'em both up by the river. They were plastered out of their minds and started blabbing about everything – including last night, which they thought was a hell of a joke, by the way. The police know you're still alive.'

'Shit!'

'Yeah, it won't take 'em long to figure out where you are, it's not as if this place is any great secret.'

As he spoke a Holden patrol car prowled along the street, scanning the other shanties for signs of life.

'C'mon, we'll have to take our chances,' Arty said.

They stuffed the remaining food and water bottles into a swag and climbed through the back window. There was no glass so it wasn't difficult. The police car pulled up and two uniformed officers started searching the shacks as Arty and Danny disappeared into the bush and headed around the town to the rail yards. They reached the railway lines and found a hiding spot inside an uncoupled freight wagon.

'Stay put,' Arty admonished. 'I'll check for trains.'

Once again he was only gone for a short time before returning with some extra food, about five pounds in coins and a decent hat.

'Don't want you dying of sunburn, do we,' he grinned. 'The cash should last until you get work and there's a train leaving for the cane fields in an hour.'

'Thanks, Arty, you're a true mate.'

'You'd do the same for me and word is out about what you did for that kid at *St Ursicinus*. You've earned it.'

And that part of Arty's plan worked fine. They found a flatbed truck piled with crates and tied down machinery. When the guard was away Danny selected a spot between two crates and invisible from outside view. The truck looked fully loaded, so as long as no one came to inspect closely, he'd be fine. Arty shook his hand and jumped to the ground as the train pulled away. He stood watching the rattler gather speed in a cloud of gushing steam. Soon the train was out of sight and Arty turned back to town. He hung around his usual spots all afternoon and well into the night before returning to his shack where two of Rockhampton's finest awaited him.

'Well, well, well, Arty Baines at last,' one of the coppers said. 'About time, laddie, we've been here for hours. Now, we'd like to know what you've been up to all day and, more importantly, where's Danny McAlister?'

With nowhere to run, Arty was nicked.

Unaware that Arty would sooner or later be forced to explain the truth, Danny settled down to enjoy the ride. It was pretty uncomfortable on the wooden floor so he made a cushion with his swag. Initially there wasn't a lot to see as the train rattled northwards. Rockhampton was surrounded by flat cattle country that was always at the mercy of summer floods and winter droughts. A couple of hours passed and they halted at Marlborough, a luckless fly-spot on the map whose only claim to short-lived fame was to mine a semi-precious gem no one had heard of called chrysoprase. The town was held in such disregard that the railway builders hadn't even bothered to lay the track past the original site, compelling the locals to up stakes and move their meagre structures, pub and all, back to the line. Needless to say the rattler didn't stop long, but the Broadsound and Connors Ranges swelled up to the west at least providing a view. Towards sunset he began to feel cold and wondered how he would make it through the night. The sky was clear which meant even chillier hours of darkness. Occasionally the train paused for no apparent reason, giving Danny a chance to check out some of the box cars that might give more protection. He found one with its door ajar and jumped inside just as the train belched into motion once more. The freight car contained a load of grain sacks that made a tolerable bed. Danny ate only a little more food, knowing he'd have to ration himself for a couple of days and then he fell asleep.

When he woke, Danny wasn't alone.

Two raggedly-dressed, foul-smelling individuals were rifling through his pockets. They must have boarded on one of the train's unscheduled stops. They'd finished off his food and pocketed the money Arty had given him.

''Andsome fella, ain't 'e?' One of the vagabonds leered and started pawing Danny's leg. Visions of Monsignor Desmond came flooding back and Danny wasn't having any of it. He jerked his knee into the man's groin sending him rolling across the boxcar floor cursing and moaning. His companion leapt on top of Danny who fought in desperate fury, flaying his fists at any target he could find. But the tramp was strong and his mate was recovering and would be back in the fight soon, zeroing the odds of Danny holding his own. His opponent landed a punch that drew blood from Danny's lip and hurt like blazes.

The vagrant hauled Danny up by his collar and slapped him a couple of times, sending his head spinning. Danny recovered quickly and drove his fist into the man's midriff, knocking rancid breath from his lungs. Danny's tenacity had caught them by surprise and undernourished, they weren't as tough as they thought. But now the other fellow was on his feet and rejoined the scrap. Danny elbowed him in the cheek and swung to land another punch, but lost his balance and slammed against the carriage wall. He was winded, allowing the vagabonds to grab him and hold him down which would have been the end of him if the rattler hadn't lurched into a bend tossing one of the attackers aside. Danny dealt out more punches before scrambling to his feet ready to meet both men again.

They charged, and seeing no other escape, Danny jumped through the car's door left ajar by the tramps when they boarded the train. He hurtled through the air and crashed onto the embankment that raised the tracks in an attempt to save the line from flooding. Danny rolled down the levee and stopped on a dirt road, little more than a couple of tyre tracks. He lay panting for several minutes before picking himself up and investigating for damage. He ached everywhere, but there were no signs of broken bones. He stared along the railway track to see the rattler disappearing around the curve until just a wisp of steam could be seen above an endless sea of sugar cane.

Great! I've no idea how far it is to Mackay. No water, no food and I'll have to walk all the way. I wonder if you can eat sugar cane.

There was nothing for it but to press on. He'd simply follow the railway and surely come to a station or maybe hop onto another freighter on a curve when it had to slow down. Indeed he might have been seriously hurt if the rattler hadn't been negotiating a bend when he jumped off. He cheered up once he realised that the people who lived in the area wouldn't know who he was. So he felt confident he'd be able to bum a meal somewhere.

About then Danny noticed grey flecks dropping from the sky and littering the path as well as covering him with a film of particles. The smell should have given it away, but he had other things on his mind.

The sugar cane grew two or three times his height right up to the roadside. A similar path ran along the other side of the railway with more cane encroaching upon it. Suddenly he heard a frantic rustling and crackling from the depths of the cane field. Then dozens of rats, rabbits and swarms of insects surged into the open. The normally shy animals paid Danny no heed as they bolted all around him and even over his feet, brushing against his legs. They were followed by bandicoots, small wallabies and a seething horde of cane toads. They all scrambled up the embankment, across the rails and disappeared into the opposite field. He jumped with surprise when snakes slithered onto the path just feet ahead of him. There were dozens of the brutes, more snakes than Danny had ever seen at one time and they were madder than hell. Some followed the other animals up the embankment, but half a dozen reared up and faced Danny, mouth agape showing venom-tipped fangs with their tongues flickering menacingly.

They surged towards Danny who froze, terrified.

'Bloody hell! What do you think you're doing? Are you barmy?' A voice yelled from behind him.

Danny didn't move.

'C'mon,' the voice called, 'before the taipans get youse or worse.'

Or worse..?

Danny came to his senses. He turned and bolted towards a truck that had pulled up behind him. As they no longer felt challenged, the snakes turned and headed over the railway. Four young men stood in the truck tray. One grabbed Danny's hand and hauled him up, plonking him onto a bench along the truck's side. All the men were covered in the same fine dust and a pile of long knives lay in the truck bed.

'Snakes kill youse for sure,' the man said with a thick Italian accent, 'but that's not the main problem, eh?'

Danny stared at him blankly then started brushing the flakes from his sleeves.

'Burdekin snow, eh?' the man smiled. 'The fire's close.'

He banged his fist on the truck cabin roof signalling the driver to crunch the gears as they lurched away. But the engine was drowned by a roar that sounded like an express train when suddenly the air erupted into flames that rose until they filled the sky. The heat was intense and the noise almost unbearable. Danny was sure the flames would overtake them, but the truck's occupants remained unconcerned. The Italian fellow even seemed to enjoy the spectacle.

'Beaut, eh?' he beamed, yelling above the fire's rage. 'You don't see a sight like that every day – well, not unless you live around here. G'day, my names Leonardo – call me Lenny.'

'Danny – pleased to meet you.'

The fire blazed alongside them until they crossed another path at right angles that acted as a firebreak, containing the flames to one section of the plantation. The truck slowed and rocked its way towards the main house and property buildings. Danny was surprised how close the buildings were to the sugar cane considering it was torched at cutting time.

'Drives the snakes out, see,' the man said.

Lenny explained they were heading for the *Zucchera di Canna* plantation owned by Giovanni and Beatrice Ricci who'd arrived in Queensland after the war as DPs – displaced persons. They'd brought their eighteen-year-old niece, Noemi with them, as her parents had disappeared into a Nazi labour camp and never returned. After arriving in Sydney the family had moved north where there were always jobs during the cane-cutting season. They'd worked hard and earned enough to buy some property of their own. Along with other farmers, some of whom were descendents of the Pacific Island Kanakas, they formed a loose cooperative that now supplied harvested cane to the CSR mill in Mackay.

The Ricci property was usually just called *Canna,* which simply meant cane, but sounded fine because it was in Italian. The main house was built in the Queensland style with timber walls, metal roof and verandas all around. A kitchen and laundry stood adjacent to the house and a labourers' barracks housing about twenty cutters was a little way off. There were also quarters for married men. Separate men's and women's lavatory and shower blocks were sited at a discrete distance.

The men jumped out of the truck and headed for a water pump and the showers to wash off sweat, dirt and Burdekin snow. They stripped where they stood with no pretence of modesty.

'C'mon, Danny,' Lenny said, 'you'd better scrub up too. You're pretty ripe, you know.'

Danny hesitated because just at that moment a striking girl flounced by, eyeing the men coquettishly.

'Don't worry,' Lenny smiled, 'that's just Noemi. Signor Ricci will take a stick to her if he sees her gawking.'

Noemi disappeared and the boys got stuck into cleaning up. Afterwards they shook out their clothes, re-dressed and boiled several billies for tea. Danny was introduced around, but couldn't remember all the names at once. He told his story without omissions. Most of the cutters were devout Catholics and they winced at Monsignor Desmond's misdeeds. They explained that, in their experience, priests were selfless and devoted men who'd risked and often given their lives for their flocks during the Nazi occupation.

'So you're on the run from the coppers,' Lenny said at last. 'I think we'd better see what Signor Ricci has to say. I'll take you up to the house.'

'The blokes steer clear of the house,' Danny observed as they approached the front veranda.

'They steer clear of Noemi, you mean,' Lenny grinned, 'and you wanna do the same or Signor Ricci will fillet your balls with his cane knife.'

Although there were other women living on the plantation who were mainly wives and daughters of the cane cutters, Noemi seemed to attract the most interest.

Signor Ricci turned out to be a hearty man with a riot of jet-black hair, huge moustache and an ample stomach he'd developed since his cane-cutting days had been replaced by a management role. Giovanni's wife, Beatrice, was in the cookhouse preparing a massive cauldron of pasta and tomato sauce that smelt delicious. She didn't speak much English, but had no difficulty making herself understood. Noemi hovered in the background, viewing Danny with interest.

'So you wanna lie low for a while,' Giovanni surmised. 'That'sa okay with me. We always gotta work to do. You looka like a strong boy.'

'What'll I have to do?' Danny asked.

'Whatta you told,' Giovanni smiled.

'I don't know anything about cane-cutting.'

'Youa learn, eh?'

So Danny went to work, and bloody hard work it was too. He learnt the back-breaking task of cane cutting, fencing, lifting, carrying, motor mechanics, welding, horsemanship and anything else needed to keep a country property operational. Giovanni advanced Danny his first pay-packet to buy spare clothes and wash gear. The police turned up after a couple of weeks. Apparently the Rockhampton constabulary wasn't fooled when Arty told them he'd put Danny on a freight truck to Brisbane.

They'd contacted the Mackay station who'd sent officers to meet the train there. Of course they'd collared the two no-hopers who'd attacked Danny and wrung the truth out of them before tossing them into gaol for vagrancy. But Giovanni shrugged and pleaded ignorance when the police made a quick search of his buildings. Danny was sweating in the cane-fields at the time so they left, satisfied that he wasn't to be found in that particular location. One runaway lad wanted for alleged assault in Rockhampton wasn't at the top of their priorities anyway. They had enough assaults of their own to deal with.

In any event the country was distracted by a looming crisis aboard. North Korea was sabre-rattling and threatening to attack Seoul, the South Korean capital. Lieutenant Colonel Charles Green's third battalion of 3RAR, stationed in Japan with the occupation force, was preparing to ship across the Sea of Japan to join the 27th British Commonwealth Infantry Brigade and face the communist threat. 77 squadron RAAF led by Wing Commander Lou Spence, also flew its P-51 Mustang fighters to join the United Nations alliance. Both units were to see plenty of hot action and both commanders ultimately lost their lives in combat.

Yes, big events were afoot as Australian once more geared up for war. So no one was interested in a wayward teenager. Danny was well under the radar...or so he thought...

Chapter 4 – Lenny, Noemi and Gladys

Noemi was bored and wilful – a naturally dangerous combination. Other than hard work, there was little social life at the Ricci property except Saturday nights when the family got together for a feast, wine, music and dancing. Unfortunately the young bachelors generally headed into Mackay after lunch to fill their bellies with beer before the hotels closed at 8pm. In this regard Queensland was better served than other states that still endured the six o'clock swill. This was generally followed by a taste of sin supplied by local working girls who'd either dodged the police or paid them off. So there was little potential romance left for Noemi to pick from.

Of course one of the young fellows she fancied was none other than handsome Leonardo Esposito who called himself Lenny because he thought it sounded cool. Lenny had been a bit of a hero in the Libyan Desert before being captured by diggers and shipped off to Marrinup in Western Australia, but the camp was overcrowded, so he was transferred to the Prisoner-of-War and Interment camp just outside Cowra in New South Wales where he sat out the war. Lenny hadn't found being a POW any particular hardship. He was cheerful, optimistic and was often in working parties employed on local farms, market gardens, orchards and building projects. Although flatter, much of the country reminded him of Italy, especially the months when he was billeted at Coonabarabran while working on roads and farms in and around the Warrumbungle Ranges. Lenny also had a way with the ladies and, with so many men fighting overseas, he was only too happy to ease a little loneliness when he could. The fact that he'd learnt English, could play a guitar and croon Italian love ballads as smoothly as Dean Martin added to his charm.

About half the POWs at Cowra were Japanese whose attitude to captivity Lenny thought was plain foolish. They had no idea how to make the best of things and spent all their time moping and feeling sorry for themselves. They were only happy playing baseball. This seemed ironic considering Americans were their arch enemies, but there was no logic to the Japanese in Lenny's view. He vividly remembered one night in 1944 being woken by the sound of Vickers machine guns crackling in the dark. He and his barrack roommates rushed to the window to see B compound ablaze with Japanese POWs running amok. Armed with makeshift knives and baseball bats they stormed the gates or formed human bridges over the barbed wire. Over two hundred were killed, and for what? They were all recaptured except the dopey buggers who committed suicide. What was the point of that? Where did they think they were going to go in the middle of Australia anyway? It was not like they blended in and the war wouldn't last forever. Worse still, they killed Ben Hardy and Ralf Jones, two guards manning one of the machinegun posts. Well, security tightened up big time after that, didn't it? It was months before things settled back to normal.

After the war Lenny applied to stay in Australian and with a glowing reference from Major Timms, the camp commandant, and the testimonials of local citizens, his residency was granted in 1947 when Cowra P.W. & I. was officially closed. Charming as he was, Lenny's luck was running out as diggers returned to reclaim their wives and girlfriends. Wisely he left central New South Wales and headed north to the cane fields.

And now he had his sights on Noemi, if not as a prospective wife, certainly a prospective bed-mate. But he knew to beware of Giovanni Ricci who'd been a resistance leader during the war and was handy with a knife and a shotgun. Giovanni was with the partisans who'd captured and executed Mussolini before stringing him and his girlfriend up by their heels to be photographed for posterity. Giovanni Ricci was not a man to be messed with or upset in any way.

So Lenny played coy with Noemi who was getting restless and she turned her sights on Danny. Granted he was a bit young, but he'd developed into a big, strapping lad after weeks of cutting cane, and he was certainly handsome enough. Noemi was a hormonal time-bomb just waiting to go off. She knew she wanted to be possessed and to possess a man at the same time and reckoned she knew just how to go about it. She certainly knew where she was responsive, especially when her fingers worked their magic at night, but it was all so confusing. Her aunt had interrupted her once and there had been hell to pay. In Signora Ricci's eyes pretty much everything before marriage was a mortal sin. During the war she'd seen too many stringy waifs sired by occupying Nazis, Yankee GIs and British Tommies alike, so she felt justified.

The Ricci Saturday evening parties were normally great fun. Beatrice and the other plantation ladies would lay out huge trestles arrayed with pasta dishes, salami from the smoke house, crusty bread, steaming meat dishes laced with garlic, cheeses, pizzas, salads and flagons of home-made wine. The tastes were all new and delicious to Danny who until then –*St Ursicinus* aside – had only eaten meat-and-two-veg. Afterwards guitars, accordions, tambourines, mandolins and violins tuned up and the dancing began. Lenny started teaching Danny to play a guitar. He practised for an hour every evening and, with a natural ear for music, soon picked up the basics. He quickly learnt the chords to many traditional Italian folk songs and was able to join in with the other players when he wasn't dancing. Noemi danced with all the men and boys, but especially Danny. She flirted outrageously and pressed against him sensually until Giovanni or Beatrice's shepherded her away, leaving Danny to endure some very unsettling nights.

Finally Lenny decided it would be a good idea to take Danny into town for a change of scene and a little fun.

'You should go with the blokes,' Lenny encouraged. 'It'll keep you out of trouble and maybe get some of that dirty water off your chest.'

'Yeah, great idea, Lenny,' Danny replied. 'I might be tall, but do I look twenty-one? They'd chuck me out of the pub or call the cops. I really need that.'

'No one will take any notice. Kids do it all the time, but stick to beer. Rum's a killer.'

So Danny allowed himself to be talked into heading for town the following Saturday. He stayed on the Criterion Hotel veranda and gave Lenny a float so the legal-age drinkers kept him supplied with pots of XXXX Bitter. Out of sight, he didn't have to worry about any embarrassing questions from publican Mrs Margaret Hoy or her barmaids. Most of the cane-cutters liked Danny and kept him company on the veranda anyway. Soon he felt pretty fast and loose.

'Whatcha do after the boozer shuts?' he slurred.

'Find some sheilas!' the boys cried in unison.

Danny was actually thinking of something to eat as beer made him hungry.

'Girls…dunno much about 'em…'

'What, you mean you never done it with a bird?' Lenny asked.

'Never done it with anyone…ha, ha, ha…It's not like I've had a lot of chances…ha, ha, ha…have I?'

Now for a teenager to confess his virginity things could go badly, and Danny probably wouldn't have admitted anything had he been sober. Either he'd be ridiculed by his mates (who were probably in the same boat, but not telling) or they'd band together to do something about it. Fortunately Lenny and his pals, being a little older, regarded Danny's inexperience with good humoured sympathy and took the latter course. As a result, at closing time they all piled into the truck and headed for a row of houses at the edge of town. Red lights glowed on the porches where cigarette-smoking girls in tight dresses and stiletto-heeled shoes lounged on the verandas. It was hardly Soho, Amsterdam, the Hamburg Reeperbahn or even Kalgoorlie's famous strip, but Mackay's constabulary was happy with its understated den-of-iniquity and tolerated its presence. The boys staggered to the front door of one place and were met by a cheerful, blousy woman called Beryl who puffed on a cheroot at the tip of a silver cigarette holder. She wore more makeup than a vaudeville performer. After a quick whip-around from the boys, Lenny explained Danny's predicament. No one seemed particularly concerned that Danny was under legal age and he certainly wasn't going to remind them. In all fairness to everyone involved, he did look a couple of years older than he was.

'I believe it's Gladys's turn do some cherry-picking,' Beryl smiled and summoned one of her colleagues who led Danny to a room with the largest bed he'd ever seen decorated with skeins of gaudy satin. She was a compassionate woman in her thirties and, after some awkwardness with a condom, showed Danny what to do. It was a brief and probably not entirely satisfactory encounter.

'Don't worry, darl,' Gladys assured him. 'First time's always a bit tricky. You'll be much better next time, especially if you lay off the grog.'

'Yeah, I'm not used to it.'

'Better stay here a bit. We want your yobbo mates to think you made a decent job of it, don't we?'

Danny thought she was nice and not at all what he'd expected. Come to think of it, he wasn't really sure what he expected. Someone younger and tartier perhaps, but one thing was for sure, he hadn't given women nearly as much attention as they deserved. Then again, as he'd admitted, there hadn't been a great deal of opportunity. They chatted for a while and he discovered Gladys had lived in Townsville and her husband had been killed during the fighting at Milne Bay. With the city full of GIs, she found turning tricks was an easy way to make ends meet. In fact she quite enjoyed the work that was so lucrative it became her vocation.

'My dad's still in New Guinea too, you know,' Danny said.

'I'm sorry…'

'He's not dead…I'm sure of it. I can just feel it.'

'How are you going to find out?'

'Dunno yet, but I'll think of something.'

She took him in her arms, in what she thought was a big sister hug, but it soon became clear Danny had other ideas.

'Goodness me,' Gladys smiled, 'ain't that just the joy of youth? C'mon then, this one's on the house…'

So as the truck rumbled back to the *Canna Plantation* Danny sat in the back with a smile that would last all night and promised himself he'd be back before too long. But things didn't quite work out that way.

*

Giovanni Ricci may have been a strict employer, but he was scrupulously honest. He ensured each of his workers opened an account at the Mackay branch of the Commonwealth Bank. He trusted the institution because a couple of years earlier it had set the Migration Information Service especially to help Italians coming to Australia. He personally deposited most of the cane-cutters' wages into their accounts and paid them the balance in cash as pocket money to splurge in town. The system worked well, ensuring his men had ample capital when they went south after the sugar harvest season. The only ripple in Giovanni Ricci's industrial relations was that he avoided employing members of the Australian Workers Union. Although he'd not been in Queensland at the time, he knew how Italian cutters had been sold out seventeen years earlier when the AWU and the CSR stitched up a deal discriminating against them. Also unionism smacked of communism to Giovanni and he had no time for reds or any other *isms* for that matter. That might have appeared odd considering his wartime partisan group was comprised almost entirely of Communists, but Giovanni only aligned himself with them against the common fascist foe. He was pragmatic and could see no point in being a communist now that he lived in Australia where you got on by simply working hard.

Canna Plantation's non-union attitude didn't go unnoticed by AWU shop stewards who were striving to tie up all the cutters in a closed-shop monopoly. So far there had only been minor shoving and scuffles between AWU members and *Canna* employees. But union bosses being union bosses, weren't going to stand still for long.

Danny was so busy at work and play that he'd not really taken any notice of industrial relations. Why should he care? He was too young to vote or be bothered about being a union member. Even now in October when the days grew stiflingly hot, he had a good life, not to mention spending-money for the first time as well as a healthy, swelling bank account. So he was in for a shock when some weeks later, after he'd saved up enough for another visit to Gladys, he joined the crew on a Saturday night excursion to Mackay.

Once again they headed for their favourite watering hole, the Criterion that they'd pretty much claimed as their own on weekends. Although Danny still stayed away from the beer taps, he now felt confidently anonymous in the crowded barroom. He was having fun although secretly yearning for closing time and a trip to the red-light district. He, Lenny and four other cutters were into a serious euchre game around a card table in the public bar. Playing sensibly for a-penny-a-point, they couldn't do too much harm. Danny had no idea how many hotels were scattered through Mackay, but there were enough to ensure harmony in the town. Rival factions tended to stay on their own turf, restricting clashes to an individual basis that were easily dealt with by the law.

For some reason that Danny never discovered a bunch of AWU boys got themselves full of grog, all worked up and in a mood to go and crack a few *dago* scabs' heads. They marched out of the Ambassador Hotel and headed for the Criterion. Their weapons of choice were mostly fists, but a couple of unionists carried lengths of 4inch-by-2inch timber and a cricket bat or two. They clattered up the Criterion's veranda steps and barged into the public bar.

'Time to clean up these wog bastards,' the leading unionist roared in no disposition to negotiate. 'C'mon lads, rip into 'em, toss the bloody greasers out!'

And the fight was on. The unionists had the advantage of surprise and with a war cry of 'Scabs out' accompanied by a host of expletives, they tore into the Italian cutters. But the *Canna* boys were tough and quickly gave as good as they got. The card players took advantage of any weapons at hand and Lenny smashed his chair into the side of the union leader's head. The man thumped to the floor and Lenny kicked him several times in the ribs so he didn't get up. One of the chair legs broke off and Danny used it to fend off an AWU man who'd singled him out.

Two unionists grabbed an Italian and hurled him at the pub's front window. He smacked into the frame and bounced back, but the force knocked out the window pane. The glass fell in a solid sheet before shattering as it hit the veranda. The unionists tackled their victim again and hurled him through the empty frame. He tumbled into the scattered glass shards and was badly cut up. As the Italians and AWU boys traded punches and insults, the barmaids screamed and ducked for cover while Margaret Hoy rushed to her phone and dialled 000. Danny faced a unionist who'd smashed a beer glass against the bar and was menacing anyone who came close enough for him to have a go at. Two of his AWU mates grabbed Danny from behind and the glass-wielder took a swing. Danny, using the men for leverage, struck the attacker in the gut with both feet, knocking the wind out of him before his pals started laying into Danny.

He felt his head spin as a jarring punch landed beside his ear and another hit his midriff with a stabbing pain. Danny spewed over his boots and onto the barroom floor now slippery with blood, rum and beer. Lenny charged to the rescue and clouted one of Danny's attackers with a XXXX bottle. But not before Danny copped another couple of blows and went down. He didn't remember much after that except a vague awareness of police whistles blowing in the distance.

Danny came to with a groan. His head was throbbing and his gut ached, but at least he was back at *Canna Plantation* barracks although he had no idea how he got there. It was daylight, but which day? He fell asleep again and finally awoke at dusk feeling only marginally better. Noemi hovered over him, regularly sponging his brow with cold water like a right little Florence Nightingale while Lenny stood at the foot of the bed looking mildly amused.

'I don't see what's so ruddy funny,' Danny groaned and winced as he tried to sit up.

'*Carissimo* Danny,' Noemi gushed, hugging Danny so tightly he winced as she squeezed his bruised body. 'You black and blue all over, *amore mio ragazzo.*'

'And she'd know,' Lenny said.

Noemi glared at him, but quickly turned her attention back to Danny.

'I will nurse you, *bambino*,' she purred. 'You are so brave. *Lei è così coraggioso, il tesoro.*'

'I don't remember a thing, how did I get back here?' Danny asked.

'It wasn't that hard,' Lenny replied glibly. 'The union blokes scarpered when they heard the rozzers coming so we had just enough time to pile in the truck and bugger off. Took three of us to toss you in the back, you weigh a ton you know.'

'*Si*,' Noemi whispered, caressing Danny's arms. 'You are a big strong fellow now, *uomo mio coraggioso.*'

Giovanni agreed that Danny would have to spend a few days recovering before he could go back to work. The *Canna Plantation* season was all but over anyway and as the AWU cutters had the other plantations sewn up as closed shops, all the boys were talking about heading south to New South Wales where good jobs were going begging on the Snowy Mountain hydro-electric scheme. Lenny asked Danny if he'd like to join a bunch of Italian lads who'd be leaving in a few days. Danny had no other plans so he agreed, much to Noemi's chagrin as she saw her window of opportunity narrowing dramatically.

So she fussed over him for the next couple of days. Soon, although he still bore some livid bruises, Danny felt he was ready to resume light duties at work. He awoke early on the last day of convalescence. Everyone else was already in the fields or performing routine jobs around the plantation out-buildings. Silently Noemi slipped into Danny's room with the stealth of a panther. She held her finger to lips to silence him because she had mischief in mind. She didn't waste time. As Danny sat up she climbed onto the bed and straddled him, pushing him back onto his pillow and smothering him with kisses.

'Noemi...' Danny gasped when he managed to come up for air. 'This is a bad idea.'

'*Segretissimo, bambino, calma,*' she whispered, all husky and urgent now. 'You lika me, no? You want me, no?'

'Well...yes...but ...Noemi...'

'I am not wearing...how you say...slip...culottes...'

'Knickers!'

'*Si, bambino...*'

About then any common sense Danny might have had in the matter evaporated. His attention was focused entirely on Noemi's breasts that heaved only inches from his nose. This was new for Danny. Whereas his experience with Gladys was based merely on technique, he now felt a different emotion altogether – true passion. The damage would have been done too if Giovanni and Beatrice Ricci hadn't marched into the barracks at that moment. They'd seen the restless signs in Noemi and were keeping an eye on her. One thing was for sure, she'd been far too long alone in the barracks with Danny McAlister.

'Traditore!' Giovanni raged. 'You rape-a my niece. I killa you now.'

Beatrice screamed, followed by a babble of Italian between herself and Noemi who leapt from the bed. Danny couldn't understand a word, but got the gist of the row. He was sure words like *slut* and *whore* were involved on Beatrice's part and, *you don't understand, I'm not a child, it's my life* from Noemi. While that verbal, tear-spattered battle raged Giovanni decided to take a more physical approach.

He stormed towards Danny who bounded to his feet and raced for the door. This was no time for false heroics or explanations. Danny dodged Giovanni's swing by sheer reflex and barged outside. A tirade of Italian oaths, threats and promises of maiming, torture and death followed him. Danny dashed across the yard past *Canna Plantation's* main house towards the storage sheds and then stopped in his tracks. Where the hell was he going? He couldn't run barefoot all the way to Mackay dressed only in his pyjamas. He looked around, but Giovanni was nowhere to be seen.

Suddenly a shotgun blast echoed between the buildings and Danny was showered with grit, wood splinters and debris as 12-gauge pellets splattered into the shed corner. Danny bolted behind the building as another shot rang out. He ran headlong into Lenny and a couple of hands who had been working close by and came hurrying to see what the fuss was about.

'Giovanni…' Danny gasped. '…He's…after me…'

Lenny stared at him blankly.

'Calm down…' Lenny began.

'Calm down! He's gonna kill me.'

'What…Why?'

'Noemi…'

Lenny nodded. No more needed to be said. The details were irrelevant. Giovanni's blood was up and nothing could be done about that except to get as much distance between him and Danny as possible then wait for things to settle down. Danny and Lenny raced for the truck and climbed aboard. They had a slight respite when Giovanni, realising he'd forgotten to bring spare shells, had to go back inside for more. The truck rattled down the driveway as Giovanni re-emerged, took aim and fired. The truck cab's rear window exploded as the pellets smashed it to micro-shards that sprayed into the cabin scaring Lenny and Danny out of their wits but doing little damage.

'You think he'll come after us?' Danny asked.

'Probably, he sure is steamed up, but we've got the truck. The other vehicles are all out in the fields, so we've got some time before he can round one of them up. I told you not to mess with Noemi…'

'Mess with Noemi? She was messing with me. She's crazy!'

'Just reached an age where she craves a little romance, I think. Beatrice will have her married off by New Year after this.'

With no other plan in mind, they roared on until they reached Mackay where Lenny had to stop for petrol anyway.

'What are we going to do with you, Danny?'

'I need some new duds for a start. I can't wander around town in my p-jays.'

They headed for a Coles 3^d 6^d & 1/- Variety Store - although the prices had inflated somewhat since George and Jim Coles established the retail chain thirty-five years earlier. Soon Danny was kitted out in new moleskin pants, a cotton t-shirt, cheap canvas shoes, a duffle bag and wash-kit.

'Look, I think I've got the answer,' Lenny said as they walked back to the truck. 'I've never seen Giovanni so mad...I mean he's never actually shot at anyone before.'

'I've never *actually* been shot at before either,' Danny retorted, 'not even by Monsignor Desmond.'

'Yeah, scary ain't it?'

'Ruddy terrifying if you ask me.'

'That's the point. I don't think we can risk Giovanni calming down any time soon and if he sees you again...who knows? You need to skip town, the season is just about over anyway.'

'What about my stuff? What about my money?'

'You can buy more stuff. It's not as if you've got much anyway. Your cash is safe in the bank and you can always arrange to have your account transferred to somewhere else. I'll leave your pass-book at the Mackay branch for safekeeping and tell 'em you'll be in contact later on. I don't think it's worth hanging about, Giovanni is hardly in the mood to give you a Christmas bonus.'

But once again the question of where to go arose.

'My mate Jack owes me a favour or two. C'mon, I'll drive you over to his place.'

*

^{J}ack Collier's place was a dockside shack next to a wharf where half-a-dozen prawn trawlers were moored. He was the skipper and owner of a particularly well-used vessel named *Lady Burdekin*. She was not a large boat, but sturdy and well maintained despite her no-frills appearance. A fishy smell imbued with diesel oil hovered over the dockside generally and Jack's boat specifically.

Lenny parked the truck next to the shack. Nets were stretched out to dry and be repaired accompanied by piles of rope, spherical glass floats, rusting bollards, winches and many other varieties of undefinable marine gadgetry.

'Ahoy there, matey,' Lenny called as he bashed on the door and winked at Danny. 'Permission to come aboard, cap'n aye.'

'Oh do shut up, you blithering idiot,' a voiced yelled back.

Lenny and Danny took that as a *welcome – come in* and opened the door. A man in his early thirties sat at a table drinking tea. He wore a plaid shirt and grubby overalls. An untidy week-old stubble grew on his face.

'G'day, Lenny,' he said in a growl, 'and cut out the smart-arsed Long John Silver crap.'

'Aye, aye, Jack m' lad.'

The Cowra library had lent books to POWs who wanted to learn English and Lenny reckoned he'd read just about everything on its shelves. *Treasure Island* was one of his favourites.

'This is my pal, Danny,' Lenny got straight to the point. 'He's in a spot of bother…'

'Oh yeah?' Jim looked suspiciously at Danny.

'Not with the coppers,' Lenny hastened to add.

'What then?'

'Giovanni Ricci is after his blood.'

Jack raised his eyebrows.

'Noemi.'

'Ah,' Jack nodded sagely.

'Nothing happened,' Danny blurted.

'Don't matter; it's all that Italian honour crap. You'd be better off on the run from the rozzers.'

'You see the problem,' Lenny said. 'I reckon Giovanni wants to chop Danny's balls off and feed them to the cane toads.'

'More than likely, but I don't see what that has to do with me.'

'You told me you're always looking for deck-hands. Well..?'

'What do you know about trawlers, Danny?' Jack asked, staring directly at Danny through eyes that pierced like knives.

'Well, nothing actually.'

'Honesty's good.'

'He's a fast learner,' Lenny added quickly. 'He's one of our best cane-cutters after only one season. Big and strong too.'

'What are you, Lenny, his agent? But, I *am* taking *The Lady* up to the Gulf this arvo. Should be away for three weeks or so and I do need another man to cook, clean up and do all the dog's-body crap. You want to take that on, Danny? I'll pay you the basic wage and maybe a bonus if you work out OK.'

Danny nodded and thought that being a fisherman mightn't be so bad. So he said goodbye to Lenny who, like Arty Baines, had turned out to be a true friend. Danny regretted there seemed to be a pattern of farewells developing in his life. Or maybe life was like that, just a series of ships passing in the night.

'See ya, mate,' Lenny said, pumping Danny's hand. 'If you don't fancy prawn fishing, come on down to the Snowy. Like I said, I've had enough of cane-cutting so I'll try my luck on the hydro scheme.'

Lenny climbed into the truck and drove away after promising to lead Giovanni off the scent if he was sniffing around in town

.

*

The remainder of the day was spent preparing *Lady Burdekin* for sea. Jack spent much of the time on the office phone ensuring the supplies arrived before they sailed. Most important were the iceblocks that had to be loaded into three holds below *Lady Burdekin's* aft deck. There were two additional crew members aboard *Lady Burdekin*. One was a rather sullen, middle-aged Aboriginal fellow called Cobar Bob, while the other was Jack's stunning young Melanesian wife, Penina. Apart from a nodding greeting, Danny learnt little more about them because he was put to work helping load the vessel. *Lady Burdekin* was less than 50ft long, but carried a stack of equipment, much of which was stowed aboard from the piles of bric-a-brac next to Jack's shack. Her bridge, main cabin, galley and sleeping quarters were all forward leaving the aft deck to support two outriggers from which the trawl nets would be deployed.

'They're Floridian style,' Jack explained, 'a new-fangled Yank system, better for small boats than single otter nets. Much easier to manage.'

He fired up *Lady Burdekin's* diesel that had its own peculiarities and required coaxing to life with the aid of several professional thumps from a large spanner. But once the engine roared to life it ran smoothly. By mid-afternoon they cruised past the Mackay breakwater towards the Whitsunday Islands. Storm clouds brewed overland behind them with the occasional lightning bolt streaking earthwards.

'Summer storms starting up,' Jack observed. 'There'll be a big 'un over town later on, it's probably best we're at sea.'

Danny didn't agree and was of little use that day or overnight when he suffered from dreadful sea-sickness. After the first few hours flat on his back on one of the cramped bunks, he'd happily have let Giovanni shoot him. He felt the frustrating nausea of wanting to heave his guts up, but somehow being unable to do so. If only he could be sick, he was sure he'd feel better. Yet he finally slept and the following morning woke feeling much better. Penina fixed him a bacon sandwich and a cup of cocoa after reminding him it would be his job to provide the meals from then on. She showed him where the rations were stored and how to use the stove.

'We eat fish mostly when we're at sea, it stands to reason,' she said. 'There's plenty out here on the Reef. Bob has a real knack for it and, being brought up on the islands, so have I for that matter.'

The rest of their supplies consisted of canned meat, fruit and vegetables, especially baked beans, along with some bread and other perishables that were kept in the ice holds until they were filled with fish and prawns. Penina explained they didn't have time for anything fancy and most food was simply pan-fried or boiled on the small galley-stove. The domestic side of boat life didn't seem so complicated.

'Just make sure you toss the waste over the lee bow,' she admonished.

Lee bow?

'Down wind, you duffer,' she grinned. 'Toss a bucket of rubbish to windward and you'll end up with a face full of, as Jack puts it, crap.'

Her teeth were sublimely white and straight and when she laughed her joy was completely infectious. Danny fell in love with her instantly and thought what a lucky fellow Jack was to have married her.

Learning the ropes from Cobar Bob was far more difficult. Cobar was an impatient and reluctant instructor, explaining how to use the trawler's equipment in terse grunts. It was just that there was so much to take in quickly and it seemed that with any mistake you risked being scarred for life, losing a limb or even your life.

'Treat your gear with respect and always wear gloves,' Cobar growled. 'Remember what I've told you or you'll be bally-well for it, okay?'

'Got it, Bob, I won't let you down.'

'Ain't a matter of lettin' me down, Snowflake. It's *you* you don't wanna let down. And call me Cobar, Bob's my mission name.'

Under Cobar and Jack's watchful eyes, Danny soon became familiar with *Lady Burdekin* and began to feel that he was being of some use. The sea was a great adventure. Danny had a grin on his face most of the time, especially when he spied a pod of dolphins that gambolled across the hull for hours. He spotted flying fish, turtles, rays and an occasional shark fin.

'Wait till next dry season when the whales arrive,' Jack said, sensing Danny's exhilaration.

Whales, now that would be something to see!

Even though she wasn't a large ship, Danny spent hours exploring *Lady Burdekin* to familiarise himself with every nook and cranny of her structure. He discovered a line of twenty golf-ball sized holes along the starboard bow that seemed to serve no practical purpose, so Danny asked what they were for.

'Jap machine gun shells,' Jack replied enigmatically, but didn't elaborate.

He navigated *Lady Burdekin* north eastwards towards Brampton and St Bees Islands before turning north to remain on the seaward side of the Whitsunday Group. At this point the Great Barrier Reef lay a comfortable distance on their starboard bow, however they'd have to be especially careful when the shoals curved closer to Australia's coastline further north passing the small fishing town of Cairns.

And so Danny's life as a prawn trawler man began.

Chapter 6 – Cobar's War

For the next month Danny learned the fundamentals of seafaring and, despite Cobar Bob's truculence, loved every minute of it. He studied charts and learnt the radio language needed to operate *Lady Burdekin's* HF transceiver that was preset to several marine frequencies. He quickly mastered the skill required to cast the prawn nets, haul the catch aboard and stow the seething avalanche of crustaceans into the ice lockers. Soon he became proficient enough to take a watch at *Lady Burdekin's* helm which he enjoyed most of all. They completed several voyages between Mackay, Cape York and beyond into the Gulf of Carpentaria where tiger prawns were the most plentiful. They off-loaded their catches into cold storage warehouses at Weipa, Karumba, Cairns and Townsville wharves. Danny took the opportunities ashore to buy spare clothes with his first pay-packet. He also bought a sketch pad, pencils and watercolours. He had a moderate talent for art and enjoyed drawing when he was young. Of course that all ended at *St Ursicinus*. Not that there was a lot of spare time, although he completed several sketches.

Prawn trawling was hard work, however there was leisure time as well. Here on the eastern Gulf coast Danny first admired rolls of sausage shaped clouds that spread for miles along the beach early in the day. Jim called them *Morning Glory* cloud,, saying they were unusual worldwide, although common enough around Cape York Peninsula. Other wonders were the huge tidal races that exposed miles of treacherous mud flats that could ground *Lady Burdekin*. Jack and his crew knew their business however and always found a deep channel to moor the trawler at low tide. Penina taught Danny how to fish for barramundi from *Lady Burdekin's* tinnie beside vast mangroves outcrops at the Norman, Gilbert and Mitchell River estuaries. It was on one of these occasions Danny spotted his first salt water croc. It looked menacing even with only its eyes and nostrils above the muddy water surface.

'They're most dangerous at this time of year,' Penina explained. 'They take black-fella kids sometimes. In the dry they lie on the beach where you can see 'em waiting for the sun to heat them up. Now it's warm enough they stay underwater and they're hard buggers to spot.'

Danny wished they had a bigger boat as the giant saurian glided past. Although it left them alone, they moved on to another fishing spot. There was no shortage of sharks either and a catch was often ripped from their hooks or they reeled in a fish with nothing but its head remaining. Sometimes they actually hooked a shark which proved good eating.

'Fish and chip shops sell shark all the time and call it something else to fool the punters,' Jack said as he showed Danny how to skin and fillet the fish. Danny hadn't really thought about sharks having no scales, but he'd come to realise just how many things he hadn't given any thought to.

When they worked in the Coral Sea east of Cape York, they occasionally found time for a spot of snorkelling beside the reefs. Jack carried masks, flippers and spears on board. This was a purely amazing experience. The underwater visibility was virtually unlimited and the blaze of coral and fish colours was beyond belief. The presence of the odd reef shark or sea snake was unnerving at first, but Jack assured him small sharks were nothing to fear. The snakes were simply curious and, as with most wild creatures, unlikely to bite unless they felt threatened. Although Jack did point out that if you were bitten it meant certain death.

The more Danny learnt and the better crew member he became, the more Cobar Bob resented him. Jack and Penina were genuinely fond of Danny and they developed a firm friendship. They exchanged small gifts at Christmas and shared a couple of bottles of beer that Jack had kept in the cold holds. Normally there was no alcohol on board, but Jack allowed a few bottles for special occasions. They obviously felt the same affection for Cobar Bob, but he steadily withdrew further into himself.

'What have I done to upset Cobar?' Danny asked at last.

'It's nothing you've done,' Penina explained. 'He's been this way with all the extra deck-hands we've employed, so they normally only stay for a trip or two. He's grumpier than ever now because it looks like Jack'll take you on permanently. I think Cobar resents that as we've been a team for so long now, especially during the war.'

'You mean he's jealous...of me..?'

Penina explained that Jack had been commissioned as a sub-lieutenant in the RANVR when *Lady Burdekin* was commandeered by Lieutenant Commander Eric Feldt for transporting Coastwatchers between Pacific islands and New Guinea during the war. She was not equipped with trawling gantries at the time and looked just like any other coastal tramp steamer.

'They enlisted Cobar too in case he was captured so he'd be treated as a serviceman and not a spy. Though that didn't make any difference to the Japs,' she said. 'We served through some hot old times during the Ferdinand ops, I can tell you. Those holes are souvenirs from one of our close calls with a Jap patrol...'

'Hang on,' Danny interrupted, 'what do you mean...*we?*'

Penina smiled.

'That was how Jack and I met.'

In July 1942, a month before the planned American landing on Guadalcanal *Lady Burdekin* had been assigned to carry a pair of Coastwatchers and resupply Major Martin Clements with new AWA 3BZ Teleradios, a generator and batteries. Clements was ashore and, aided by native volunteers, monitored Japanese naval movements. Unfortunately Kempeitai secret police captured several of his Islander group and tortured the unfortunate men until they revealed the truth before bayoneting them to death. Penina, who was only seventeen at the time and a member of Clements's team, witnessed the atrocity and rushed to the beach to warn the boat crew, but the Japs got there first.

She saw a rubber dingy being rowed ashore in the moonlight and sensed Japanese soldiers were moving towards the jungle edge. There was a sinister click-clack of rifle bolts as they loaded their first round. She knew the Japs were waiting for the Coastwatchers to reach the beach where they'd hopefully capture and interrogate them. They would certainly be an easier target as well. Until then she'd spoken mainly German and Pidgin, although she had studied a little English at a Honiara mission school. She only needed one word – *Japanese* – though it sounded more like *Japanee*.

Racing across the beach yelling for all she was worth would only attract Japanese gunfire so, crouching as low as she could, she crept towards the shoreline. She reached the water unnoticed as the Jap's attention was on the dingy and its occupants. It glided silently towards her and was only yards away – the Japs were holding their nerve.

'*I gat samting nogut!* (Dangerous place)!' she hissed, '*Japanee soldia, haitim ol insait long bikbus!* (Japanese soldiers hiding in the jungle)!'

The two Coastwatchers in the dingy were former district policemen and understood perfectly. So did Cobar Bob at the oars. The Japs saw her and started shooting. The crack of rifle fire sounded deafeningly close as muzzle-flashes spat from the palms and the reek of cordite filled the still night air. Coral debris sprayed around her bare heels as bullets slammed into the white beach. Penina splashed into the sea as the dingy turned and she thought she was to be abandoned. To their credit, one of the coast watchers reached from the stern while the other opened fire into the jungle with his Lee-Enfield .303.

'*Kam hariap, meri, swim kalap long bot!*' the voice hissed.

She dived forward and swam for her life. Like all Islanders, she'd played in the sea and spear-fished since childhood so she was an excellent swimmer and quickly reached the dingy. The Coastwatcher hauled her dripping body in as Cobar paddled desperately towards *Lady Burdekin*. Several Japs reached the shoreline and took aim, but were cut down by machinegun fire from the Bren manned by Jack on the trawler deck. The dingy slammed into *Lady Burdekin's* hull and everyone scrambled aboard not forgetting their precious radio equipment. Penina was practically thrown into Jack's waiting arms and clung to him with sheer relief and fright.

'Not now, Jacko,' Cobar yelled as he dragged the dingy over *Lady Burdekin's* gunwales. 'Time for ladies later, mate.'

Just then the Japs manhandled a Type 99-1 machine gun onto the beach. It weighed thirty kilos and took a moment to set up on a tripod. That gave Jack enough time to dash into the wheelhouse and fire up *Lady Burdekin's* engine. Then a burst of lead blasted into *Lady Burdekin's* bow. Jack swung the wheel to full lock and they powered away to sea at max revs with Cobar and the Coastwatchers firing rapidly astern to discourage the Jap machine-gunners. Fortunately they were able to make another rendezvous with Major Clements' team and resupplied them with new radios and batteries.

Penina and Jack hit it off right away and she stayed with *Lady Burdekin* for the duration, serving as interpreter and turning into a pretty good shot too. Penina was the daughter of a German coconut plantation manager and a Melanesian girl. Her parents fled Guadalcanal for Germany, abandoning their native workers to whatever fate held when the Japanese arrived. Although Germany and Japan were part of the Axis Alliance, Penina's father had heard of Japanese impartial butchery in China and other Far Eastern countries they'd conquered. He wasn't prepared to chance his luck with the Imperial Army. Penina stayed, Honiara was her home and from what she'd heard, the Third Reich was no place for a black girl. Her father may have been of sound, Arian stock, but marrying a Pacific Islander wasn't well received by Nazi purists and they disappeared without trace after reaching Europe. Penina had witnessed enough Japanese atrocities to eagerly join Major Clements' Coastwatchers team.

'Jack married me after the war when we knew it was safe enough to expect a future together,' Penina said coyly. 'Now that we've paid off *Lady Burdekin,* we're planning to start our family. We still have the Bren gun, .303s and ammo from the war. They come in handy occasionally when we're in croc territory.'

After all the danger they'd faced for three years it sounded so incongruous for Jack and Penina to be calmly planning domestic bliss. Danny wasn't sure how Cobar would react to any new arrivals either.

'But it doesn't explain why Cobar doesn't like me,' Danny said.

'Not you, just the world in general. You know he was awarded the Distinguished Service Medal for bravery during the war, but he's not allowed to vote – he's not even an Australian citizen. He can't get a drink in most Queensland pubs or RSL clubs and he's a war hero! He's still just another Abo no-hoper to them no matter what he did for his country. His people live somewhere along the Ross River, but he doesn't see them often. We're his family now. He's nasty on the grog and gets into trouble all the time, but he's okay when we're at sea. That's why Jack doesn't like to keep booze on board.'

Danny nodded. What could he say? Cobar was way too deep for him to understand. It didn't really worry Danny that Cobar called him *Snowflake*. It was an American term he'd picked up from US Marines. Although, if Cobar was so touchy about his own name, he could at least call Danny by his. But, Danny wasn't going to push it.

Feeling on common ground with Jack and Penina as they'd both served around New Guinea, Danny told them about his father. They were sympathetic and even a little encouraging.

'A lot of blokes went missing and turned up months – even years later,' Jack said. 'The Fuzzy-Wuzzies helped 'em as often as not. Hid 'em from the Japs and kept them alive, but how're you going to find out?'

It suddenly occurred to Danny that he'd been slowly creeping north for six months and New Guinea wasn't so very far away. Why hadn't he thought of it sooner? He'd find a way there somehow and start searching.

'Get up there and ask questions, I guess.'

'It's a ruddy big place,' Jack went on, 'highlands, jungle or swamp. It's not that easy to get around.'

'The district officers and police patrols should be able to help. It's somewhere to start.'

Jack wasn't as sanguine, but kept his thoughts to himself. He'd heard from diggers who'd fought through the hell of Kokoda that a man could have fallen only metres from any of the tracks and been instantly swallowed by jungle. There were stories of dead and wounded soldiers being eaten by starving Japanese troops as they retreated to the Buna-Gona beachheads where they'd first landed. Totally out of food and ammunition, cannibalism seemed the only survival option for many of them.

'I suppose if I make it to New Guinea the worst that can happen is I'll get to see the place.'

Around New Year they docked at Townsville. After offloading their catch and completing the endless paperwork, Jack announced they'd be in port for a while. He needed to order replacement parts for their generators. It'd be a few days before they could be freighted by road-train from Brisbane, so Penina and the boys were at a loose end. They slept aboard *Lady Burdekin* except Cobar who spent much of his time ashore. No one asked where he went or what he got up to. Jack was forever on the phone with mounting frustration as he discovered that, due to flooding, there would be a week's delay before his spares arrived. Danny started another bank account with his wages and arranged for his Mackay funds to be transferred to Townsville. After a phone call the teller established Lenny had been true to his word. Danny's pass book was at the MacKay branch and the manager said he'd post it to Townsville straight away.

Danny kept a few pounds in his pocket and wandered around town although there wasn't much to explore. He decided to climb Castle Hill and check out the view. Even though the sky was overcast, the day was still oppressively hot and humid, but Danny didn't mind. The panorama was stunning. Danny scanned past the city sprawl across Rowes Bay to Magnetic Island where Jack promised to take him spear-fishing. Danny looked north-westwards to Garbutt Airfield then south to the Ross River that straggled past the town and beyond to Oonoonda where several bomb craters were still visible after a Japanese air raid in 1942.

By then he was getting thirsty and started down the track to town and a cold drink. As he approached Gregory Street on his way to The Strand he saw Cobar in a deep discussion with two rather untidy white men outside a seedy looking hotel. Cobar spotted Danny and scowled for a moment, but then to Danny's surprise, stepped to meet him as if he was a long-lost pal.

'Danny,' he beamed.

Not Snowflake or Whitey?

'You wanna earn a couple of quid while we're stuck here?'

'Jack was gonna take me over to Magnetic Island for a spot of fishing…'

'You can do that any time. Ya wanna make some extra cash, don't ya?'

True enough, I'm building up a nice, fat kitty, but the more the merrier.

'What have I got to do?'

'You know how you're always banging on about going to New Guinea?'

Danny nodded.

'Well, my two mates Lou and Sid here are flying a freighter up to Moresby tonight and they need help with the loading and unloading. They're comin' back night after tomorrow – plenty of time before *the Lady's* ready to go. There's a fiver in it for you.'

'What about you?'

'Naw, gonna see my mob down the river before the coppers move 'em on. Dunno about flyin' anyhow.'

That was the clincher. Danny had never flown before and neither had anyone else he knew. This was an adventure not to be passed up. He had nothing else to do anyway and, as Cobar had pointed out, he could go spear-fishing any time. Not only was he going to fly, but he might even have time to scout around and find some clues about his dad.

Chapter 7 – Gooney-Bird Trail

Cobar neglected to tell Danny what particular business Lou Brennan and Sid Donovan were in. You'd think Danny would have been less trusting by now, but he didn't give it a thought even though both men looked shifty and ill at ease much of the time. They both lounged against the pub's veranda post with a glass of rum in one hand and each had a durry butt dangling from their lips. They were uniformly dressed in grubby, gabardine overalls, blue singlets, work boots and slouch hats.

'Bob says you're a good worker,' Sid said.

Danny simply nodded, noticing Cobar didn't object to Sid calling him *Bob*.

'Okay mate, meet Lou and me here at closin' time and we'll get cracking.'

As they walked back to the *Lady Burdekin's* mooring, Danny quizzed Cobar about his mates, but gained little extra information. Cobar also neglected to tell Danny that Lou's and Sid's service careers had been less than spectacular. Lou had been a RAAF sergeant pilot who flew C-47 transport planes with 36 Squadron in 1944. However his performance was mediocre at best as his CO, Squadron Leader Purvis succinctly stated in Lou's PP-29 conduct report – *This NCO is spending his RAAF career pushing doors marked 'pull'.* Needless to say the air force had no difficulty demobbing Lou immediately hostilities ceased.

Sid was a similar *square peg* although no one knew precisely how he spent his wartime service, but it appeared to mostly involve black marketing, KP and strife with MPs. He was never elevated above probationary aircraftman, but he and Lou made their pile with one scam after another. So much so that, after the Japanese surrender, they were able to buy a plane and continued their nefarious business enterprises.

Another essential point Cobar failed to mention was he'd slipped Lou and Sid a couple of quid to take Danny to New Guinea, but not bring him back. After all that's what the kid wanted, wasn't it? So Cobar was only doing him a favour, right? Then things could get back to normal aboard *Lady Burdekin.*

Jack was unaware of Cobar's unsavoury mates so could see no harm in Danny's northern sojourn. Penina however voiced her concern about air travel. Jack said it was probably no more hazardous than seafaring and certainly safer than driving. So

Danny arrived at the pub at closing time. The regular drunks were lined up along the veranda, each systematically quaffing the half-dozen beers set in a row beside them. Other winos staggered away from the bottle shop carrying their plonk home, 1/- bottles of sherry and port being the beverages of choice for those connoisseurs.

Lou was driving an ex-army covered lorry when he and Lou arrived and told Danny to hop in the back. He squished in beside the cargo consisting entirely of liquor crates, cigarette cartons and boxes containing less-than-savoury publications. Lou and Sid didn't feel the need to inconvenience Townsville's customs authorities with an inspection of their payload, thus dispensing with any duty payments. As a result they didn't head straight to the airport, but parked at the edge of town until well after midnight. Danny joined them as they sat beside the lorry guzzling rum from a hip flask.

Danny declined a swig, but found hanging around pretty boring.

'Get used to it,' Lou said. 'The flight is over four hours.'

'Why can't we go now?'

'No one to switch the runway lights on at Moresby. We'll have to arrive in daylight.'

That sounded reasonable enough although Lou didn't mention that when you're smuggling it's best to wait until all the customs officers are fast asleep and the coppers thin on the ground before you load contraband onto your plane. Arriving in New

Guinea didn't pose any problems as they weren't going to Jackson's Field, Port Moresby's international airport, but one of several satellite airfields built during the war where no customs officials would meet them.

Townsville's Garbutt Aerodrome was a joint civil-military facility. The RAAF tarmac and terminal were sited at the southern end of the airfield where a flight of Lincoln Bombers was parked ready for deployment to Butterworth in Malaya to help the RAF against insurgents there. It seemed that commies were cropping up everywhere. The bombers were guarded by military guards with dogs. Other military installations and fighter revetments stood way off to the northern tip of the field, but the civil terminal was situated about half way down the longest runway pretty much smack in the middle of the aerodrome. That's where the truck headed. The runways had all been sealed and lengthened for US bombers who had carried out raids over New Guinea, the Bismarck Archipelago and Solomon Islands throughout the war.

A Douglas DC-3 was parked among a group of other transport and training aircraft beside three Nissen huts that were used as hangars, met-briefing office, passenger terminal and maintenance sheds. There was also a sprinkling of Ansett, Trans Australian Airlines and Australian National Airways commercial airliners parked close by, yet all the buildings were closed with their lights switched off. A single padlocked gate barred the road leading to the buildings. Sid jumped from the truck and easily picked the lock, opened the gate and reset it after the lorry had passed through. There was no other security at this part of the field so they drove the truck right into the complex. Also known as a Dakota, C-47 or, as Lou preferred, gooney-bird, the plane had a careworn, down-at-the-heel appearance and questionable airworthiness. As Danny had no knowledge of any aspect of aviation, he saw nothing amiss in the darkness, only an impressively massive shadow. He'd never been close to a plane and hadn't realised how big they were. It was at least as long as *Lady Burdekin* and the wingspan was even greater with an oily-metallic-leathery smell pervading the tarmac.

This particular old war-bird was a veteran of countless hazardous flights over New Guinea where mountains and bad weather were as dangerous as Jap Zeros and ack-ack. She'd carried soldiers to drive the invaders back and dropped paratroopers to reinforce the beleaguered militia. She'd flown through flack barrages to drop supplies and ammunition into tiny, bitterly contested jungle clearings. She was a proud work-horse who'd fallen on hard times.

'Where are the lights?' Danny asked as he jumped from the truck tail-gate.

'No lights!' Lou whispered urgently.

Sid silently opened the plane's cargo door, pulled down a set of metal steps and climbed aboard. The three of them then formed a relay loading team and Danny saw why they needed an extra man. Lou handed the contraband crates to Danny who carried them to the plane and passed them to Sid who stowed them in the fuselage. It would have taken over twice the time for two men to complete loading and Sid and Lou seemed in such a hurry. And the risk of an accident or dropping something was also greatly reduced, although if you'd asked them, Sid and Lou wouldn't have placed health and safety high on their list of priorities. There were a couple of large crates on the cargo compartment floor and Sid loaded much of the contraband into them. Once they were full they stacked the remaining boxes in piles wherever they'd fit.

After they finished loading the plane, Lou made a quick inspection that mainly involved kicking the tyres while Sid drove the lorry behind one of the Nissen huts. Lou appeared satisfied and scrambled over the freight to the cockpit. Sid returned and pulled the chocks from the plane's main wheels. He hustled Danny aboard, showing him a canvas seat that unfolded from the fuselage wall. Beside it was a yellow pack marked *life-raft* about the size of a large rolled-up tent. Several floatation-jackets were piled randomly on top. Apparently they came with the plane as it was unlikely Sid or Lou would have bothered with spending cash on safety equipment. Sid then threw a tie-down strap over part of the load, but didn't bother with the large containers, reckoning they'd be heavy enough to stay put. It didn't look too secure to Danny, but Sid didn't seem concerned. He gave a *thumbs-up* just as the 1100hp of Pratt-&-Whitney Wasp S1C3G engine coughed, wheezed and then roared to life on the starboard wing. Danny nearly jumped out of his skin.

'Welcome to aviation!' Sid yelled, but Danny couldn't hear as the port engine burst into action amid gouts of blue smoke.

Danny found a canvas seat-belt and buckled up.

There were problems involved with smuggling, some of which involved a lack of pre-flight preparation. The meteorology office was closed so Lou had no recent forecasts. The refuelling truck was back at its depot in town, forcing Lou to fill the gooney-bird's tanks earlier that day. They made no weight-and-balance calculations and, as a result with a maximum fuel load, the plane was seriously over-loaded. The haphazardly stowed cargo paid only lip-service to the correct C-of-G, making the plane's stability and flying characteristics even more problematic.

Lou and Sid's *close-enough-for-a-government-worker* attitude had worked in the past and they weren't about to change now as they taxied to the nearest runway. Fortunately there was little breeze, so take-off direction didn't matter other than the fact that Garbutt field was surrounded by hills including Mt Louisa, Castle Hill and Magnetic Island. On a dark night you had to know your away around them, but Lou seemed confident enough and he wanted to be airborne before anyone took any notice.

Using only the gooney-bird's landing lights and his local knowledge to guide him, Lou taxied the plane to runway 01. He lined up about half way along the strip because back-tracking down the runway and using its full-length would take him too close to the military compound and suspicious RAAF guards. He made no calculation to determine whether the remaining runway length was enough for take-off. He simply pushed the mixture lever to full rich, the prop-pitch control to fine and slammed the throttle fully forward.

The gooney-bird lurched ahead. Danny thought the plane would shake itself to pieces as it lumbered down the runway. He'd seen planes fly by and they seemed to glide smoothly through the air, but on take-off the vibration was alarming. The C-47's sound-proofing had been stripped to reduce weight for its military service, so the noise was painfully intense forcing Danny to ram his fingers into his ears to shut it out. He leant forward and was just able to make out the back of Sid's head in the co-pilot seat. Sid was certainly unconcerned. He lit two cigarettes, sucked them into life before handing one to Lou.

The tail lifted and swayed considerably as the plane gathered speed. Lou held the gooney-bird on the ground as the runway end rushed towards them. Just as it seemed they'd plunge into Rowes Bay, Lou eased back on the control column. Nothing happened. So with a grunt he yanked the stick into his belly. The plane finally inched skywards, bounced once and then became airborne just as the last metre of tarmac flashed past below them. Lou immediately called for Sid to select the undercarriage lever up to lessen the wheels' drag as soon as possible. The plane staggered only feet above the waves for agonising moments as the main wheels slowly withdrew into their wells. With the slipstream now flowing smoothly past the underside of the wings, the gooney-bird found a new lease of life and accelerated away. Lou banked to the left avoiding the peak on Magnetic Island and retracted the flaps. He reduced the throttles and set the mixture and propeller-pitch to their climb settings. The noise and vibration reduced significantly much to Danny's relief.

Once airborne the plane took on an entirely new characteristic. It seemed to float effortlessly over the air currents, which of course it was designed to do. The gooney-bird had a massive wingspan that bore the plane with ease as they climbed into the night. After about twenty minutes Sid left the co-pilot seat and fumbled around a crate and dug out three cans of military-issue bully-beef and some spoons. He handed a can and spoon to Danny.

'Breakfast,' he yelled over the engine noise.

Danny twisted the can-opener and peeled off the top. He was hungry and soon polished off the bully-beef. There was a choice of beverage from the contraband, but Danny stuck to water from an army water-bottle the Americans called canteens.

'Wanna go up front for a look?' Sid said after a while. 'I'm gonna grab some kip for a couple of hours.'

Danny nodded and scrambled forward, easing into the co-pilot seat. Lou smiled, gave another *thumbs up* and drew deeply on his cigarette. The flight deck was a maze of dials, levers and winking red lights making Danny wonder how anyone could remember what they were all for. Lou pointed out the flight instruments in front of him: artificial horizon, gyro compass, airspeed gauge (ASI), vertical speed indicator (VSI), turn-and-bank indicator and altimeter. Most of the gauges were duplicated on the co-pilot's panel. In the centre panel were the engine instruments for each motor, RPM, boost, oil temperature and pressure and a few others whose functions were a bit obscure so Danny soon forgot what purpose they served. There was also a VHF and HF radio, but Lou hadn't bothered to switch on either set. On the roof above him, Danny was aware of a host of switches. One thing was for sure, Danny liked sitting in the cockpit and he liked flying – or so he thought.

They cruised on through the night at 8000 feet with 120 knots on the ASI, but Lou said they were actually going about twenty knots faster. It had something to do with the air being thinner up there – it was certainly colder. Lou was okay in his fur-lined, leather bomber-jacket, but Danny began to shiver.

'Hey, before you nod off, grab the lad a blanket, will ya Sid?' the pilot called and, moments later, Sid thrust a rough, grey service blanket through the cockpit doorway. Rough maybe, but Danny felt much better with the blanket wrapped around his shoulders.

'Wanna have a go?' Lou beamed.

What kid would say no?

'Take the controls. Keep her wings-level at 8000 and steer 351°,' Lou said pointing the various instruments. 'Just little control movements. Use the ailerons to stay on course not the rudder pedals or you'll spoil Sid's nap. Pull back on the elevators if she starts heading down and push forward if she goes up. Simple. Nothing to it.'

It took a bit of practice before Danny settled down. The controls were heavier than he expected, but then they were lunking thirteen short tons of aeroplane though the sky at over 150 miles an hour, so wind resistance had to count for something.

'The control surfaces are connected by cables,' Lou explained. 'They move the ailerons on the wings, the elevators and rudder on the tail. The disruption of the slipstream causes the plane to change direction. Air acts the same as water. Just think what it would be like if you stuck your hand out of a boat into the sea going this fast? It's the same thing only air is much thinner or it'd be impossible. See what I mean?'

Danny nodded. He'd been a bright kid at school, even *St Ursicinus*, and caught on fast. As he gained confidence, he found if he concentrated hard, he could stay on course and height.

'There you go, you're a natural,' Lou beamed.

Lou relaxed and even fell asleep at times. He awoke at intervals, made a quick check and reset the directional gyro to the magnetic standby compass to deal with something he called *precession* before nodding off once again.

So they cruised on through the night. After an hour, when they'd burnt off enough fuel to lighten the plane, they climbed to 12,000 feet for better range. Strictly speaking they should have worn oxygen masks above 10,000, but although the masks were stowed beside each pilot station, the tanks had been depleted long ago. The air was smooth for the next couple of hours, but as time passed they flew through some turbulent patches and Danny spied lightning flashes ahead.

Chapter 8 – Cyclone Season

When they hit a patch of stronger turbulence, Lou jogged awake. He was a little groggy due to lack of oxygen and it took a few minutes before he focused ahead. The sky was black except for a faint smudge of purple on the south-eastern horizon heralding dawn. The hum from the propellers changed tone as fluctuating air currents interrupted their revs. Lou adjusted the pitch levers to try to compensate, but realising it was an endless and thankless task, gave up in the end. They'd just have to put up with the props' out-of-sync droning.

'Looks like rough weather ahead,' Danny observed as another few more flashes sparked ahead.

'Naw, she'll be right, mate,' Lou replied. 'There're always storms around this time of year. They settle down in the morning and it'll be light by the time we reach 'em so we'll be able to fly around 'em.'

Normally that might well have been true, but Lou did not have a recent weather forecast. Had he obtained one, he'd have been aware of a brewing tropical low that had now reached cyclone strength and had drifted across their flight path. Although the Americans started naming typhoons in the Western Pacific just after the war, Australia hadn't got around to it and this one was simply designated by a number that no one remembered. In daylight Lou would have recognised the huge, continuous cloud mass ahead rather than what he thought were isolated storms and avoided the cyclone. However the gooney-bird flew right into the swirling, hostile sky and was immediately enveloped by cloud. Then the turbulence intensified in earnest.

Being shaken by high winds, while uncomfortable, wasn't fatal as the gooney-bird was a solid plane built to ride out storms. The sound from torrents of rain lashing the windscreen was deafening, and other problems began to affect the flight. Holding the compass heading was difficult enough as the plane was buffeted from all sides, but the swirling winds posed another risk. The plane was pushed off its planned track by an eighty knot easterly gale. Lou had tuned into Port Moresby's radio beacon so a needle on one of the gauges pointed directly to the station, guiding them along the correct flight-path. The hitch with that technology was that it responded badly to electrical storms. Lightning flashed constantly from all quarters and the needle spun randomly lured by huge voltage spikes, making it useless. So as the gooney-bird lurched around Lou struggled with the controls and hoped he wasn't blown too far awry. There wasn't sufficient fuel left in the tanks to turn back, so they had no choice but to press on into the storm.

The danger of being off course when they reached New Guinea was that mountain peaks reared almost from the shore-line and they risked flying into them. But that wasn't the greatest threat right now. Ice started coating the wings and tail. The extra weight slowed the plane as did the drag caused by ice interfering with the smooth airflow over the wings. Lou activated the carburettor heat so the engines wouldn't freeze up and cut out.

'Switch that on,' he yelled pointing to a lever beside Danny's seat.

Danny moved the selector which opened a valve that channelled hot air surrounding the engines into rubber tubes called *boots* along the front edge of the wings. The air pressure expanded the rubber, heated the wings and in turn shed any ice. The plane began to vibrate as ice built up on the propellers, but similar rubber strips filled with anti-freeze were fitted to the blades' leading edges. Lou switched on the system that pumped out anti-freeze and dislodged the ice. Suddenly Danny heard a number of crashes against the fuselage.

'Ruddy hell, Lou!'

'It's okay,' Lou replied. 'It's just the ice breaking off the props and bashing into the side. We'll have to descend though. Ice won't stick to the wings and props where the temperature's warmer.'

Lou hadn't tested the de-icing system for some time and failed to notice that only one wing was operating correctly. Routine maintenance would have picked up the fault, but routine maintenance wasn't one of Lou's strong points. If Danny'd had time to consider the point, it might have puzzled him that, considering Lou flew the plane, he was singularly blasé concerning the safer points of aviation. But there were plenty of gung-ho pilots worldwide who thought they're indestructible. The valve on the port wing had frozen shut, preventing any warm air entering the wing's leading edge on that side. At that moment the ice build-up on the starboard side broke off and was whipped away into the slipstream. Now the ice-covered wing was dangerously heavy, forcing the plane to roll left with Lou straining to regain control. To make matters worse, as the plane lurched onto its side, Sid's lack of care took its toll. The cargo tumbled from under the tie-down straps and clattered to the side, destabilising the gooney-bird even further. The large, heavy containers that Sid hadn't bothered to secure at all, slid forward and to the port side. Like the cargo, Sid was tossed around the fuselage and ended up among crates, boxes and sacks in the corner just behind the cockpit.

The plane's C-of-G was now hopelessly out of balance and it almost rolled onto its back before plunging into a spiral dive. While Lou frantically wrestled with the controls, the flight instruments went berserk. The altimeter spun wildly and the airspeed built up far beyond the plane's maximum design limit. The gooney-bird rattled so violently Danny thought it would shake apart and the sound of the slipstream screamed in his ears.

'Give us a hand…' Lou yelled above the howling gale.

Danny grabbed the control column and heaved back with all his strength, but with no success. Anything they did only seemed to steepen their ballistic descent.

The altimeter flashed through 10000 feet…

9000 feet...

'Do something, Lou..!'

8000 feet…

'I am, bugger it…'

7000 feet…

'It's not working…'

6000 feet…

'Shut up, Danny…Just pull the stick back…'

5000 feet…

'It's still not working…'

4000 feet...

'Bloody hell…'

3000 feet...

'Shit..!'

When the gauge spun passed 2000 feet the outside air had warmed sufficiently for the ice on the port wing to melt. It probably would have melted around 7000, but the gooney-bird shot through that altitude so quickly the ice didn't break away until they'd nearly dropped to sea level. The plane suddenly responded to the controls and Lou yanked the wings level, but the speed was 100kts above the plane's structural limit. Trying to counter the force on the ailerons and elevators was like paddling in cement.

At last the plane slowly responded just as they broke clear of cloud only feet above the waves. Lou closed the throttles and the airspeed needle zipped back around its gauge. They might just have made it too, but at that moment the plane burst from the swirling maelstrom of cloud and rain into the dead calm of the cyclone's eye. Affected by a sudden eighty knot wind shear, the airspeed dropped to below the stall before Lou could react and the plane slapped onto the water surface. It was like hitting solid rock. There was hardly a ripple as the gooney-bird bounced once before splashing down again with bone-jarring force. This time a ton of spray and a heaving bow-wave surged ahead of the stricken plane. Lou gunned the throttles, but the propellers had ripped away on the first impact. One shattered blade sliced through the upper fuselage just behind the cockpit before streaking away somewhere into the ocean. Another foot lower and it would have taken Danny and Lou's heads with it. Above the screech of torn metal the engines screamed in their death throes before seizing altogether. The plane slithered to a halt with only the air in its wings keeping it afloat.

Lou and Danny sat rigid in their seats in total, numbed silence. The wind was calm and the engines still. Only a faint lapping of sea-water could be heard. At least morning had dawned long enough for them to see what they were doing.

'Bleeding hell, someone give us a hand!' Sid's muffled voice cried from somewhere in the fuselage.

It was enough to galvanise Lou and Danny into action. Danny tried to climb from his seat and tugged against the shoulder harness before remembering to undo his seat-belt and clamber out. The cargo was just wreckage. Smashed bottles, cases shredded to splinters and cigarettes strewn like confetti littered the entire plane. Sid was pinned behind one of the large crates that had skidded across the fuselage floor during the crash. Lou and Danny tried to heave it away from Sid, but they couldn't seem to manage it. Every time they tried to gain some leverage, they slipped in the slick oil-water mix that now slopped over the floor. The engines had jarred so savagely during the crash they'd ripped cracks into the wings and punctured the fuel tanks. Aviation gasoline was leaking out and water was leaking in. There were cracks in the hull where seawater seeped in as well.

'We're ruddy-well sinking,' Lou said and raced to open the cargo door. 'Danny, grab the life raft!'

'What about Sid?'

'Yeah, what about me?'

Lou stared at Sid, although all he could see was one flailing arm. He looked uncertain for a second, but he'd made his decision.

'Get the raft first...and the life-jackets,' Lou ordered, glaring at Danny.

Lou wedged the cargo entrance open revealing the door-sill was just above the water line. In seconds sea began pouring in and the plane's floor was instantly awash. The life raft was one of the few things properly stowed aboard the gooney-bird and was easy to find in the dimness. Danny released its straps and dragged it to the door. He raced back and found the life jackets amid the general flotsam, now floating in ankle deep water. He only found them because they were yellow. He put one on and buttoned the front then handed another to Lou who did the same. Meanwhile Lou had tethered the raft to the fuselage with a lanyard to prevent the pack drifting away.

Then they turned their attention to Sid. Danny reached over the crate and handed him the last life-jacket even though Sid wasn't in a position to put it on right then. They wrestled with the crate that proved just as intractable as before and water now lapped past their knees.

'It's no good,' Lou gasped. 'We can't budge the bugger. Danny, we've gotta go. She'll sink any second now.'

'Don't leave me!' Sid begged.

'Sorry, mate,' Lou replied. 'We can't lift the ruddy crate.'

'We can't leave him,' Danny said, pushing the crate as hard as he could, but it made no difference.

'There's nothing we can do. If we stay here, we'll *all* drown.'

Lou waded to the door as Sid screamed hysterically, but Lou simply unlatched the lanyard and yanked the cord to release compressed air from a gas cylinder in the pack. The raft swelled to life and bobbed on the ocean surface.

'Come on Danny!' he yelled.

Now waist-deep in water Danny could see no hope for Sid. Jammed as he was, water was almost to his nose and he wailed in despair. Just then the plane lurched as more water flooded in changing the C-of-G. Her nose started to drop below the surface. The crate that trapped Sid now floated inches above the fuselage floor and drifted a little way from the wall.

'Grab my hand!' Danny yelled, spitting out a mouthful of seawater.

He hauled Sid free and they swam to the door, now almost completely swamped with only a thin sliver of light visible at its top. Lou's hand reached through the opening from outside. He grasped Sid's arm and heaved him upwards. Unfortunately Sid's head cracked against the door's edge and Lou lost hold. Danny pushed Sid forward and Lou grabbed him again.

'Duck your head, you bloody idiot,' Lou shouted.

Sid was dazed, but understood. He bobbed below the water allowing Lou to drag him clear just as the gooney-bird gasped its last, tortured groan of escaping air, fuel, disintegrating components and shredded equipment. It sank to its watery grave with Danny trapped inside.

The fuselage tipped forward and, like a diving whale, started its long, dark plunge to the ocean floor. The plane was now vertical with Danny up to his neck in water at the tail section with only a small air pocket to breathe. He tried to dive for the door that was submerged below him, but the cargo floated to the surface and blocked his way. It was impossible to struggle through the jammed wreckage that acted as a total barricade. Danny panicked. He frantically battered the fuselage knowing it was useless.

No, not drowning. I don't want to die this way. No, please!

As the plane sank the wedged cargo was forced further and further into the fuselage walls while ocean pressure squeezed the hull from outside causing immense stress. The tail structure was notoriously the weakest part of any plane and the gooney-bird's fin and rudder had been seriously damaged during the crash. The strain took its final toll. Initially as small cracks, but seconds later the entire aft-fuselage broke away taking Danny with it. The tail then tumbled downwards flinging Danny clear. It was pitch black and he was totally disorientated. Nevertheless he managed to grab the inflation toggle on his life-jacket and pulled. The jacket collar bloated with air and Danny shot upwards, but it was so far to go.

Danny's lungs were bursting and he still hadn't reached the surface. He grew faint and started to exhale from pure exhaustion. It saved his life in the end. Had he held his breath to the surface his lungs would have expanded and probably ruptured as sea pressure reduced. It was a close run thing and he gasped out his last scrap of air as he burst from the sea. He sucked for breath that would have been sea water only a second earlier. His life jacket held him afloat while he panted for air. The ocean was no longer calm as the storm had caught up with him. Waves splattered over his head and rain lashed his face. It took a while for him to recover his wits and take a look around. The storm had darkened the sky and waves blocked his vision, but one thing was for sure.

There was no sign of Sid, Lou or the life-raft.

Part Two – Beyond the Coral Sea

The storm raged all day and there was nothing for Danny to do but ride it out. Once he'd established the direction of the ocean swells he turned his back to them, avoiding continual mouthfuls of brine. He simply floated with the waves. The only disadvantage was occasionally an extra large wave broke over his head, but other than a few doses of salt water, he coped pretty well all things considered. The sea was about the same temperature as the surrounding air so hypothermia wasn't an immediate problem and rain squalls at least provided Danny with drinking water.

Jack Collier had explained that tropical lows were unpredictable at best and this one was no exception. Some brew for days and hang around even longer. Sometimes they re-intensified just when you thought the worst was past. The one Danny was trapped in had formed in hours and died just as quickly. As the day wore into evening the wind dropped and the sea calmed to a smooth, regular wave motion. By late afternoon conditions had eased to the point where Danny found himself bored to sobs as time idled along. Fortunately the sky remained overcast, shielding him from the sun. As night fell he knew there was no hope of anyone spotting him in the dark. He was resigned to another ten hours in the ocean and even then there was no guarantee a ship was going to cruise by. He had to face the fact that most vessels would probably have stayed clear of the storm or been wrecked by it. The sheer emptiness was pretty scary and disheartening, but as darkness closed around him things grew plain spooky. The worst feeling was the absolute isolation and utter loneliness.

Sooner or later there is no way anyone cast adrift in tropical waters isn't going to start thinking about what is swimming around with them. Poisonous jellyfish, sting rays, giant squid, sea snakes, killer whales and most of all – sharks! Everyone knew the Pacific Ocean was swarming with them. Just before the end of the war, an American cruiser, the *USS Indianapolis,* was torpedoed and sunk by Japanese submarines in the Philippines Sea. It was headline news and, along with the rest of the world, Danny had read all about the tragedy. Around a quarter of the *Indianapolis'* 1200 crew members perished in the explosion, while the rest jumped overboard and spent five days in the ocean. By the time the survivors were finally rescued nearly 600 more seamen had died from exposure, sunburn, dehydration, hunger, salt water madness and mostly – shark attacks. They'd been the world's unluckiest 900 men because the Japanese surrendered two weeks later. The heartbreaking irony was that *USS Indianapolis* had shipped a secret cargo from San Francisco to Guam before she was torpedoed. She carried components for the atomic bomb that the *Enola Gay* would drop over Hiroshima the following week. *USS Indianapolis* had also survived a kamikaze hit in the battle for Okinawa and her crew thought they were at last on a cushy assignment in safe waters.

So with vivid images of panic-stricken sailors growing in his mind Danny faced encroaching darkness as a castaway, alone in the Coral Sea. The night was pitch black and totally silent apart for waves lapping against his neck. But after an hour or so the clouds peeled away revealing a starlit heaven that seemed so close Danny thought he'd be able to reach up and touch the galaxies. Later a half moon rose in the east. Its D-shape indicating it was in its declining phase, but still cast a reassuring iridescent beam across the sea surface. Danny judged the time to be midnight. Jack had explained a full moon rose at dusk and about an hour later each night after that as it waned.

Danny felt reassured by the moonlight and relaxed a little. He raised his legs and pointed his toes out of the water. He floated more comfortably in a lying position and his head stayed higher above water. By this time he was thirsty, hungry and, above all, exhausted. He fell asleep.

He awoke at dawn and he was cold…so cold he shivered uncontrollably. With only his clothes for insulation, the sea had finally lowered his body's core-temperature. The chill was mind-numbing, but before he could fully come to his senses something thumped into his back and pitched him face down into the sea. He jerked back upright and spluttered a mouthful of salt water before being nudged again. A shadowy object brushed past him

What the..?...Shark!

Danny swung his fist and thumped into something solid sending agony spasms up his arm.

God, that's hard. Are sharks that solid?

Then Danny looked up and saw a shadowy silhouette that was far too high to be a shark fin. Many coconut palms had been uprooted in the storm, blown into the ocean and swept out to sea. Danny had drifted into one of them. He dragged himself onto the trunk and draped his arms and legs around it. That didn't entirely lift him free of the water, but he was now exposed enough for the morning sun to dry him off and warm him up. Although his feet and arms still dangled under water, he felt greatly encouraged now he was floating on top of the sea and not in it. Unfortunately, although some fronds remained there was very little shade and the very sun that was saving him from hypothermia grew blisteringly hot. Gradually he became very parched indeed. As moisture evaporated from his clothes and skin, he was caked with a salty residue with a taste that only made him thirstier. Considering the trauma the palm tree had suffered it still bore several coconuts filled with life-giving, thirst-quenching milk. Unfortunately Danny had no way of opening the husks.

The heat soon became unbearable so Danny often dropped into the water and swam around for a while. It cooled him off nicely, although clambering back onto his raft was sapping his strength. He knew he'd soon be burnt to a crisp so he unbuttoned his life-jacket, pressed the air release valve to deflate the floatation chambers. He could always blow the jacket up again if the palm sank. Placing the jacket over his head wasn't ideal, but offered some shady relief. As the day wore on he felt an urgent desire to gulp down sea water and only resisted the urge with images of going crazy just as a rescue boat arrived. By mid-afternoon his craving became almost unbearable and his resistance was just about up. Danny grew delirious, hallucinating about shady trees and a beverage he'd only tasted once or twice, but thought it the finest drink in the world – ice-cold *Coca Cola*.

And that was when the first dorsal fin appeared. A black triangle sliced through the water surface about a hundred yards away. Occasionally a smaller tail fin broke the surface. The shark wasn't too eager to close in, but happy to keep its distance as it sized up the situation. Initially it didn't seem so menacing, just curious and really very graceful. It wasn't even particularly big, maybe the size of a man. After a while it was joined by another shark and then a third, much larger one. These creatures now attracted more and before long a dozen sharks were prowling around Danny's palm tree. As they circled they inched closer and every now and again one would slip towards Danny before darting back into the pack. At first they cruised with a fluid slickness, but grew alarmingly agitated.

One shark glided within feet of Danny and he only drove it away by clouting it with his life-jacket. The problem with that was the splashes attracted the other sharks and they closed in. The life-jacket deterred them, but it was only a matter of time before Danny tired or a shark sneaked up unnoticed. As the largest shark rolled away it bared rows of savage teeth just waiting to rip Danny to shreds.

So this is it...shark bait. I wonder if it'll hurt. Of course it'll ruddy well hurt! Look at those flaming great teeth! Bugger off, you bastards.

Suddenly the sharks went into frenzy and swirled around the palm, churning up the water surface. But they didn't attack and formed a pattern that moved away rather than towards Danny. He knew he was going mad when he heard a rhythmic drumming and chanting accompanied by a rattling noise in the background. The cacophony grew louder by the minute.

Three outrigger canoes approached across the water. Each one was manned by three Papuan natives. Two men paddled the canoes while the third crouched in the bow, armed with a spear, machete and a club. The natives had painted their faces with white, yellow-ochre and red dye and the spear bearers wore feathered head dresses that seemed unnecessarily ornate for a fishing trip. That is, if they were on a fishing trip. Everyone knew, even in modern times, there were cannibals and head-hunters around New Guinea and the surrounding archipelagos.

Just my luck – if the sharks don't get me the head-hunters will.

Initially the canoeists ignored Danny or hadn't spotted him. Their attention was focused on the sharks. The leading native on each boat splashed the water with a coconut shell rattle while the entire group chanted and paddled into the centre of the pack. Danny peeked between the fronds, trying to be as inconspicuous as possible. One man (it looked like the smallest to Danny) from each boat leapt into the sea, but stayed close to their canoes. The sharks were drawn to the rattles and disturbed water, but were cautious at first. Finally their curiosity overcame them and they swam right up to the canoes nudging the dugout hulls while the swimmers clambered back on board in a hurry. It appeared their job as human bait had succeeded. The Papuans who splashed the rattles had nerves of steel as their hands were now only inches from the sharks' jaws.

Why would anyone want to attract sharks?

Sharks were now circling all three boats at a frenetic pace. They swirled and shoved each other and even breached the surface. The natives remained unfazed and continued chanting almost as if they were entranced. While still splashing his rattle, one of the boat leaders drew a wooden board with a vine noose and line attached to it. As a particularly curious shark brushed the edge of his canoe, the native looped the noose around the sharks head and pulled the line tight. The shark was caught as the twine dug into its gills. The board acted as a float so the animal couldn't submerge and the line was securely tied to the canoe preventing the shark from swimming away. It thrashed so violently it looked as if the canoe would capsize. Indeed if it hadn't been for the stabilising outrigger that would have been the case and all the occupants would have been pitched into the sea.

The shark-catcher drew a massive club from the canoe hull and stilled the shark with several thumps to its head. Unfortunately this drew a great deal of blood and the three canoeists had to quickly manhandle the carcass aboard. Even so one of the frenzied sharks rushed in and took a lump out of the dead beast's tail. That was a mistake because the shark-catcher lassoed it as well and it also ended up being dragged aboard. The other boat crews were now also trying to snare sharks, but the leading crew seemed the most proficient. After an hour they had landed three sharks while the other boats had one each. Once the dead sharks were on board the canoes and the blood dissipated through the water, the other sharks appeared to sense the danger and swam away.

Shark catching was a risky and physically taxing business in stifling heat and the natives were exhausted. They slumped back into their canoes, sliced the tops of some coconuts with their machetes and shared the milk. They seemed pretty pleased with themselves and chattered away, but after a short rest it looked as if they were ready to head for shore. Danny wasn't quite sure how he felt about that. He had no idea who the natives were or how they were disposed to castaways. Everything he'd read wasn't too promising on that score, but on the other hand, he'd never reach dry land without their help. One thing was certain he couldn't last much longer out here. His thirst was raging and he'd soon be sunburnt to a crisp.

There was only one thing for it. He raised his hand and waved his life-jacket above his head.

'Help!'

He had to admit that sounded pitifully inadequate, but the natives turned and became very excited indeed. They all babbled at once, pointing rather unnecessarily at the palm. As the three canoes approached the natives became more agitated and, to Danny's dismay, brandished their clubs, machetes and spears. The outriggers circled Danny's floating palm and their occupants were far more menacing than any old pack of sharks. At close quarters the natives were fearsomely imposing. Not only did each man wear what Danny interpreted as war-paint, but they were all tattooed with swirling designs over their faces and their bodies. Most sported some sort of object made of bone, wooden shard or shell through their noses and ears. They were naked except for long, protruding cones that covered their penises.

'It's okay, I don't mean any harm,' Danny stammered, but of course they couldn't understand a word he was saying. They continued to challenge him with spears, but were loath to venture too close until they knew exactly what they were dealing with. Danny knew perfectly well that they were up against a single teenager with no warlike intentions whatsoever. He wondered what a peace sign might be. In all the western movies he'd seen the hero raised his right hand and said *how*, so he tried that, but it didn't seemed to make any impact. He tried smiling, but that turned out more like a nervous grimace. Maybe a gift would help, you always gave natives a bauble or two, but what did he have? The only thing at hand was his life jacket. Being yellow and judging by their war-paint, it was a colour the natives favoured.

He put the inflation tube to his lips and blew up the jacket. That intrigued the natives and caused more gestures and verbal consternation. When he'd finished Danny placed the life-jacket in the water and pushed it towards the closest dug-out. This was not without its risks. Danny was well aware that the palm tree might become waterlogged and wouldn't float indefinitely. Straddling the trunk was fine in calm water, but altogether trickier should larger waves build up. It was possible the natives would simply take the jacket and paddle away.

The tribesmen were delighted with the gift and again all chattered at once. The spearman of the leading boat fished the jacket aboard and waved it aloft. He then dropped it into the water and tried to push it under. There were shrieks of laughter from his colleagues as the jacket kept bobbing to the surface. He compared it with their wooded boards and had already decided it was an altogether superior float to use on their next shark-hunting expedition. Any hostile tendencies they harboured vanished. They all grinned and looked pretty happy about the present. Danny took that as a good sign.

Finally the canoe with the smallest shark on board drew alongside Danny's drifting palm. The natives beckoned to Danny, indicating he should climb aboard behind the paddlers. As he was out of options, Danny carefully stepped across to the outrigger. The natives seemed friendly enough although they smelt a bit organic, but Danny didn't hesitate when one of them offered him a coconut shell. He gulped the milk in seconds and thought nothing had ever tasted so good – even an ice-cold *Coca Cola*.

Without any further delay the natives turned their canoes for shore and paddled home.

They made good time to shore, especially when the third man in each outrigger took up a paddle and helped out. Danny had nothing else to do other than admire the scenery around him. The water was a deep, royal blue, even indigo at its depths then morphing to dazzling turquoise as the canoes cruised over coral reefs. He glimpsed flashes of rainbow colours from thousands of fish dancing beneath him. They passed one final reef where the water became a little cloudy. Danny had no way of knowing, but they were approaching the Fly River estuary. This was a labyrinth of channels adjacent to mangrove swamps and small palm-shaded beaches where groups of naked children played in the shallows. Danny smiled, thinking how wonderful it must be to grow up here

– no school, no monsignors, no union thugs, and no cares – just fun in the sun.

They paddled on until they reached a larger cove where a dozen huts had been built on stilts surrounding a larger, communal long house. A fresh water stream flowed through the village centre and opened into the brackish, tidal main river. Smoke drifted aloft from cooking fires and women were busy about their tasks. They were all nude except for the barest loin cloths and masses of shell jewellery. Most were tattooed and some nursed infants, but one was suckling a piglet. Danny wasn't sure how he felt about that. Children were everywhere along with small pigs and chickens. Racks of fish and meat strips hung drying in the sun and under each hut baskets of sweet potatoes, bananas and coconuts lay in the shade, guarded by youngsters to make sure village livestock stayed clear. Several men were re-thatching the long house roof, but there was no other sign of cyclone damage.

Blimey, it looks like a Johnny Weissmuller movie.

Everyone downed tools and dashed to the beach as the canoes paddled up. There was great excitement over the sharks that would feed the villagers for some time, but even more interest in the white boy who'd come along with that good fortune. They swarmed around Danny which was daunting at first, but they appeared curious and cautious rather than menacing. No one seemed to know what to do next. There was an intense babble as everyone talked at once. Several bolder souls felt the need to touch

Danny to see if he was indeed flesh and blood. He started at first and that caused a chorus of laughter so he simply grinned back.

The focus was taken from Danny when the leading canoe-man shouted gruff instructions to a group of young women who immediately heaved the sharks from the outriggers and began carving them up by the shoreline. Obviously the order-giver was a man of some importance around the village. He wasn't the head man though, because three elders emerged from the long house and climbed down the ladder. They were tattooed from head to foot and wore magnificent head-dresses decorated with coloured beads, gemstones and bird-of-paradise feathers. Each man was practically weighed down with necklaces, bangles and earrings made with shells, beads, and small animal skulls. Danny wondered whether they wore so many ornaments all the time or just on special occasions, like meeting a castaway white boy. One sported a carved cassowary bone through his nostrils while the other two had managed to attach large discs to their noses and ears. To Danny it seemed a painful process just to look weird, but guessed the idea was to appear warlike. He had to admit they did look pretty scary. More formidable still were the canes they carried festooned with more colourful feathers, shark's teeth and what looked suspiciously like wrinkled human heads. They had been shrunk to a size little bigger than a fist and attached to the poles by the victim's hair.

The three chieftains edged close to Danny and started scrutinising his every detail along with the occasional prod with their canes. Danny was starting to wonder whether he was being examined for his suitability for the dinner menu and sincerely hoped they'd prefer shark meat. One chief glared unnervingly into Danny's eyes.

'Hello,' Danny said as calmly as he could and hoped he wouldn't stutter. 'My name is Danny. Pleased to meet you...'

It was the chief's turn to jump back and looked startled.

'Dispela wait manki, em nat toktok pisin. Wanem toktok?' The chief demanded, at least Danny thought his tone indicated he was demanding something. He couldn't understand what the chief said, but it seemed strangely familiar. A deal of discussion followed until the leading shark-hunters said *'Em spik ol waitman.'*

Once again a debate ensued until it seemed the headmen were satisfied. They turned around and climbed back into the longhouse. The other men appeared to lose interest in the proceedings and turned their attention elsewhere leaving their women to finish butchering the sharks. Most of the children still clustered around Danny, who they'd determined wasn't dangerous. Danny felt a bit of a goose just standing in the village centre with no idea what to do. He understood primitive people often had customs and taboos they felt very touchy about and he didn't want to upset anyone unintentionally – or intentionally for that matter. About then he noticed dozens of human skulls hanging in skeins like bundles of French onions and knew he'd have to be on his best behaviour – whatever that was in Papuan terms.

Shortly the woman who'd been nursing the piglet approached and started talking to half a dozen teenage girls. After more chatter accompanied by a lot of giggling two of the girls who Danny estimated were about his age approached shyly and held out their hands. Danny was perplexed and shrugged with his palms up as he had no idea what they wanted. It turned out to be the right response and the girls held each of his hands and led him towards one of the huts. There was plenty of room between the hut stilts and the shade was an enormous relief. The girls unrolled a palm mat and indicated Danny should sit on it. Once they determined he was comfortable they brought him a meal of sweet potato, dried fish, bananas, a rather bland sago gruel and coconut milk.

Danny hadn't eaten for two days and after all the excitement realised he was starving. He didn't care that the sweet potato needed salt, he wolfed it down. The gruel was a little more unappetising, but okay when he mixed in some coconut milk. In any event he was hungry enough to eat almost anything. The girls were getting pretty friendly too and didn't seem the least bit embarrassed about stroking his arms and any other bits they could reach. Remembering the trouble he'd got into with Noemi, Danny thought it best to play coy. He had no idea of local customs and a village full of irate tribesman armed with war-clubs, spears, machetes, bows, arrows and goodness-knows-what-else would be far dodgier than Giovanni Ricci. Eventually he decided their intentions were therapeutic rather than carnal and, after he'd eaten, he lay face-down on the mat while they massaged his back.

In any event he was exhausted. Although he'd slept the previous night, it was a short and unrewarding rest as the ocean's coldness had sapped his energy. Despite his fitness, he was both physically and mentally spent. Now with a full belly and lying in a comfortable, warm spot, not to mention a brace of lovely masseuses, all he wanted was sleep. In minutes that's exactly what happened. He lapsed into oblivion, without dreaming or any other distractions. Darkness was approaching anyway and he slept throughout the night.

*

He woke at dawn feeling totally refreshed and ready to take on whatever fate was going to throw at him. The girls had covered him with a blanket woven from palm fronds and now lay asleep beside him. It appeared they'd been posted there to look after him day and night. Danny was wondering what to do next when a native man strode towards him. Although he was as black as the villagers he wasn't a native. His features were quite different. He was in his mid-twenties maybe and dressed in a white t-shirt and denim jeans cut into shorts. He wore a Stetson hat just like the cowboys in western movies. He was barefoot, but had a pair of boots draped over his shoulder tied by their laces with his socks stuffed into them. His belt was made of military-style webbing with a leather holster containing a US Army 1911 model Colt 45 automatic pistol. He also had a canvas pack strapped to his back.

'Howdy,' the man said.

Howdy? He's gotta be kidding.

'Howdy yourself,' Danny replied uncertainly.

'Pleased to meet ya pal, the name's Mad Monty,' the stranger said, extending his hand. He spoke in a drawly sort of American way.

'G'day, Danny McAlister. *Mad* Monty..?'

'Yeah buddy, more like a state of mind than a name actually. Got it when I was in the military during the war. Army Air Corps, they were good at making up nick-names. Y'all an R-C, right?'

'Not really, but I got shoved into a Catholic school. It was crap.'

'No. *Are-See.*'

Danny was wondering what religion had to with anything before the penny dropped.

'Oh, you mean Aussie.'

'Yeah man, that's what I said. You ain't simple or nothin', are ya?'

'Sorry, language barrier I guess. What are you doing here anyway?'

'I came to check on y'all. I'm a bush pilot, got my *Goose* stashed in a creek up-river. I parked her there for shelter until the storm passed. Turned out it only brushed by us here with no damage done. Some of the local lads fetched me to talk to you, magic boy.'

'Magic boy?'

'Oh yeah, man, are they pleased to see you.'

'Why?'

'You brought the sharks back. They say you have *shark spirit*.'

'Why would anyone want sharks back, and where did they go in the first place?'

'One shark's gonna feed a lotta folk and I hear they caught a whole parcel of 'em.'

'Five.'

'That'll keep this lot going for a while, so you're *Mr Popularity* right now.'

'They didn't need my help to catch them. I didn't do anything.'

'What y'all gotta understand is these guys are living in the Stone Age. They're superstitious as hell. Their shark hunters ain't had a peck o' luck for months and then, hey presto, you pop up and they bag five. You're one lucky omen I reckon, pal.'

'But why did the sharks disappear?'

'No mystery there Danny Boy, there's a whole mess of estuarine crocs hereabouts. That is there *were* until I flew in a team of hunters six months ago. They culled 'em out pretty good to make shoes and bags for fancy folk back state-side. Stands to reason, the crocs ate all the fish so the sharks looked elsewhere. With the crocs gone the sharks have gotten their feeding ground back. Simple really, but the locals don't understand that. They think it's all down to you.'

'What? Do they think I grew out of a floating palm tree?'

'Something like that. Fell from the sky, swam out of the ocean maybe. So how exactly did you come to be floating around?'

'Fell from the sky is about right. On a flight from Townsville our plane ditched in the cyclone.'

'*Our* plane?'

'Yeah, there was the pilot and crewman. They escaped in a dingy. Blimey, they're probably still out there. I've got to get to Port Moresby and tell someone to start searching.'

'Moresby's a couple hours flying from here, but I should be able to get 'em on the HF radio. I don't suppose you know the location where you went into the drink, do you?'

Danny shook his head.

'Don't worry. They'll be able to check the route from your flight plan.'

'Flight plan?'

'Yeah, you did file one when you left Australia, didn't ya?'

'I don't think so. I certainly didn't see our pilot do anything like that. All the buildings were closed when we left anyway.'

'Okay, what were the guys' names? We'll start from there.'

'Lou Brennan was the pilot and Sid Donovan his crewman.'

'Yeah, well that'd explain the lack of a flight plan.'

'You know them?'

'I've run into 'em a couple of times, can't say I'm surprised they crashed their plane. Look, let's grab breakfast and we'll jaw some more.'

'Well, actually…'

'Yeah, spit it out man.'

'I really need to take a bog.'

Mad Monty stared at him — another language barrier and Danny gave him a pained look.

'Oh, a dump!'

'Yeah and my mouth tastes like the bottom of a cocky's cage.'

'I'm not even gonna try and translate that one, but I take it you've got a bad dose of bum-breath. I can fix that.'

He fished a tube of toothpaste from his back-pack and handed it to Danny.

'Sorry I ain't got a spare brush. No drug-stores close by, so you'll have to make do with your finger. It'll freshen you up, but there ain't no out-houses round here, just jungle. C'mon I'll show you where.'

A crowd of chattering, beaming children had gathered around the hut and appeared to be once again intrigued by their village stranger.

'*Dispela, em laik long go monigtaim pekpek.*' Monty informed them.

Kids are scatological the world over, give them a fart or poo joke and they'll dissolve into peals of laughter, even if it's not particularly funny. The village children were no different, but unlike westerners who'd built artificial taboos around bodily functions. There were no such reservations here. They led Danny into the bush and indicated a spot and considerately left him to his privacy. The local protocol appeared to be: find a stick, dig a hole, cover it up afterwards, choose your leaf wisely and watch out for snakes, spiders, ants, giant beetles and anything else that would bite, sting or otherwise harm you.

Greatly relieved, Danny washed up in the creek and rinsed out his mouth with toothpaste and fresh, cool water. With his morning ablutions complete, he felt he could now tackle breakfast with the enthusiasm it deserved. He strolled back to the village surrounded by the noisy gambolling children who'd adopted him as their new friend. He couldn't understand a word they were saying, but that didn't seem to matter and only added to their amusement.

Mad Monty met him accompanied by a middle-aged white man. Standing between them was a golden-haired girl about Danny's age. She was a sublime beauty with a figure that filled out her spotless white dress nicely. Her legs were smooth, tanned perfection with dainty, sandalled feet. A silver crucifix hung from a chain around her neck. Danny thought she was simply the most beautiful person he'd seen in his entire life. She was indeed an angel.

Danny simply stared as the middle aged man extended his hand.

'Reverend Doctor Gordon Holyman,' he greeted rather formally. 'I'm pleased to make your acquaintance.'

Danny pulled himself together and dragged his eyes away from the girl. He took the reverend's hand and shook it firmly. Someone had told him you could tell a lot about a person by their handshake. If it was limp they were probably queer, a politician or someone wanting to make a commission by selling you something you don't need or want. The reverend's grip was fair-to-middling, but as Danny had a pretty poor opinion of clerics anyway, he was cool, suspicious and a little distant.

'And I'm Doctor Holyman's daughter, Angela,' the girl said, taking Danny hand. Her voice had that sultry bedroom quality English girls can put on when they want to.

'H…h…hello,' Danny finally managed pitifully.

'And you are..?' she insisted.

'Seems a bit simple, don't he?' Mad Monty said. 'Understandable really after a plane crash and a couple of days playin' shark-bait in the Coral Sea.'

'Goodness, how awful,' she seemed genuinely concerned. 'You must tell me all about it over breakfast, but first, please tell us who you are.'

'Danny…Danny McAlister,' he finally managed although it was still an effort.

Breakfast was eaten around an open fire. Danny was happy when Angela took his arm, led him to a spot on a large palm mat and sat beside him. Several village dignitaries, including the three chieftains and the canoe leader took their places and started chatting to Doctor Holyman, Mad Monty and each other.

'Damn, I wish I could understand what they're saying,' Danny said. 'It's almost like something I know but…'

'They're speaking Melanesian pidgin or *tok pisin* as they pronounce it. And please don't swear!'

'*Damn* isn't swearing,' Danny said defensively.

'Yes it is,' she replied primly. 'God will punish you for profanity and then you'll be sorry. So best stop now and pray for forgiveness.'

'I don't think God listens to me, not if my past experience with his representatives is anything to go on.'

'Dear, dear me, 'she said patting his arm. She seemed to like touching him, which he didn't mind. 'Daddy and I shall just have to change your mind, won't we?'

Breakfast was a fine affair. Angela produced a cook pot and, after some discussion, a woman who appeared to be one of the chieftain's wives supplied a basketful of eggs and tropical fruit. Angela filled the pot from the stream and placed it on the fire. Once the water was boiling she dropped half-a-dozen eggs into the pot.

'Call four minutes please, daddy,' Angela said and the reverend checked his watch.

As they dined on fresh boiled eggs and fruit, Danny discovered a little about his new acquaintances and why they happened to be in a remote Papuan village at the mouth of the Fly River.

It appeared Dr Holyman had found God while serving with the Royal Army Medical Corps in Northern France after the D-Day invasion. Danny was at a loss to understand how amputating shattered limbs and digging bullets from gunshot wounds would draw anyone spiritually, but hey, what did he know? After the war Gordon Holyman joined a Baptist Christian mission and he was soon posted to enlighten poor, ignorant New Guinea savages who'd managed quite well with the gods they had until then. Angela was fired with the same Christian spirit that compelled her father, but her mother preferred Chelsea and headed home after a steaming row only a couple of months after arriving in Port Moresby. So the good doctor and his devout, devoted daughter travelled around the highlands and remote village settlements. They helped medically where they could and attempted to replace the indigenous, ancient religious mythologies with another, more perplexing one. In all fairness they'd had some success and Dr Holyman put the villagers' health before their spiritual well-being. Angela however was unflinching in her missionary zeal.

'Yeah, but you gotta lot of help from the Cargo Cult crazies,' Monty said.

'Cargo Cult..?' Danny hadn't heard anything about that.

'Sure,' Monty explained, 'tribes throughout New Guinea and the Pacific Islands love all the western junk colonists have. You know, metal tools, electricity, planes, ships, automobiles, stuff like that. So they think if they believe in the same god, then all those civilised goodies will fall from the sky just for them. Watching planes air-drop supplies to troops during the war kinda reinforced that notion. Not all tribes have the same handle on how it works, but that's the general idea. Sort of God bribing converts.'

'We have to try to teach these people to love God for his mercy and goodness alone and not material gain,' Angela preached sincerely, massaging her crucifix. It was something she did often especially when she was hell-bent on a bout of muscular Christianity.

'Best of luck with that then,' Monty replied. 'After the big war these folk ain't seen a whole mess of *mercy and goodness.*'

Mad Monty's arrival in New Guinea was altogether more interesting. Monty wasn't even his real name, but a cut down of Montgomery, Alabama where he was born and raised.

'All a nigger boy had to do to get along was keep his head down, mouth shut, sit at the back of the bus and remember to give up his seat for white folks.'

Danny saw Angela looking uncomfortable.

'I didn't think you liked being called niggers,' he said.

'Nope, we just don't like *honkies* calling us niggers,' Monty smiled.

'I think you're all talk, Mr Montgomery,' Angela said. 'Why the American deep south is a very devout place by all accounts.'

'For a lot of 'em prayin's all they got, ma'am. But, I'll allow I purely love the music.'

Monty's childhood had not been particularly happy although he'd received a solid education at an all-black school. You either went to an all-black or all-white school in Montgomery. Trouble was brewing though. The Negro population was tired of sitting at the back of the bus and wanted equality, but white people were having none of it. Black teachers, students and anyone else who spoke up for justice were regularly beaten up by red-necks who felt it was their Christian duty to keep niggers firmly in their rightful place. Many city officials and police officers were ardent

Ku Klux Klan members so Negro bashing, even lynching and murders, failed to be investigated.

All that changed for Monty after Pearl Harbour. Just over fifty miles down the road from Montgomery lay Tuskegee Airfield where an all-black flying unit, the 99th 'Red Tails' Pursuit Squadron, was preparing for war. Monty hitch-hiked to Tuskegee and, because of his fitness and sound education in maths and physics was accepted as a cadet pilot. When he graduated he served in North Africa on P-40 Warhawk fighters. Later he was based in Italy flying P-51 Mustangs on bomber escort duty. The Mustang vied with Britain's Supermarine Spitfire for the title of 'Greatest WWII fighter plane'.

'Man we had a high old time,' Monty said. 'We even had a crack at them Kraut Me-262s in '45. Piston versus jet and we did okay too. Got the name *Mad* during some of them dogfights. I ain't braggin', but I was mighty good at shooting down Kraut planes, it sort of came natural to me.'

It was as if he regretted the war ending.

'I left the unit after the war. I loved flyin', but not the Army. Everything was windin' down and they still hated niggers. Y'know the danged gov'ment only de-segregated the military a couple years back. Hell, I'd had my taste of true freedom and I wasn't lettin' no Army take that away from me again. No way. My daddy was born in a swamp shack and his daddy was born a slave.'

However that same, racist army offered Monty his chance. After the war the Pacific was a logistical mess. Stores of weapons, ammunition, equipment and military hardware were stockpiled on islands from Guadalcanal to Okinawa. Uncle Sam wanted to get stuff back home as cheaply as possible or sell it to anyone interested. Much of it was shipped to China by General Claire Chennault's Civil Air Transport (CAT) to help Chiang Kai-shek's Nationalists repel Mao Tse-tung's Red advance. Chennault's Flying Tigers had seen hot action against the Japanese over the hump from Burma to China during the war. CAT's Curtiss-Wright C-46 transport planes were still receiving plenty of bullet holes, but from Communist gunfire now.

Quartermasters held fire-sales all over the Pacific. Their brief was to get rid of it or get it back to the States and then get rid of it. Army and marine units were reduced to a tenth of their wartime size. Every stateside-bound vessel was loaded to the gunwales with war surplus and they didn't take half of it. With discharge papers staring him in the face, Monty volunteered to ferry planes back home and, at least earn a few extra months pay. And at a remote strip in Bougainville he discovered the *Goose* stranded with no pilot to fly it home.

The marine gunnery-sergeant left in charge of the airfield claimed General Macarthur had used the plane as his personal air-taxi. That may well have been true, it was certainly well maintained. The last freighters were gone so the plane waited to be ferried. But, with a range of 600 miles and no hope of obtaining extra internal fuel tanks, there was no way it could make the leg from Hawaii to California. This left the option of hopping via US bases in the Philippines, Taiwan, Japan and the Aleutian Islands then down the west coast of Alaska. It all seemed very tedious, but Monty and the gunny got to talking over a bottle of Kentucky sour mash.

'There should be no trouble getting fuel, lieutenant,' the gunny said after sending signals to en-route bases checking for AVGAS availability. 'But what ya'll gonna do when you get back to the States? No offence, I'm a good ol' southern boy myself although I ain't got no axe to grind with Nigras, but I don't see much waitin' for ya back in Alabama.'

'None taken, because you're damned right. Maybe I'll take this bird as far as China and join up with Gen'rl Chennault's CAT outfit. I hear they're always looking for pilots.'

'Maybe I got a better idea.'

'I'm listenin'.'

'How much money you got comin' to ya, son?'

Monty noted that, while friendly enough, a white gunnery-sergeant still couldn't bring himself to call a black officer 'sir'. At least the gunny hadn't called him 'boy', so he let it slide. The war was over, he was nearly out of uniform and life was just too damned short anyway. After checking with his pay book and tallying up his back-wages, the gunny seemed satisfied.

'Tell ya what, lieutenant,' he declared with largess, 'I'll sell ya this here airplane for what ya got and throw in a full fuel load to boot. What d'ya say? There's plenty of call for a small freight plane around the islands.'

Monty was hooked immediately.

'Won't the Army have something to say about this? And how do I get the money to you?'

'Don't worry about that. I'll have the papers transferred to you all legal, signed and sealed and I'll fix it with the paymaster. The gov'ment'll get a few bucks for scrap and everyone's happy.'

'I hope you'll wangle a small gratuity for yourself,' Monty said finishing the whiskey.

'Naturally, it's the American way,' the sergeant drawled while fishing around for another bottle.

'What about my discharge? Technically I'm still an Army Air Corps officer. You won't get any money if I'm charged with AWOL.'

'No sweat, just leave it to me. I'll send your demob and service certificates over to Rabaul and you can pick 'em up next time you're passin' through.'

'You can fix that?'

'I'm a marine gunny, I can fix anything. That's what we do. Ya'll really think a buncha gen'rls run the Corps? No way, lieutenant.'

So Monty became the proud owner of a Grumman *Goose* in mint condition. He hadn't the faintest idea how to run a charter business or licence his aircraft, but after a lot of trial and error and a degree of good luck he found plenty of work. The BHP, Billiton and Rio Tinto mining giants had prospectors clambering all over New Guinea looking for oil, gold, copper and zinc and Monty had just the plane to ferry them around. They paid top dollar on time so Monty had funds to lease hangar space at Lae airport and hire a mechanic to keep his plane airworthy, thus satisfying Australia's Department of Civil Aviation. As flight was the only practical way of moving around New Guinea's mountains and swamps, Monty secured many other contracts as well. Some were with the local missions and that was precisely what he was doing carrying Dr Holyman and Angela, from one settlement to another where they could perform their good deeds.

Danny told Monty and Angela his story, although Dr Holyman was only half listening because he was engaged in an intense conversation with the village elders. When Danny said he was looking for his father who'd been fighting along the Kokoda Track, Monty beamed.

'Hell, no sweat, man,' he declared, 'you can hitch a ride with me in the *Goose*. There're dozens of war-time guys who never went home. There're scattered all over the north coast and islands. We can start asking around, someone'll know something. What d'ya say?'

Danny couldn't believe his luck.

'Don't forget we have to start a search for Lou and Sid.'

'Sure thing, kid. We'll let Moresby know and they'll get the RAAF out of Townsville right away.'

'You don't mind, do you ma'am?' he added, turning to Angela as her mission had chartered the plane.

'Please be our guest, Danny,' she said graciously, patting his hand once more.

It was then that Dr Holyman turned his attention from the chiefs.

'It may not be as easy as that,' he said quietly. 'I think we might have a hitch.'

Actually he could have a left out 'think' and 'might', because he knew perfectly well they had a hitch.

'These chaps want you to go fishing with them next time, Danny, and with the lot they caught yesterday that'll be about a week from now. We'll really have to be back on our rounds by tomorrow. The cyclone down time has already put us behind schedule.'

'I'll say sorry then, maybe next time,' Danny replied. 'I mean I'd like to go on a fishing trip, but I wouldn't be much use. I didn't do anything last time. It was their rattles and the blokes jumping in the water that attracted the sharks and I sure don't fancy trying to lasso one.'

'They don't quite see it that way, Danny,' Dr Holyman explained. 'They believe you brought the sharks back and they want you to stay. They're happy and friendly right now, but if we upset them there could be serious trouble and we don't want that. If you don't believe me, just take a look at those skulls hanging from the long-house. District commissioners send police patrols to keep law and order, but it's a hopeless task with so few men over these vast areas. There are still brutal clashes between tribes and plenty of deaths as well.'

'What can we do?'

Dr Holyman shrugged. He hadn't thought that far ahead.

'And of course we don't know how they'll react if they don't bag any sharks next time. A good-luck charm can turn into a bad omen pretty quickly around here.'

'I might have a plan,' Monty said with a wicked grin. 'First I gotta get some stuff from the *Goose*. We're gonna have a party tonight.'

'No, Mr Montgomery,' Angela wailed. 'I forbid it. You know our rules.'

'Special circumstances, ma'am. What d'ya say, Doc?'

'Maybe just this once, Monty, but I can't say I approve.'

'Okay, who's ready for a dandy sing-sing?'

Monty took a canoe upriver and Danny went along to help him. They were accompanied by four native paddlers to make sure everyone returned. The *Goose* lay moored in a protected creek about a mile away. There was nothing particularly handsome about the plane, but there was a rugged, business-like quality about it. The high-winged, stubby nosed craft sported two Wright radial engines mounted with their props almost abeam the cockpit.

'She's gotta be noisy,' Danny opined cautiously. 'A bit,' Monty conceded, 'but she's as tough as old boots, reliable and can go just about anywhere. And she's all mine. I just love the ol' gal.'

As the outrigger pulled alongside the *Goose*, Monty unlatched its side door. He clambered aboard and soon returned with a case of unmarked bottles filled with clear, slightly brown liquid. Danny looked at the bottles suspiciously.

'Are these what I think they are?' he asked.

'Absolutely,' Monty beamed, 'A-grade hooch, aged for at least two weeks. You don't think Lou and Sid are the only ones who dabble in a little contraband, do you?'

'And Angela has a bit of a downer on booze, I take it?'

'It's a Methodist, Baptist, Lutheran thing – whatever. I like a beer now and then, but this stuff is strictly currency.'

'The district commissioner would take a dim view if he caught you with this lot.'

'Maybe, but I've done the administration a favour or two so the patrol officers leave me alone. Jim Taylor up at Goroka is a pragmatic fellow. He scratches my back, I scratch his. We get along fine.'

'Is Angela always so formal, why doesn't she call you *Monty*?' Danny asked.

'Maybe it's her way of keeping the hired help in their proper place.'

'I see that's working well, then.'

It was pretty obvious what Monty was up to and from the looks of the native paddlers who eyed the crate expectantly, he'd found an easy mark. Monty was reluctant to crank up his long range HF radio because it drained the plane's battery unless the engines were running. So he transmitted on the *Goose*'s VHF band radio. Although Port Moresby was out of range, he was able to relay a distress message on Sid and Lou's behalf through a passing Ansett airliner bound for Cairns. He mentioned he'd found a teenage survivor, but lost contact with the plane before he could identify Danny.

'Doesn't matter,' Danny said. 'There's no one who really needs to know and we can always call back later. But, why don't we just take the *Goose* down river to the village, jump on board and bugger off?'

'Wouldn't work, I need to back-track up here for a straight take-off run. There's a bend in the river just past the village and by the time I get enough space to take off the water will most likely be full of canoes. Flying boats take ages to get airborne, it's all that drag from the hull. I really need to start from here, trust me.'

'Trust me', yeah right, where have I heard that before?

A night take-off was not an option as they risked hitting the jungle on the riverbank and no one in their right mind flew through the New Guinea highlands at night in the wet season. The mountains were littered with the wreckage of those who'd tried.

So they paddled back to the village with their contraband and unloaded it on the beach. Angela met them sullenly, revelling in a good old dose of low-church morality. Although Monty's plan was simple it required timing and that was not without its risks. If the Papuans started boozing too early no good would come of it as they'd also sober up too soon. But Monty was a showman at heart and knew how to work a crowd. Advertising was the answer. He put the word around that there was a great celebration that night in honour of the *shark-boy* so everyone had better get ready. This took attention away from the grog as the whole village surged into top-gear preparation for a party.

Everybody got out their finest clothes, painted their faces with intricate patterns, dressed in bird-of-paradise headgear and crocodile skin skirts. They adorned themselves with bling made from shells, animal bones, beads, coloured glass and polished stones. To supplement barbequed shark fillets, they slaughtered a pig and roasted it with vegetables wrapped in palm leaves over hot coals covered with sand. A couple of hours after sundown they were ready to party and Monty was happy to accommodate them. Again there were risks. The villagers' reaction to grog was variable at best, which probably didn't make them different from anyone else. But the plan worked and soon, much to Angela's disapproval and dismay, the whole village was roaring drunk and dancing for all they were worth. Towards midnight the pig was cooked and the oven uncovered, singeing quite a few fingers in the process. While the shark fillets were seared over the coals, the roasted meat was laid out on palm leaves and, without further formalities, everyone tucked in for a grand feast.

With their full bellies the bootleg liquor began to take its toll on the villagers. Fortunately there were no fights this time and around two in the morning nearly everyone had staggered back to their huts and fallen asleep. Many of the women and children set off along the beach and hunkered down for the night some distance away. They knew most of the men would wake up with miserable hang-overs and they didn't plan to be on the receiving end of any bad tempered back-handers in the morning.

Although he wisely hadn't touched a drop, Danny must have nodded off because the next thing he knew Monty was nudging him awake. Dr Holyman and Angela had packed up and carried their belongings in knapsacks. Apart from the occasional snoring reveller who'd crashed before he'd made it home, the village was deserted. The four fugitives crept past the long house and found a dug-out large enough for them and their gear. They stowed their packs and passed out paddles. After they all boarded, Monty shoved off and leapt onto the stern as they paddled upriver in the last of the moonlight.

'You were lucky, Mr Montgomery,' Angela hissed when she thought they were out of earshot. 'That could have been a disaster!'

'Nothing ventured, ma'am...' Monty grinned.

They reached the *Goose* as dawn's scarlet glow shimmered just above the tree line. The morning air was balmy and still but alive with the chirp of insects and awakening bird life. Danny wondered at the beauty of the jungle silhouette, but there was no time for sight-seeing. They loaded everything aboard and Monty cast the canoe adrift.

'It won't drift far,' he explained, 'and someone will find it pretty soon. Come and sit up front with me, Danny.'

Danny clambered uncertainly into the co-pilot's seat while Angela braced herself between the pilots' stations. Dr Holyman strapped himself into a passenger seat in the cabin. Angela's position wasn't particularly safe, but she liked to watch the take-offs and normally sat at the co-pilot's position. Monty knew better than to argue with her. Danny fastened his harness with some ambivalence, which was understandable considering his last aviation experience. His enthusiasm for air travel may have been dampened somewhat, but it was that or an uncertain fishing trip with a bunch of volatile, sore-headed natives. The engines roared into life and Monty water-taxied the *Goose* into the main stream. He turned the plane upriver as far as he could before they reached a sharp bend.

'This should be far enough,' he said, 'a nice long, straight take-off run.'

Monty rattled through a checklist and flicked switches that mainly turned red lights green as far as Danny could determine. He set the mixture and prop-pitch levers before revving both engines and checking each magneto in turn. He tapped a dial here and there and set the altimeter to read zero. Danny understood from Lou that daily changes in air pressure affected the altimeters, which had to be reset before every flight to give an accurate reading.

'All set back there?' Monty yelled into the cabin and got a thumb up from the good doctor in reply.

The plane spun on its floats and faced the take-off path, but the river wasn't clear. A line of out-riggers stretched from bank to bank. They would have been difficult to spot except one crew member in each canoe held a flaming torch to light their way.

'Ah, now that's going to be problem...' Monty sighed.

'What'll we do?' Danny asked. 'They're blocking the whole river. There isn't enough room to take off now, is there?'

Monty turned to Danny and grinned.

'Nope, there ain't, but those guys sure look mean and we can't let 'em eat you, now can we?'

'They're not cannibals,' Angela insisted.

'Can't take that risk,' Monty replied and pushed the throttles fully forward.

The *Goose* surged forward, ploughing up the glassy surface with its bow wave. They seemed to have travelled way too far before the airspeed needle flicked from zero and slowly moved around the gauge.

'Mr Montgomery...Stop! I demand you stop!' Angela screamed, clutching her crucifix, but Monty ignored her.

The *Goose* surged on and in seconds the canoes and their paddlers grew so distinctive Danny could make out details and he didn't like what he saw. The warriors were armed with axes, bows and clubs that they brandished in rage. Their heads were probably pounding after the night's carousing which didn't make their disposition any happier. A couple of arrows even came their way, but sliced into the river ahead of the charging *Goose*.

Monty pulled on the control column and, to Danny's dismay, nothing happened. He felt the fuselage lift slightly as the *Goose* started aquaplaning across the water surface, but still with insufficient pace to fly. There was no way they'd make it. The ASI needle still flickered below the green arc that showed the minimum take-off speed. The boats were now impossibly close. They were sturdy craft made from solid, hardwood trunks. Whatever damages the *Goose* might do to the canoes, its hull would be ripped apart for sure as soon as it hit any of them.

Then Monty hauled on the controls once more and started pumping the yoke back and forth. Just yards before the line of canoes the *Goose* leapt into the air, but only for a foot or two and then bounced back to the surface. Monty's timing was exquisite. As the plane hit the surface for the second time Monty heaved on the controls and the *Goose* soared over the canoes in its path. The plane's hull shot through the cordon only inches above the dugouts. Paddlers dived aside and hit the water just avoiding decapitation by the props.

The *Goose* may have been airborne, but didn't have the speed to stay there long. Not enough air rushed over the wings to produce sufficient pressure to keep the plane aloft. The *Goose* shuddered as the airflow broke away from the upper wing surface in turbulent eddies. The plane crashed back to the water with the engines still roaring at full power. The prop wash blasted several canoes pitching more warriors into the river while other furious natives screamed and tossed missiles after the *Goose*. Although no one had been seriously hurt, their pride was wounded as they bobbed in the water waiting for the other canoes to pick them up.

The *Goose* charged on and normally that would have been no problem as Monty simply had to accelerate to safe flying speed before taking off. But, in skipping over the surface like a flat pebble, the *Goose* had lost half her speed and the next river bend loomed ahead. Monty would never be able to control the plane and negotiate the turn at high speed. It was the same dilemma all over again – not enough distance to get airborne – stop or go?

'Go!' Monty yelled to no one in particular, pushing the throttles into the console firewall, hoping to get an extra inch of boost from the engines. To make matters worse the roaring engines unsettled a squadron of pelicans that flapped upwards in front of the careening seaplane. Hitting a bird the size of a pelican would be disastrous. The birds flashed past around the *Goose*, but miraculously they all missed the plane. At the last second Monty pulled the *Goose* skywards as the river curved away to the right. They sensed rather than heard the scraping sound as the *Goose's* hull brushed the jungle canopy. The airspeed needle hung precariously at the bottom edge of the green arc as Monty gently lowered the plane's nose and they skimmed only inches above the trees. More birds scattered from the tree tops and swarmed in panic. One smacked into the windscreen with the crack of a gunshot before bouncing away in a mess of crimson pulp and mulched feathers.

'Shit!' Monty muttered.

Angela screamed again while Danny was simply riveted to his seat.

But, other than a messy windscreen, it seemed that the *Goose* had survived unscathed as the plane slowly gained airspeed and finally climbed away. Monty drew the throttles back and reset the mixture and pitch levers for climb. The vibration settled to a comfortable purr and everyone breathed a sigh of relief – well, everyone except Angela who, despite her recent terror, was as cantankerous and judgemental as ever.

'Are you crazy, Mr Montgomery?' she wailed. 'You could have killed us all.'

'Yes ma'am, that's me. Crazy for sure, didn't get my name for nothin',' Monty grinned and she had no answer for that. He always agreed with everything she said and proceeded to do exactly as he pleased.

'I hope all take-offs aren't like that,' Danny ventured nervously. So far aviation was proving far more hazardous than he cared for.

'Around here they're mostly interesting, I'll say that,' Monty admitted.

Doctor Holyman poked his head into the cockpit to check everything was okay, but didn't seem particularly concerned about Monty's piloting technique. It must have felt awful, but as he couldn't see clearly through the windshield, it mightn't have looked too bad. However Dr Holyman was sanguine. In his opinion if he died suddenly he'd meet God sooner and if not, he'd make himself useful here on earth in the meantime.

'Daddy, Mr Montgomery tried to kill us,' Angela complained.

'I see he hasn't succeeded,' Doctor Holyman replied calmly. 'Next stop Goroka, I believe Monty?'

'Yessir – can't wait. Ain't had no coffee this morning. Can't fly worth a damn without coffee – it's one of them pilot rules, you know. And if you want coffee, ain't no better place than Goroka to get some. I hope Jim Taylor's home.'

Chapter 13 – Trouble in Paradise

Danny thought spectacular was a bit of a cliché. Everyone said this or that was *spectacular* when what they really meant was *nice*. The Gulf of Papua stretched away endlessly to the right disappearing into the Coral Sea. Dissipating maritime thunderstorms disgorged their last lightning bolts as they melted in the morning light to be replaced later by overland afternoon storms. As the *Goose* climbed above the Fly River delta and headed inland, the Eastern New Guinea Highlands reared up before them and the view was truly *spectacular*. Flying through mountain passes with peaks towering above the *Goose* was exhilarating if a little scary.

Mist patches still hung over some of the valley floors and rain showers shrouded many of the gorges to either side. Danny thought all the terrain looked bewilderingly alike and soon lost his bearings. Monty often referred to a topographical map clipped under the cockpit side window frame, but appeared completely at ease. They cruised over ridgelines from one breathtaking valley to another.

'You've gotta keep clear of rain patches,' Monty said. 'They may only look light, but you'll lose all visibility if you fly into them – and then splat – right into a mountainside.'

'That's comforting,' Danny replied. 'There seem to be a lot of showers around.'

'Yep, it's the nature of the beast. It's okay in the morning, but wait for the storms to brew up later on and then you're really working.'

Monty explained he always needed to see over at least two ridges ahead so he knew he had a clear valley to turn around in if the weather turned nasty. Danny asked what would happen if rain formed behind them and felt a little concerned when Monty suggested they'd just be having a bad day. Danny couldn't get over the jungle density, the steepness of the mountains and lack of any signs of tracks let alone roads, or human habitation.

'There are still huge unexplored areas and people who've probably never seen a white man,' Monty said. 'Jim Taylor's been policing, exploring and gold prospecting since way before the war and he reckons we'll never discover it all. There are hundreds of tribes all with their own dialects. These valleys are so isolated some people never leave the one they were born in. They still use bridges made from jungle vines.'

Radio messages crackled in Danny's earphones and he was able to determine a search was underway for Lou and Sid. Monty confirmed he had one survivor which pleased the RAAF Lincoln crew who were combing the Gulf of Papua. Danny gave them the gooney bird's departure time and approximate crash time so they could narrow the search area considerably.

As the morning progressed much of the cloud burnt off and the skies cleared. It was a common, calm prelude to the afternoon cumulonimbus build-up. They reached Goroka in a couple of hours of zigzagging through passes and skimming ridge-lines. Making a last minute diversion along the beautiful Asaro River Valley, Monty turned the *Goose* north to line up on Goroka's airstrip. The runway was short and, at an altitude of 5000feet. thin atmosphere made landing and take-off more critical as a plane had to fly at higher speeds while its engines produced less power. But that was aviation in New Guinea for you, and Monty was a seasoned expert. The *Goose* was primarily a flying boat, but equipped with wheels that fitted flush into the fuselage and were lowered like a conventional aircraft.

Monty radioed the tower that was just a shack erected on stilts and not always manned. He told the controller Dr Holyman was on board if anyone needed him. No other planes were in the circuit area so Monty was cleared to land straight in from his position a couple of miles south of the runway.

Much of the jungle around the plateau where Goroka town lay had been cleared. The local people were mostly subsistence farmers although some, like Jim Taylor, had started cultivating coffee. The Eastern Highlands climate was perfect. Rainfall was ample even in the dry season and the temperature never varied from 25° Celsius or 77° Fahrenheit, which was the system used at that time.

Monty clunked the *Goose* onto the ground and taxied beside a couple of small hangars that housed light planes. There was a British Auster Autocrat and a new Yankee Cessna 140 parked close by, but no large planes. As Monty cut the engines a small crowd of men, women and children surged towards the *Goose*. Dr Holyman was well known and was soon surrounded by noisy, excited people who needed attention for complaints ranging from cuts and bruises to advanced pregnancies, serious infections, ulcers and that unfortunate European import – venereal disease. Dr Holyman carried a supply of Bayer Penicillin which was unknown before the war, but now the villagers saw it as a miracle cure for common complaints that had once proved fatal. They were unaware that the marvel was due to an international triumvirate of scientists who shared the 1945 Nobel Prize for Medicine by refining penicillin to a usable state. It was just in time to save thousands of lives during WWII. Ernst Chain, a Jewish refugee from Nazi Germany, joined Australian Howard Florey who, with the help of Scotsman Sir Alexander Fleming brought the wonder drug into production. Of course that was precisely the kind of evidence cargo-cult devotees needed and Angela was quick to exploit, explaining how great God was to have produced three such fine fellows. No one questioned why He'd waited so long after the birth of mankind to bestow this benefit. Indeed Angela ascribed to a disturbing belief that creation all happened in less than a week about 6000 years ago, but Danny was sure it must have taken much longer than that.

The local people set up a table and chairs in a shady spot where Dr Holyman conducted his clinic. They all sat around patiently for him to deal with them one by one while Angela acted as nurse and secretary, recording all their medical histories on cards and filing them in a shoe-box. Danny helped unload the doctor's supplies while Monty checked the *Goose* for damage. He was pleased to report it was in good shape other than a few scratches along the hull. It looked like Dr Holyman would be busy all day and Monty soon grew bored. Fortunately a few minutes later an ex-US military Jeep sped along the track to Goroka Field. The driver was a rangy Australian who jumped out and strode across to Dr Holyman and vigorously shook his hand. Angela stopped what she was doing and hugged him fondly. The newcomer was about fifty and bore that rugged, *Chips Rafferty* look many outback Aussies have. He left the medical team to it and approached Monty and Danny with an outstretched hand.

'G'day, Monty,' he drawled, 'nice to see you again. Who's your chum?'

Danny introduced himself, submitting to the stranger's crushing fist.

'How're y' going', sport, I'm Jim Taylor, nice to meet you.'

'G'day, I'm fine, but I'd kill for a cuppa,' Danny said.

'We can do better than that,' Jim beamed. 'Hop in the Jeep and we'll head for my place. Looks like Gordon and Ange'll be here for a while.'

Jim Taylor's coffee plantation was only a short way from town and soon they pulled up outside his comfortable-looking home surrounded by a broad veranda. Jim had married a local girl, Yerima and she met them on the front steps holding her baby daughter, Meg, in her arms. Jim introduced Danny as Yerima already knew Monty.

'I heard your plane,' she said, 'so I knew Jim would bring you over for a brew. How do you like your coffee, Danny?'

Danny didn't know. He was a tea-drinker like most Australians and had never tasted coffee. Stanley Hallet had once brought Mavis a bottle of *Bushell's Coffee & Chicory Essence*, but hadn't felt inclined to share any with Danny.

'Well, you're in for a treat,' Yerima said.

They settled into high-backed cane chairs on Jim's veranda while Yerima fixed the coffee. The home was simple and Jim seemed perfectly satisfied in the idyllic setting. The view was stunning, looking out over mountains and rain-forest filled valleys.

'I came here as a young man,' Jim explained, 'and fell in love with the place. I've tramped all over the highlands, using ancient tracks most of the time. It seemed impassable at first, but with decent guides you can get around. My first big trek was back in '33 with Mick and Dan Leahy and Ken Spicks, but the bigun was in '38 with Jack Black and Pat Walsh. We took over 200 native police and bearers and found people who'd never seen white folk before. Some of 'em thought we were ghosts from the past. Our mission was to try and bring these people into the modern age. It seemed a good idea at the time, but I'm not so sure now. I think we've just complicated their lives for 'em.'

'It must have been dangerous,' Danny suggested.

'We were a big enough force to deter most aggression although we were challenged by spear-wielding warriors at times. A rifle shot in the air normally stopped them. I had to shoot a pig once to show the locals our fire-power. That calmed them down and we all enjoyed a feast afterwards. A lot of the men leave their villages and go to work in the gold mines now. They make good money by their standards, but the working conditions are shocking and quite a few die in mine accidents. This naturally causes resentment from their families left at home. There're no social services like back in Australia.'

'Do you miss Australia?'

'Why? I've got everything a man could dream of here. Goroka is paradise. I have a good wife and we've started our family, the coffee business is kicking off and I think it'll do well. I've been a district commissioner, police officer, gold prospector and was civil administrator during the war. There have been some exciting times, but now I'm happy just to be a farmer.'

He certainly had a point especially when Yerima returned with the coffee tray. Danny found the drink bitter but enjoyed it after she added goat's milk and sugar. They chatted pleasantly for a couple of hours while Yerima prepared a lunch hamper for Angela and Dr Holyman. Monty drove the Jeep back to the airfield taking the hamper with him. He needed to refuel the *Goose* for their flight to Lae and ensure it was properly chocked and bedded down for the night. That entailed locking the plane's control surfaces to prevent them flapping in the wind. He also placed leather covers over the instrument probes and rubber bungs in the engine inlets to prevent insects, rain and what he called *foreign objects* finding their way into the plane's systems.

Dr Holyman' surgery was normally an all-day affair and the Taylors prepared their spare room for Angela. The men would bunk down in their guest lodge close to the main house. It was an airy, two-room bungalow that could sleep half a dozen people. Jim lent Danny a change of clothing after Yerima insisted his own gear was long overdue for the laundry. She intended to rectify that deficiency straight away. With nothing else to do after lunch, Jim took Danny sight-seeing. Goroka was a small town and it didn't take long to cover it. What struck Danny most was the contentment of everyone he met. They all greeted Jim with broad smiles and waved happily.

'I see why you like it here,' Danny observed.

'Yep, we're lucky here everyone gets along. In other parts tribes are always at odds with each other and blood feuds are common. But, don't be fooled. Give 'em an excuse and these people can be pretty fearsome when they have a mind to be.'

That evening they all sat out on the Taylor's front lawn and enjoyed the sight of lightning flashing from dozens of thunderstorms hugging the mountain peaks. They were forced inside by a sudden downpour, but it was time for bed anyway. Everyone was dog-tired. Just before they turned in a group of locals arrived at the house and spoke to Jim. Danny couldn't understand what was being said, but saw the messengers were concerned. Jim nodded and the villagers disappeared into the night.

'Is there a problem?' Dr Holyman asked.

'Could be, there's a disagreement between two families who live close by. Seems a girl is pregnant and crying rape, but the boy involved says she consented. It'll boil down to a matter of compensation. They want me to adjudicate, but there's nothing I can do tonight with this rain anyway. I'll sort it out in the morning.'

They said *good night* and headed for bed.

*

'**B**limey, what's all the noise about?' Danny cried as he tumbled out of bed.

There was a hullabaloo outside. Screams and wails came from everywhere. Danny dashed to the door and grabbed his pants as he went, not wanting to confront a crisis stark naked. Dr Holyman and Monty were close behind him. Beyond the doorway they saw grey forms dashing past eerily illuminated by moonlight and lightning flashes. The ghostly figures were all armed with long spears and huge shields and yelling for all they were worth as they charged by. Some of the warriors had attached long bamboo sticks on their fingers. The bamboo was shaved to wicked points making the sticks into vicious weapons. Other than loin cloths they were naked and, unlike other native people, they wore no shell jewellery at all. They were completely covered with what at first sight looked like talcum powder.

'Dammit, mud men,' Monty hissed. 'I'd say they're looking for trouble.'

'Mud men..?'

There was no time to answer Danny's question. In the wake of the mud men Jim Taylor raced across the lawn towards the guest bungalow. He carried a Webley service revolver.

'Get dressed,' he yelled. 'Bring your bag, Gordon, I think you'll need it.'

They were ready in seconds when Angela joined them dressed in slacks and a t-shirt.

'Stay here,' Dr Holyman told her. 'This might be dangerous.'

No,' she cried, 'I can help.'

There was no time to argue, so the small group jumped into the Jeep and raced after the mud men. When they arrived at the Goroka showground they halted as they looked in dismay. The mud men had formed a line and faced another equally large group of warriors who were also well armed with spears, axes, machetes, clubs and shields. Many of the men carried burning torches so the showground was clearly lit up. There were at least a hundred men in the arena, all chanting, stomping their feet and lunging aggressively at their opponents.

'Looks like they couldn't wait for you to settle things, eh Jim?' Monty drawled.

'Seems that way. Those blokes must have taken half the night caking that mud on. Usually it means they want to sneak up and ambush someone, but either word got out or this is an arranged killing zone. They're probably tanked up with home brew and betel nut as well. It makes no difference now. Both sides mean business.'

For the present the two gangs were content to yell abuse at each other. Danny was intrigued by the mud men. Whereas the other warriors were dressed traditionally pretty much as he'd seen the Fly River people, the mud men were smeared completely grey and wore domelike helmets with round eye and mouth holes. Some masks were grotesquely sculptured with vicious faces. Danny thought if they set out to be intimidating, they'd succeeded.

The roaring reached a crescendo and it was clear the warriors were only moments away from an all-out brawl.

'What'll we do?" Angela cried.

'Get help,' Jim replied. 'I'll rouse the police, although I reckon a few of them are in that lot already. Tribe before duty it seems.'

'No time,' Dr Holyman said, as the two groups edged forwards within striking distance. He raced between the warriors' lines waving, yelling for them to stop, but his timing couldn't have been worse. As he dashed between the lines of men, someone hurled the first spear and a shower of missiles followed. Dr Holyman didn't stand a chance in the middle of such a volley of airborne weaponry. A spear-point pierced his chest and sliced through his torso. He dropped with a grunt and fell beneath a stampede of milling feet.

'Daddy!' Angela screamed.

Jim Taylor raised his pistol and fired a single shot skywards.

Chapter 14 – Showground Showdown

Jim's pistol shot made no difference and he was loath to fire another into the crowd. They were doing enough damage to each other as it was, but Dr Holyman lay stricken in the heart of the melee. If they barged in they'd likely suffer the same fate although there appeared no choice in the matter. In the rush Monty had forgotten to bring his Colt 45 automatic, but Angela was already leading Danny and Jim pell-mell into the fight, so he followed. They ducked through the tussling, screeching warriors who seemed to know they were not the enemy and concentrated on their own opposite numbers. But clubs were flaying hell, west and crooked and Danny caught a glancing blow that sent his head spinning. Monty broke his fall and dragged him forwards until they joined Angela and Jim who huddled over Dr Holyman.

The fight continued as warriors broke into small groups or engaged in individual tussles. A few old scores needed to be settled and the warriors made the most of the opportunity. Yet in all the confusion and turmoil they still avoided Danny, Angela and Jim, possibly because they were white, but they sensed Monty wasn't part of the argument either. Their traditional dress and mud man masks acted as indentifying uniforms and they left non-combatants alone. That might have been so, but it was a messy business all the same and blood spilled everywhere.

The doctor was in a bad way, the spear had driven clean through his chest and blood seeped from both the entry and exit wounds. Moving him needed care and even dragging him clear of the mob might only injure him more. The fight was intensifying with several axes and knifes drawn ready to do serious damage. At that moment they heard police whistles as twenty native policemen charged into the showground. They were all armed with truncheons and led by a sergeant who carried a Lee-Enfield .303 rifle.

'Protect Gordon!' Jim yelled and fought his way through the pack.

He met the patrolmen head on and, although no longer officially a policeman, immediately took charge. Such was Jim Taylor's reputation that the sergeant and his men deferred to him without question. The sergeant had done a sterling job getting his men together in such a short time. Jim ordered him to fire two shots into the air and did the same himself. This time there was a reaction. About half the warriors hesitated, which gave Jim his chance. He led the police into the centre of the fight. The warriors split apart under the truncheon wielding onslaught. The extra combatants confused the warriors. Suddenly the battle frenzy faded and both sides fled in all directions, disappearing into the night. Half a dozen men were left writhing in their own blood. The sergeant asked Jim if they should give chase, but Jim thought not. He knew both clans and could round up the ring-leaders in the morning, but what would be the point? Although his wounding was accidental, Dr Holyman wasn't the only major casualty. Those left on the battlefield were badly slashed about and would need medical care. The trouble was that however the original feud had started this fight would spark many more grievances that must be avenged.

'Dopey buggers stabbed the only doctor in town,' Jim muttered.

Angela was distraught as she cradled her father in her arms.

'We must get him to hospital,' she sobbed. 'Right now!'

Goroka Base Hospital was hardly up to the task. It was little more than a sick bay staffed by a pair of local nurses. They were competent and well respected, but ill-prepared for major surgery. Periodic locum visits were down to dedicated medicos like Dr Holyman. Unfortunately there was no one left to tend him.

'We'll have to get that spear out before we move him,' Jim said.

'We can't,' Angela said in barely a whisper. 'The shaft is acting like a plug. If we pull it out he'll haemorrhage to death.'

'Fair call,' Jim conceded, 'but we can't shift him with that dirty great thing sticking out of his chest. It'll only have to snag against something once and there'll be hell to pay.'

'We could saw it off,' Monty suggested.

'No,' Danny urged. 'The vibration will open the wound. We need bolt cutters.'

'Good idea, lad,' Jim said.

Jim told the sergeant to clean up, take the wounded tribesmen to the base hospital and rouse the nurses from their beds if the night's ballyhoo hadn't already done so. They'd have to manage as best they could. Then he leapt into his Jeep and raced off to get a set of bolt-cutters from his tool shed. Before he left, Angela reminded him to pick up Dr Holyman's medical bag which contained antiseptic, gauze, bandages and most importantly, morphine. Danny was at a loss and felt helpless. His head ached abominably from the blow he'd received, but he made himself useful helping the other wounded, one of whom was badly slashed from elbow to wrist. Blood was oozing from the wound accompanied by arterial spurts. The man would be dead in minutes.

Danny tore the sleeve off his shirt and, to his amazement, it ripped away cleanly.

Try doing that when you're calm, he thought.

He tied the sleeve around the man's upper arm and knotted it as tightly as he could. He noted with satisfaction the blood flow stopped, but knew the wound need suturing. This man was almost in as grave a condition as Dr Holyman. The police sergeant took over and ordered two of his men to carry the wounded fellow away.

Jim was gone for an interminably long time, but when he returned he brought a canvas stretcher. Yerima was with him, having left baby Meg with a neighbour. Angela still sobbed, but was all business now. Dr Holyman groaned feebly as she laid him on his side. Jim wasted no time and quickly severed the spear shaft as close to the wound as he dared. Angela used gauze to staunch any seeping blood and then bandaged Dr Holyman's chest. The spear stumps hindered her work, but she did a pretty neat job under the circumstances.

Monty, Jim and Danny gently lifted the doctor on the stretcher, taking care to leave him on his side where he was most comfortable and less likely to aggravate his wound by disturbing the spear stumps. Angela injected a syringe-full of morphine into her father's arm that took effect within minutes although he shivered continually. Fortunately Yerima had the sense to bring blankets and covered him up.

'We must get him to Moresby,' Jim said. 'We don't have the facilities to deal with anything this serious. We'll probably need to take a couple of those other chaps too. They might need some blood.'

'It'll be dawn soon,' Monty said. 'We can take him straight to the *Goose*. Jim, get anyone else you think we'll have to medivac outa here.'

Jim headed for the hospital while Monty and Danny laid the stretcher across the Jeep's wide, flat bonnet that seemed to have been designed exactly for that purpose. Monty drove at a snail's pace, but Danny leant over the windscreen and held onto the stretcher in case they hit a bump. A jolt might be enough to kill Dr Holyman not to mention the danger of him being tossed off the stretcher. They dropped Yerima at home to pack up their kit including Monty's gun. She was practical enough to realise there was no way of knowing when they'd be back and they'd need a change of clothes.

When they reached the *Goose*, they immediately loaded Dr Holyman aboard. His stretcher just fitted in the aisle, wedged between the two rows of seats. Shortly afterwards Jim and Yerima arrived in Goroka's 1948 Holden police car. They reported that those wounded in the fight were stable. The nurses had stitches the most serious wounds, dressed the rest and set one broken arm. They felt their patients be safer waiting until another doctor made his rounds rather than risk being bounced around in the Monty's *balus*. Unless of course they started fighting again, but Jim said he'd station a policeman in the ward to avert trouble. Danny's tourniquet had worked on the fellow whose arm had been badly gashed and it looked like he'd pull through after all. Danny was pleased he'd been of some use even if he hadn't started the fight and now his shirt only had one sleeve.

After stowing their gear, they said a brief farewell to Jim and Yerima, who were left to sort out the feuding tribes. Monty fired the *Goose*'s engine into life. Danny once again occupied the co-pilot's seat while Angela looked after her father. It was first light when the *Goose* roared skywards and headed south-east into weather that looked far from promising. Huge storm clouds still billowed above the peaks and heavy rain poured into many of the valleys. Monty contacted Port Moresby as soon as they'd climbed high enough to get radio contact. The forecast for Moresby was no better: low cloud, poor visibility, heavy rain and thunderstorms in the area: just about everything pilots avoid if they possibly can. As the first flecks of rain splattered the windscreen, Monty banked the *Goose* and turned sharply to find clear weather, but there wasn't much around. He flew along one valley after another, but each way was blocked sooner or later. Monty knew the names of all the river valleys and mountain passes, but he was growing concerned that even he would become disorientated before too long.

Angela sensed the manoeuvres and poked her head into the cockpit.

'What's happening, Mr Montgomery?' she demanded.

'Sorry ma'am, I don't think we can get through. The weather's total crap ahead.'

'Mr Montgomery, I insist you get through to Port Moresby. My father needs urgent attention. And please do not use profanities.'

'Sorry ma'am, but right now we have to make split-arse turns every two minutes to stay clear of rain squalls and that's a great way to hit a mountain. Is that what you want?'

This time she ignored his *profanities.*

'You must find a way. Please Monty.'

It was the first time Danny'd heard her address Monty with any familiarity.

'I may be nuts, but I ain't suicidal.'

Meanwhile clouds swirled close to the *Goose* and Monty was having trouble picking a safe flight path. There was no alternative; they'd have to back-track, much to Danny's relief. He had no wish to repeat his flying experience through thunderstorms, especially surrounded by high terrain.

'Look, 'Monty said, 'we'll head for Lae. The weather's clear to the north. I know the hospital isn't as big as Moresby, but they have a resident doctor and an operating theatre. This might be a good time for you to do a bit of that praying you're so keen on, ma'am.'

Angela nodded and returned to the cabin to nurse Dr Holyman.

A common meteorological phenomenon of New Guinea was that if the weather was appalling south of the Central Highlands, it was often fine to the north and vice-versa. Of course sometimes there were torrential downpours just about everywhere. But, on this occasion Monty was able to pick his way back through the passes. He had to fly almost all the way to Goroka before turning east and heading for Lae. It was his home base and he knew the area well so navigation wasn't a problem.

He radioed ahead for an ambulance to meet them when they landed at Lae airport. It was a short east-west grass strip with a couple of hills close by, but posed no difficulties for Monty. This was the very airport where Amelia Earhart and Fred Noonan took off in 1937 only to disappear into the Pacific en route to Howland Island.

Angela accompanied her father with a nurse and a rather careworn doctor who'd been up half the night, but responded readily enough when duty called. After the ambulance sped away Monty taxied the *Goose* to a hangar with a sign bearing the name *Alabama Aviation* on the wall. They were met by the duty engineer from Ansett Airlines, who sub-contracted to Monty. It was a good arrangement because Monty was able to access the airline's spare parts store and ordering network. That way the *Goose* was always maintained to a first-class standard. Monty wrote up the maintenance log and discussed the *Goose*'s needs with the engineer before leaving the plane in his capable hands.

Danny stood in front of the hangar at somewhat of a loss. He was now on the north coast of New Guinea as a result of matters that were completely beyond his control. He had no idea what he was going to do next. Monty tossed him the satchel containing his freshly laundered clothes and a couple of crumpled quid notes and some coins that had survived all the way from Townsville.

'Yerima's a pip, ain't she? Mothering you to death. The trouble about living in the tropics is personal hygiene. You gotta stay clean. I'm surprised she didn't iron your bank-roll, but I guess there wasn't time. C'mon, you can stay at my place until you figure out what to do.'

'Thanks, Monty, but I don't want to be a pain. And like you say, I've got some cash for rent somewhere.'

'Don't sweat it. I'm not doing anything until we find out how the doc is faring. His mission chartered the *Goose* for a month.'

Monty owned a 1926 Morgan Aero 3-Wheeler and it was a bit of squeeze for two people especially when Monty deposited his knapsack onto Danny's lap. They drove to Monty's beach shack that looked a bit rundown, but on close inspection had all the comforts Monty needed. The place consisted of a lounge room, two bedrooms, a kitchen and a bathroom. He'd rigged a shower to a large rainwater tank, but the toilet stood a short distance inland connected to an underground septic system. Coconut palms shaded the shack, but Monty had erected a lattice-roofed pergola in front of his home for extra coolness. His other furnishings were fine as well. The beds had decent mattresses and mosquito nets while his high-backed, cane lounge chairs were padded with soft cushions. A generator chugged beside the house powering a few lights, ceiling fans and, to Danny's amazement, a small refrigerator. No one back home owned a fridge. Anything that needed to be chilled was kept in ice-chests that were replenished by a delivery truck driver who made his rounds every few days.

'I know you can get ice from town, but hey, I want a cold beer any time I choose.'

'Struth Monty, you're well set up,' Danny commented.

'Sure am. Hell I checked out half the stock piles in the Pacific after the war. I picked up all the mod-cons. Island hopping was sure tough for those marines right up to colonels, but generals like their home comforts. I picked up the stuff for my still as well. It's kinda hidden under the palms yonder.'

Monty owned a portable wireless he called a radio, a library of crime and western novels and a hand-cranked phonograph with a collection of crackly blues and country music records. There was a stove attached to a gas bottle in the kitchen, but Monty preferred to use a portable barbeque fired by charcoal briquettes. Monty's most prized possessions were a Gibson ES-150 acoustic guitar with an electric pick-up, a 1948 Fender Broadcaster and a tweed-amp. Both guitars were protected in black cases while one of Monty's girlfriends had made a decorative cover for the amplifier.

But there was no more time to admire Monty's home.

'C'mon.' he said, 'I'll show you around later. Right now we need to get over to the hospital and see how the doc and Ange are doing.'

The Morgan 3-Wheeler felt only slightly less squashed without any baggage, but it barely took a few minutes to reach the hospital. The building consisted of a single ward, consulting room, OR, reception and waiting area, bathroom and toilet. They found Angela sitting in triage with her head in her hands. Monty sat beside her, placing his arm around her shoulder. He could be quite tender and empathetic when he put his mind to it. Danny sat on a seat opposite them feeling equally sympathetic, but also a little uncomfortable. He had no idea what to say that might comfort Angela, so he wisely remained silent, hoping that just being there helped.

They waited about an hour. Angela had stopped sobbing, but her cheeks still glistened from her tears. Danny saw a box of Kleenex paper handkerchiefs on the admittance desk and took some to dry her eyes. *What a beaut idea,* he thought. Tissues had only been available outside the USA for a short time and he'd never used them before. Old news print was still the toilet-paper of choice for most regional Australian households.

'Thank you,' she sniffed to which he simply nodded and smiled.

A doctor appeared a short time later. He was still dressed in a theatre cap and gown with a disturbing amount of blood on his sleeves, but at least he'd peeled off his rubber gloves before he shook hands. He introduced himself as Stephen Graham.

'He's stable, but still serious,' he announced. Dr Graham was not known for his bedside manner and thought it important to tell the truth as briefly as possible.

'We've stopped the haemorrhaging and we'll operate to remove the projectile shortly. I'm afraid it will be a long and risky procedure.'

Angela gasped.

'You did very well, my dear,' the doctor actually managed to smile. 'Stopping the blood-flow was the most important thing. You've no idea how many patients have bled to death while being transported here simply because no one thought to stick their thumb into the wound. You saved your father's life, and now you must do one thing more.'

'Anything,' she murmured. 'Please, I don't know what I'd do without him.'

Dr Graham cleared his throat.

'He has still lost a lot of blood and will need a transfusion. Our supply is low because we don't have a large stock of anti-coagulants or storage facilities. So I'd like you to make a donation. We'll transfer your blood directly into your father, but...'

'What?'

'It probably won't be enough. We can only take a pint from a girl your size.'

'What about us?' Danny said.

'Us..?' Monty added hastily.

'Too right, you and me Monty, we've got a pint or two to spare.'

'I'll have to test your blood group and see if you're compatible with Dr Holyman.'

It turned out that Monty didn't have to contribute his part of the 'us' offer. His blood group was A+ which was incompatible with Dr Holyman's O+ type. Danny's blood was O– which pleased Dr Graham because it was a universal blood group and could be used with all other blood types.

The upshot was that Danny and Angela donned hospital gowns, washed up thoroughly and entered the OR. Dr Holyman lay deathly pale on the operating table covered by a sterile sheet. A local GP had been called in to administer the anaesthetic and three nurses were assisting, along with a wardsman to do the heavy work. Dr Graham asked Angela to lie on a gurney that was wheeled beside her father. One of the nurses inserted a needle into Angela's arm while she held her crucifix in the other. It was her only piece of jewellery and Danny had never seen her without it. Almost immediately blood flowed through a tube into a Walter & Murphy plastic bag.

'They're brand new,' the nurse beamed under her surgical mask. 'So much better than our old glass bottles. These only arrived last month.'

It took about fifteen minutes for the bag to fill after which the nurse immediately removed the needle from Angela's arm. She inverted the bag and attached a new, sterile point to the tube and injected Dr Holyman's vein, beginning the transfusion. Dr Graham gave a nod of approval and got to work.

Danny stood beside Angela and held her free hand. She gripped him tightly and smiled while he tried to look reassuring in return. He also tried to ignore what was occurring on the operating table. Fortunately Dr Holyman was screened by sheets and although Danny sensed the activity and urgency, he didn't see much. He simply heard Dr Graham grunting terse instructions to his team like *swab, clamp,* and *suture* as the operation progressed. After about fifteen minutes the wardsman escorted Angela from the theatre with instructions to find her a cuppa and a sandwich. Then it was Danny's turn to lie on the gurney. They didn't take his blood straight away, but waited until the spear had been removed which took over an hour. His experience was the same as Angela's and once the second bag was full he too was escorted to the waiting room. One of the nurses examined the livid club wound Danny had suffered during the fight. His head still throbbed, but the bruise had so far been ignored in all the excitement. She declared there was no evidence of serious injury and applied a cold compress that eased the pain. Other than that, Danny felt okay and enjoyed a corned-beef sandwich with a cup of sweet tea.

And then they waited.

Angela sat close to Danny and held his hand once more.

'Thank you,' she whispered.

She kissed him lightly on the cheek and rested her head on his shoulder. Danny sensed her lips moving and realised she was praying silently to her crucifix. He hoped her prayers would be answered, because so far his hadn't been.

Monty was asleep and they must have nodded off too, because the next thing Danny felt was Dr Graham shaking him gently. He reported the operation was over and, although Dr Holyman was not yet out of danger, he was resting quietly and the prognosis was optimistic.

'Look,' Dr Graham advised, 'I think the best thing for all of you is to go home and get some proper rest. We'll telephone as soon as we have any news.'

'Angela's staying at my place, doc,' Monty said, because her home was actually in Port Moresby.

'Good, leave your number at the reception desk.'

The doctor smiled as reassuringly as he could and returned to the OR without another word.

As there was no room in the Morgan with Angela and her suit case, Danny said he'd walk back to the beach hut. He remembered the way and it'd only take him about half an hour. So after Angela and Monty sped away, he followed in their tracks. Lae was still a small, but multi-cultural town in those days. Although most of the population was Papuan, there was a fair smattering of Chinese merchants, Filipino and Malayan fishermen as well as European expatriate prospectors and administrators. He passed shop fronts with their wares displayed out front accompanied by a lot of cheerful haggling going on between traders and customers. He left the town centre, walking towards a row of small houses and shacks made from fibro sheeting and local material. He came to a garden where a woman tended hibiscus bushes that bloomed in a riot of colour.

She noticed him staring.

'*Yupela laikim plaua?*' she asked, pointing to the plants

'They're brilliant,' he beamed.

'*Yu laik mi katim wanpela sampela.*'

Danny nodded thinking a bunch of colourful flora might cheer Angela up. One of the few things he knew about girls was that they all liked flowers. The woman used a small knife to cut a generous bunch from several of her bushes. She pruned the excess leaves and handed the flowers to Danny. He fumbled in his pocket and produced his change. He'd no idea how much to offer her, but she shook her head.

'*Yupela gatim nais meri?*' she smiled.

'Something like that,' he replied still proffering a palm full of change. In the end she took only a half-penny, so he pocketed the rest, bid her good day and headed for Monty's shack.

Monty had brewed coffee when he arrived and Angela was just finishing hers. She was exhausted and feeling the effects of her blood donation so she thought she'd turn in. An afternoon sea-breeze cooled the shack, so sleeping wasn't a problem.

'I brought these for you,' Danny said with a little embarrassment as he'd never given a girl flowers before, but Angela was delighted.

'That was very considerate of you, Danny. Thank you, they're lovely.'

So are you, Danny thought, *even if you're such a God-botherer.*

'Ain't got a vase,' Monty said, 'but I'll stick 'em in my beer pitcher.'

While Monty went to fill the jug, Angela kissed Danny again, but this time on the mouth with her lips slightly parted that promised something more than a chaste peck. Then the moment was over before it had really begun and she went to her bedroom. Monty returned with the flowers. There was no door to Angela's room, so he knocked on the frame and placed the jug on a cane bedside table. Monty took the mattress from the other spare bed and leaned it against the lounge-room wall.

'Normally you could bunk down in the spare room, but I bet Angela's kinda tight about that sorta thing. You'll be comfortable right here.'

'I'll be fine. I know we've been up all night and I'm shy a pint of blood, but I don't feel tired yet.'

'I know what you mean. The adrenaline must still be pumping. You wanna beer?'

'Ripper, I reckon we deserve one.'

Monty pulled two bottles of *San Miguel* Manila lager from his fridge while Danny pushed a couple of chairs onto the front porch. They sat for a while and chatted a bit before Monty got up and brought back one of his guitars. It differed from the flat-top flamenco style instruments Danny had played at *Zucchera di Canna*. Other than the electric pickup, volume and tone controls it was also made with a curved top, *f*-shaped sound holes and steel strings. Monty quickly tuned the instrument, strummed an *E*-chord with a tortoise-shell plectrum and nodded approvingly.

'Sweet tone,' Danny observed.

'You play?'

'A little – mostly Italian folk songs.'

Monty handed the guitar to Danny who strummed some chords and finger-picked *O Sole Mio*.

'Not bad, but you're kinda stiff.'

'Stiff..?'

'Yeah, you gotta slide around the fret board more. Here, I'll show you.'

Then Monty showed his stuff. He ad-libbed within a chord progression that reminded Danny of Glen Miller's *In the Mood*. But rather than placing his fingers directly behind the frets he often slid from one to another.

'Fiddle players do it all the time because they ain't got frets, but it don't mean we can't do the same. Black folk down the Mississippi play nothin' but blues. It's a 12-bar progression. Just three chords and dead easy to remember so then you can concentrate on making the music happen. It ain't a straight tempo either, but a lazy shuffle; you sorta ooze four half-beats into three.'

Monty explained the relationship between chords and scales and showed Danny how to play the blues by adding and deleting notes from the chords. He also tapped the strings at times in what he called *hammering-on*.

'*A* and *E* are great keys for the blues 'cos you can use open strings which have a good ring to them,' Monty said. 'Guys like Muddy Waters, Howlin' Wolf, B. B. King and John Lee Hooker have been doin' this stuff for quite a few years, but are only just getting air time from Sam Phillips at WREC station in Memphis. Phillips is a white boy, but he sure understands black music. You never know, more white folk might starting digging it too. Tell you what, you play the rhythm and I'll get out the Broadcaster and I'll teach you some black licks.'

This guitar was like nothing Danny had seen. It was the first of its kind, a beautifully designed, solid bodied instrument, but the sound was unimpressive. Then Monty plugged in the amplifier and the guitar came to life.

'You'll wake Ange,' Danny hissed.

'Oops, sorry.'

Monty peeked into her room and happily reported she was sleeping soundly.

'It'll take a sabre jet to wake her,' he smiled, but turned the volume down nevertheless.

So Monty showed Danny a boogie riff he'd been working on that would become the basis of so many rock'n'roll tunes of that decade. Surprisingly Monty could read sheet music whereas most self-taught pickers tended to simply play by ear. Monty could do both. He laid out some scrappy pieces of paper and although Danny couldn't make head or tail of the melody and bass staves, he could follow the chords.

'It's like math,' Monty said. 'Everything is connected. Each scale has three basic chords and what they call a relative minor chord. You can learn by just knowing those facts, but you've gotta feel the music or it's dead dull.'

Monty explained a little more music theory to Danny and they jammed until sunset when Angela awoke. She was concerned about her dad, so they checked with the hospital and were relieved to hear he was sleeping peacefully. He'd been pumped full of penicillin to stem any infection. Angela wanted to visit him right away, but Dr Graham suggested they wait until the morning. Also she was hungry so they went to the Chinese emporium in town where the owner cooked Cantonese style that was new to Danny and a delicious surprise. As they strolled home Danny wondered whether he should hold Angela's hand, but thought better of it.

She could be infuriatingly prissy. He was sure she liked him and had kissed him twice, but he didn't want to push his luck. She might just have needed comforting and Danny was pretty sure she wasn't ready for Noemi's kind of passion. At least with Noemi he knew where he stood even if it was on shaky ground.

Back at Monty's place they picked up the guitars and strummed some more. They asked Angela to sing, but she only knew hymns that sounded a bit dreary, so Monty taught her some hand-clapping, foot-stomping, southern gospel tunes. After a little uncertainty, she joined in enthusiastically. Danny was happy to see her finally let her hair down and have some fun.

It was a beautiful, balmy tropical night with the song of waves lapping against the shoreline only yards away and the buzz of insects in the trees. Danny was having a great time, but as the evening wore on fatigue finally took its toll, so Monty and Danny turned in and immediately fell asleep. Despite her siesta, after a pretty solid prayer session Angela did the same.

In the morning they went to see her father.

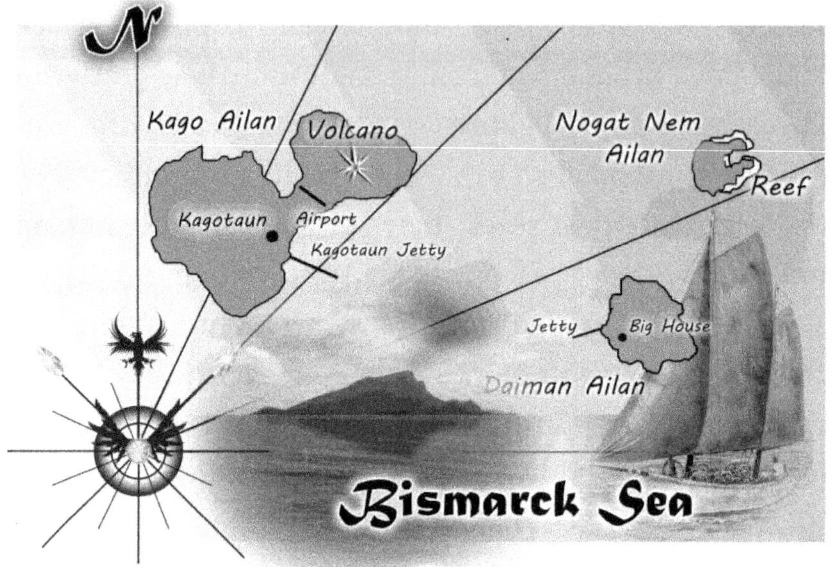

They entered the hospital with trepidation. Expecting the worst but hoping for the best, they were pleased to find Dr Graham in an almost jolly mood.

'Your dad's doing fine,' he told Angela. 'He's very weak of course and he'll be sore for a while, but he should make a full recovery. He'll be with us for at least a fortnight.'

'Can I see him,' she begged.

'I don't see why not, he's pretty groggy, but awake at the moment. Just you, Angela. Nothing personal, boys,' he added to Danny and Monty, 'but a room full of people can unsettle patients. It's the movement and extra noise you see.'

So Danny and Monty waited in reception while Angela visited her father in his private room that served as the hospital

ICU. She was gone for no more than ten minutes, but seemed concerned when she returned.

'Everything okay?' Danny asked.

'Daddy's fine,' she replied, 'but he's so stubborn.'

They stared at her.

'He can hardly speak and all he's worried about is continuing our rounds.'

'Fat chance,' Monty said. 'You heard Doc Graham, he's in here for at least two weeks and it'll take a while after that before he's fit for duty.'

'You tell him that! The trouble is daddy will fret if he doesn't know the job's being done.'

'Yeah, but I don't see how...'

'We'll carry on without him. Your plane has been chartered for another month Mr Montgomery, so we'll just do the best we can. It's mostly routine vaccinations and antibiotics that I administer anyway. What we can't deal with, we'll contact Dr Graham and there's always Port Moresby and the naval station on Manus Island.'

'Yeah,' Monty agreed, 'Manus is crawling with brass at the moment, and I bet they've got all the medics they need. Some hard-arsed Jap general called Takuma Nishimura is on trial there for war crimes. Apparently massacring innocent bystanders and POWs was his speciality. He'd been sentenced to gaol by the Brits, but some Aussie redcaps snatched him in Singapore and brought him back to Australian jurisdiction to face the noose.'

Angela shuddered.

'There is no excuse for the death penalty whatever he's done,' she protested.

'Tell that to his victims.'

'I believe they are beyond judging and rest in the arms of our Lord.'

'Even the heathens..?'

Danny cleared his throat as he saw the theological discourse getting heated.

'Might be an idea to continue this back at Monty's place,' Danny suggested.

'Good idea,' Monty agreed because he'd become bored with the whole debate anyway.

He and Angela continued arguing back and forth as they walked back to his shack, while Danny thought it wise to shut up. Religion and politics always seem to get people agitated, so it made him wonder why the human race bothered with either.

'You're going to be short handed, Ange,' he said during a sulky lull in the dispute. 'Would you like me to come along and help out?'

'Thank you, Danny,' Angela replied, still a little miffed with Monty. 'But, I won't be able to pay you.'

'That's okay. All I need is food and a place to sleep.'

'I'm sure we can arrange that, and I would appreciate *some* help,' she said eyeing Monty peevishly.

'Be nice to the pilot now, ma'am,' Monty said.

'I'm surprised a man who spends much of his life so close to the heavens isn't more Godly,' she retorted.

'Spirituality is one thing, religious dogma quite another and who says God is up there anyway..?'

And they were off again, arguing all the way home. Luckily they were all busy during the day. Monty refuelled the *Goose* while Danny was sent to town for supplies on the mission's account. Angela was in charge of medical needs and replenished them from the hospital pharmacy. Dr Graham was ambivalent about Angela proceeding alone, but had no power to stop her. He realised he'd not only be dealing with a recalcitrant young woman, but her father as well. The last thing he wanted was Gordon Holyman relapsing after all the Lae medical team's hard work. By mid-afternoon the *Goose* was loaded and ready to go.

'We'll leave at first light,' Angela announced when they returned to the shack. 'So please don't drink too much beer tonight, Mr Montgomery. I'm going to see daddy now. Can I bring anything back from the emporium?'

'It's okay. I'll pick some stuff up. I'll give you a lift in the Morgan.'

Danny was pleased to see Angela and Monty had made up or at least agreed on a truce. He hung around until Monty returned with some mincemeat he called ground beef, onions and bread rolls. He put the meat in the fridge and suggested they do a spot of diving. He gave Danny a spare pair of goggles and a spear that looked a bit like Neptune's trident. Monty's place was far enough from the harbour so the off shore lagoon was crystal clear and protected by a reef teeming with fish. A couple of adolescent turtles had also made it their home and were quite tame. Monty and Danny bagged several fish that would make fine appetisers before supper. Danny was a little concerned when a white-tipped reef shark darted past, but Monty said they didn't bother swimmers. He failed to mention anything about salt-water crocs until they were safely back on the beach and then said they preferred the muddy mangrove swamps further up the Markham River estuary

'Smart move, offering to go with us tomorrow,' Monty said when they returned to the beach shack and they had showered and dressed. 'It'll be nice to have your company. We'll cover a lot of territory and might find out something about your daddy.'

'Don't tell Angela I have an ulterior motive. I'd like to keep in her good books.'

'I'll bet you do. You sure that ain't the real ulterior motive?'

Danny just grinned and kept his thoughts to himself while Monty sped off to collect Angela. She was in a good mood when they returned as her father's condition had improved and he'd been reclassified from critical to serious, but stable.

A couple of local girls turned up with two crates of clean, empty bottles that they deposited behind the house and Monty gave them half-a-crown each. They seemed very friendly with Monty and Danny thought 2/6d was pretty fair wages for washing Monty's moonshine bottles. Their relationship was never defined beyond merely assisting Monty's boot-legging, but evoked Angela's disapproval especially as they were brazenly bare-topped. The girls chatted so quickly in *Tok Pisin* that Danny failed to keep up. They flirted shamelessly until Monty finally sent them home with a good-natured pat on their respective bottoms. They eyed Angela and giggled some more, but Monty shook his head and sternly wagged his finger. As the girls flounced home arm-in-arm Angela glared at Monty.

'What?' he said with his hands on his hips. 'I sent them away didn't I?'

'And you told them you'd see them again when you get back next week.'

'Sure did,' he said with a wink.

'Oh, you're impossible, Mr Montgomery. Your soul is in for some serious judgment when the time comes.'

'Better enjoy myself while I can then.'

'I hope those two hussies don't think I'm going to have anything to do with you enjoying yourself.'

'No ma'am, you can be sure I put them straight on that matter. But tell the truth, ma'am, I'd rather be a lover than a fighter.'

'I believe you have done your share of fighting in the past. I suppose you'll tell me the same about loving...'

'Not me ma'am, ain't gonna kiss and tell, but you handled yourself pretty good back at the showgrounds.'

'I disapprove of violence in any form.'

'What about self defence?'

She hesitated.

'You know the one good way to stop a man is a swift kick in the gonads.'

'Mr Montgomery..!'

It seemed to Danny that Angela spent rather too much time thinking up ways people *shouldn't* enjoy themselves instead on concentrating on ways they could. Evangelists often tended to be like that. Danny thought Monty was giving sound advice, especially as New Guinea had turned out to be so hazardous. Then again Monty might just have been baiting Angela for the fun of it.

That night, along with filleted fish starters, Monty barbecued beef rissoles he called hamburger patties and served them in a bun with Heinz tomato ketchup.

'There's a bloke who runs a fish and chip shop in Mackay that makes these,' Danny said. 'He puts beetroot slices in 'em if you don't stop him. I hate beetroot slices. It's a pity we don't have lettuce and tomato.'

'Sorry, lettuce wilts in the tropics. But I'll roast some yams.'

'I wonder why they're called hamburgers when there's no ham in them.'

'Because they were invented in Hamburg, silly,' Angela said.

'There're all the rage back stateside,' Monty said. 'Just before the war Maurie and Rich McDonald started a swell joint in San Bernardino, California. They make burgers real fast to compete with them nifty little White Castle sliders.'

The night wore on without further friction and, after phoning the hospital to confirm Dr Holyman was okay, Angela turned in. Danny and Monty were not far behind her.

*

The *Goose* was airborne at first light heading north-east over the Huon Peninsula and across the Vitiaz Strait en route to the countless islands scattered across the Bismarck Sea. As she was only qualified to perform the more basic medical tasks, Angela decided to concentrate on the most remote villages. Although she'd visited larger towns like Madang and Wewak with her father, they had some health facilities, so she thought she'd attend to those places that had none. There were no runways on many islands, but Monty knew all the lagoons where he could land safely.

They were generally met by a flotilla of canoes and a cheerful welcoming committee. The settlements were mostly fishing villages with subsistence plots growing yams, bananas, pineapple and sago as staples. Occasionally they stopped at a coconut plantation where a few imperial Europeans clung to the last vestiges of colonialism. There were one or two missions run by well-meaning clerics and nuns of various denominations. Danny was surprised to see how strongly Christianity had been adopted by the islanders.

Angela was all business and efficiency, but had an empathy with her father's patients so they trusted her. She administered pills, injections, bathed and dressed wounds with antiseptic solution. Danny simply made himself useful whenever he could. He carried the bags, set up tables and chairs, cleared away the waste and acted as crowd-controller. Monty lent a hand, but stayed with his plane when he felt it needed mechanical attention or refuelling. This often involved manhandling 44-gallon drums onto an out-rigger and using a hose to hand-pump the AVGAS into the wing tanks. Where the approach to the beach was clear of reefs, he could lower the wheels and taxi the *Goose* ashore then return to sea, raise the landing gear and moor the plane using an anchor he stowed in the nose compartment. Hoskins was one of the few places with an airstrip where the *Goose* could carry out a safe landing, but mostly they took off and landed at sea.

Food and accommodation were never a problem as the small communities overflowed with hospitality that included a nightly feast and sing-sing. After a week their supplies were almost exhausted and it was time to return to Lae. Danny had made inquiries, but had discovered nothing to locate his father other than the fact that many allied soldiers had remained in New Guinea and the islands. The reasons varied from marrying local girls to treasure hunting on sunken wrecks or simply wanting to stay in paradise. Some had changed their names for fear of being identified as deserters even though they'd served in combat until war's end. They'd just ignored the formal discharge process. Many of this group were from unhappy marriages and this was an ideal, if inconsiderate, option to *get-while-the-getting-was-good*. A bunch of American marines from California and the Hawaiian Territory stayed simply to surf the Nusa and Nago reef breaks off Kavieng.

One of the greatest thrills for Danny was learning to fly. Monty was a patient instructor and encouraged Danny to take the controls as often as possible to the point where he could take off and almost land by himself. Danny'd overcome his original misgivings regarding aviation and now embraced the concept wholeheartedly. Monty called it *bootlegging* flying hours, but made Danny record all his flight-time at the controls in a notebook, explaining they'd copy the hours as *dual* or *co-pilot* into an official log book when they returned to Lae. That way, with a little paper-work manipulation, Danny was half-way to obtaining his pilot's licence.

Their last stop was at one of three isolated islands in the Witu Group, thirty miles north of New Britain. Two of the islands were known locally as *Kago Ailan* and *Daiman-Sikmanmeri Ailan,* while the third was unnamed (*Nogat Nem)* and uninhabited. The islands, along with a scattering of tiny atolls, were in sight of each other although beyond the horizon of the rest of the archipelago. All three islands and the atolls were covered with lush jungle and surrounded by sparking lagoons and coral reefs. *Kago Ailan* was by far the largest of the three islands with a smouldering volcano that rose from its eastern shore. The volcano belched sulphurous magma regularly, but had seldom caused any serious damage.

Kago Ailan was a massive Japanese base during the war. They'd built an airstrip right across it for their bombers to conduct raids over Port Moresby and allied positions on the north coast of Papua after the Japs had been beaten back along the Kokoda Track.

There was a town on *Kago Ailan* where a long pier stretched from the shore into deep water to facilitate supply ships. The place was known as *Kagotaun*. The dirt main street was lined with stores, cafes, bars, brothels and a shabby hotel. Angela called the town a den of iniquity and magnet for thieves, cut-throats and harlots, every bit as wretched as Sodom or Gomorrah and a place to be avoided if possible. Previously Angela and Gordon Holyman had come by boat or with other aerial charters, so although he'd heard of the place, Monty had never been there, but insisted it really sounded like his kind of town. The name *Kago Ailan* was relatively new. It came about after the US Marines had taken *Kago Ailan* from the Japs and island-hopped to their next bloody battlefield, leaving thousands of tons of precious 'cargo' behind. The locals, who had suffered hideously during the Japanese occupation and subsequent struggle for the island, felt justified in commandeering what supplies they could. So wartime ravaging aside, the cargo-cult was alive and well on *Kago Ailan*.

But the large island wasn't their destination. Angela said they only called there if time permitted as the only health risks were barroom brawl injuries, liver cirrhosis and STDs. Monty put the *Goose* down inside a reef on the western shore of *Daiman-Sikmanmeri Ailan* and moored on a small jetty leading from a beach shack. Fishing dugouts were drawn up on the beach and several nets hung out to dry on wooden frames. The ground rose steeply for several hundred feet with huts scattered along the hillside. There was a larger building half-way up, but no cheerful welcoming committee, in fact – no sign of people at all.

As Danny moored the *Goose* to the jetty, he noticed a silent tension between Monty and Angela, but shrugged and put it down to their usual animosity. An industrial wheel-barrow stood on the jetty and they filled it with Angela's supplies. As soon as they had unloaded the equipment Monty returned to the cockpit and didn't come back.

'Come along please, Danny,' Angela said rather stiffly.

'Isn't Monty going to help?'

'No, he says he needs to fix the plane. We shall have to manage without him this time.'

She strode away leaving Danny to follow with the barrow. As they reached the tree line a rather haggard-looking priest in full cassock and an equally careworn nun in a crisp white habit met them.

'Welcome, Miss Holyman,' the priest greeted, 'but where is your father?'

'I'm afraid he's had an accident. He's in Lae hospital.'

'Oh dear, nothing too serious I hope.'

'It is serious, but I believe with our Lord's grace he'll pull through.'

'We shall all pray for him at Mass.'

'This is my friend Danny. He's been such a dear and gave blood to save daddy. Danny this is Fr Kennedy and Sister Celeste.'

'G'day,' Danny said, but noticed neither the good father nor sister offered a hand in greeting or to help with the barrow. But, they both smiled politely.

'Everyone's waiting in the big house,' Fr Kennedy said and they headed up the hill.

When they reached the building a group of people were sitting along the veranda. Some were in chairs while others were on the floor. They all had some sort of deformity varying from missing fingers and toes to terrible skin lesions, festering sores and bloated facial disfigurements. They were mainly adults, but there were a few children as well.

Danny gasped.

'Bloody hell, Angela...'

'Yes Danny,' she sighed, 'these poor people suffer from Hansen's disease. They're lepers.'

Chapter 17 – Tremor

Danny stared dumbfounded. *Of course, how could I have been so flamin' thick? I didn't even ask. Daiman-Sikmanmeri Ailan...* Dead and Sick People Island!

'You should have told me!' he hissed.

'You wouldn't have come if I had, would you?'

'Too right I wouldn't. No wonder Monty was so cagey. Struth Ange, you lied to me!'

'No I didn't.'

'Okay, you may not have lied, but you were still dishonest.'

That cut like a knife, he could see it in her eyes.

'Leprosy isn't highly contagious, Danny. We'll wear surgical masks and gloves.'

'*You'll* wear them. Sorry Ange, count me out of this one. I've lugged your stuff up here and now I'm gonna wait with Monty.'

'You're such a coward,' she stormed with un-Christian venom. 'Mr Montgomery is just a selfish mercenary, but I thought so much better of you.'

'Maybe, but that's the way it's going to be. You had no right to bring me here without warning me first.'

'Please...'

'No.'

Had he thought about it he probably would have reconsidered, but he was so furious nothing would change his mind whatever she said. Dammit, he wasn't her flaming slave. He turned in fury and hurried back down the track to the wharf.

What a nerve calling me a coward after everything I've done for her? She's just a silly, stuck-up cow and to think I fancied her. I must have been bonkers!

Monty was playing a harmonica as he lounged against a pylon on the jetty. He'd checked the *Goose* and was ready for a quick getaway. Maybe he should have gone before Danny got back, because Monty bore the brunt of his rage.

'...Of all the self-righteous, infuriating, opinionated, manipulating, deceitful...'

Monty pocketed the harp. He stood with his arms folded and a mildly amused look.

'That went well, I take it,' he said.

'You're no better,' Danny snarled. 'You could have told me.'

'More than my life's worth, buddy.'

'Don't "buddy" me...'

As if reflecting Danny's rage, *Kago Ailan's* volcano rumbled ominously before disgorging an ash cloud followed by a tremor that rattled along the jetty. The pier actually wavered like a snake tail as the water surged out to sea.

'Oh shit,' Monty hissed.

'What?'

'Tidal wave...c'mon...we've gotta move....fast!'

Monty unhitched the mooring cable.

'Get in!' he yelled.

'What about Angela?'' Danny asked a he clambered aboard.

Monty was already starting the engines

'No time, she'll have to fend for herself. They're all half way up the hill. They should be okay,'

Monty was taxying past the reef as Danny slammed the cabin door closed and dashed to the cockpit. The current was racing away and carrying the *Goose* along with it.

'We've gotta get clear before this ebb exposes the reef and cuts the hull to shreds.'

Approaching the coral they saw the surface break up as the water level dropped. Monty gunned the throttles and the *Goose* flashed over the reef where jagged bomboras now reared above the surface. The *Goose* shuddered as its hull grated against the coral outcrops with a sinister growl.

'That sounds bad,' Monty muttered, but they'd cleared the reef.

Made it, Danny thought then looked ahead and wondered if that was true. A three metre high wall of water reared ahead and surged towards them. A tsunami had exploded from the seabed and was forced upwards by the earth tremor. The *Goose* was right in its path.

'Can we outrun it?' Danny yelled.

'No way, our only chance is to get past it before it breaks. I hope we ain't taking on water through the hull.'

The wave was just a smooth wall of water at that stage, but the outgoing swell dropped the water depth dramatically. As soon as it was shallow enough the tidal wave would break forward in a devastating maelstrom of white surf. A tsunami was less dangerous in open water as surface vessels simply rode over the swell, but as soon as it reached the shallows or made landfall it wreaked merciless havoc on anything in its path. The wave seemed to grow as the *Goose* powered towards it. The peak was beginning to ripple and curl over and was on the point of breaking when the *Goose* roared up the wave face. It felt almost as if they were travelling vertically when the *Goose* surged over the crest and staggered into the air. Monty shoved the control-column forward to maintain airspeed and the *Goose* skimmed down the back of the swell, but they were airborne although still not free of the tsunami. A secondary wave welled up towards the plane's hull. Monty raised the nose once more. The *Goose* now had enough airspeed to climb, but still clipped the crest. The *Goose* shuddered, but they were clear and the wave surged away behind them.

Monty banked the *Goose* back towards *Daiman-Sikmanmeri Ailan*. They were just in time to see the wave smash over the reef and into the lagoon. The jetty was swept to splinters in seconds along with all the canoes and any equipment on the beach. Shacks along the wharf disintegrated and vanished. The tidal surge gouged up dirt, rock, coral and vegetation indiscriminately, turning the crystal turquoise water to a filthy grey sludge. The waves were past the island in seconds and from their vantage point Monty and Danny could see it charging away in a huge arc eastwards across the Bismarck Sea.

'Mayday, mayday, mayday,' Monty yelled into his radio mike. 'All traffic in the *Kago Ailan* region sea hazard warning. Tidal wave moving east at high speed. Approximate height ten feet followed by a secondary swell. Shore stations get to high ground. Sea vessels get to open water.'

He was relieved to hear Rabaul air traffic control respond and relay the message although the wave speed made him wonder whether they'd have time to act. It was really all they could do, the tsunami was long gone and, even if the *Goose* could overtake it, there was no way of warning people on the ground. So Monty circled *Daiman-Sikmanmeri Ailan* to see if there was any sign of life. The sea level had receded remarkably quickly and had returned to normal with equal speed. There was nothing left along the shoreline though. Some of the forest remained, but the lower trees were decimated. Debris floated all around the island, but at least the big building and surrounding huts had survived.

'They can't have been swept away,' Danny said. 'They were well above the wave.'

'I dunno...' Monty replied and took the *Goose* down for a closer look.

At first they didn't see what was happening, but after flying past several times it became tragically clear. The tsunami had gouged out a great slab of terrain below the main building which began to shift almost imperceptibly. Then it was slowly slipping away. As it gathered momentum down the slope it dragged anything in its path, including trees and huts. Pieces of masonry and timber were flung sideways as the walls buckled and the roof vanished in shards of palm thatch. The big house lumbered on until it finally crunched to rest on the shoreline with shredded vegetation heaped on top of it.

'Take her down, Monty,' Danny said. 'We'll have to give 'em a hand.'

'Sorry, I dunno whether the hull is damaged. If it takes in water on landing it'll break up and that'll be curtains for us.'

'But Angie's down there!'

'You think I don't know that, but we're no use to her dead.'

'I left her before...We can't just leave her now.'

'You didn't know this was going to happen. We'll head back to *Kago Ailan* and get help. I can land on the airstrip.'

'If it's still there.'

'I reckon the wave started at *Kago* so all the damage is ahead of it, not behind. We've no other choice.'

'Those poor blighters down there didn't have much going for them, and now this...'

Monty headed the *Goose* towards the big island. It was easy to pick out because the volcano still spewed out a cloud that rose thousands of feet above them. As they approached they saw the ash cloud drifting away with the occasional splash as a lump of magma plunged into the sea. The mountain appeared satisfied for the moment as less and less molten rock hurtled up and the volcano simmered down almost as quickly as it had erupted.

'It's done that a few times since I've been flying up here,' *Monty* said, 'but this is the first time I've heard of it setting off a tidal wave.'

The runway flight path was clear so Monty manoeuvred for his approach. There was no ATC service at the aerodrome so Monty simply made a VHF radio call letting any other planes in the area know he was landing at *Kagotaun* cancelling his Search-and-Rescue watch on the Rabaul HF radio. The touch-down was bumpy with the runway in disrepair and Monty had to dodge potholes and tufts of vegetation that sprouted from every crack in the tarmac. No other planes were parked at the strip so Monty taxied the *Goose* beside an abandoned Nissen hut. While Danny chocked the main wheels Monty looked over the fuselage. He'd made the right decision to return to *Kago* because the hull bore several tears that would have leaked so badly that even if the plane hadn't broken up on landing it certainly wouldn't have been able to take off again.

'She's a land-based aircraft until I get that fixed,' Monty tut-tutted.

'Bad?' Danny asked.

'Bad enough, but not terminal. She'll get us back to Lae okay. C'mon, let's get into town and tell 'em what's happened on *Daiman.*'

It was about a mile to town and the day was the usual scorcher. The air was filled with acrid sulphur fumes, but Monty estimated it'd clear in a few hours. It seemed a long way, but they hadn't gone far when they saw someone trotting towards them. He was a diminutive Chinese fellow pulling a rickshaw. The heat didn't appear to bother him, but he was shaded beneath a huge coolie's hat. He stopped in front of Monty and Danny grinning with far more teeth than his mouth could hold.

'You wanna number one lide to *Kagotaun*?' he beamed. 'Jorry good top-hole lide. Onry harf-a-clown. Number one lickshaw lide.'

'Half-a-crown for half-a-mile,' Danny said. 'I'll give you a zac.'

'Two shirring.'

'A bob.'

'Two shirring.'

Monty drew his Colt 45 automatic and waved it menacingly in the Chinaman's direction.

'One shilling, we're wasting time,' he snarled.

'Okay dokey, one shirring. But you no jorry good ferrow, you bad-bum Yankee, worse than sook ching japanee.'

'Yeah, I'm a gun-totin' bad-arse so you'd better hop to it.'

They clambered into the rickshaw and the Chinaman scampered away.

'Talk about an opportunist,' Monty said with more than a hint of admiration. 'He must have seen the *Goose* land and got the taxi service rolling.'

'Did you see the wave?' Danny called ahead.

'Oh yesee. Me see velly big rave.'

'We need to get help to the people on *Daiman Ailan.* Take us to the police station.'

'No porice station. No porice on *Kago Airan.* Jorry good too. I take you to pub.'

'We don't need a drink...'

'Not you maybe,' Monty said.

'Barman, he toughest guy in town,' the coolie said. 'You wanna something, he fix it.'

It was as good a place to start as anywhere. They'd need able-bodied men to help clear the wreckage, but whether they'd be prepared to go to a leper colony was another thing. Monty's pistol might be needed for persuasion. Danny had rather forgotten his own prejudice. Now all he wanted was to find Angela. He'd been a bit of a wimp really, but she'd taken him by surprise. Of course had he stayed he'd be in the rubble pile at the foot of *Daiman-Sikmanmeri* Hill too.

They entered *Kagotaun* Main Street. It was a colourful thoroughfare lined with stalls selling everything the town needed. There was a greengrocery market, fishmonger, butcher and French patisserie. Every second doorway looked like a grog shop and working girls touted from second floor windows. The street was full of people who seemed unconcerned about volcanic eruptions or tidal waves. Apparently *Kago* Volcano suffered from indigestion every few months, so it was no longer remarkable. Like the big house on *Daiman* the town was situated well above sea-level and had remained intact through cyclones, thunderstorms, tidal surges, earth tremors and volcanic eruptions.

Kagotaun was a multi-cultural Mecca. People of all nationalities had gravitated there after the war. Ex-colonial landlords, soldiers-of-fortune, Chinese gold-diggers, Filipino merchants and pirates, European adventurers and ex-servicemen all contributed to the mix. There was even a group of Japanese geishas left over from the occupation who'd diversified and lowered their standards considerably. They fused with the local islanders in a mutually-dependant society. There were no constables and, although the district commissioner had visited once, he'd not been seen since. Some places were best left to their own devices.

The coolie stopped outside a large three-storey veranda-fronted building. A sign above the doorway read *Imperial Hotel,* although most of the paint had peeled away. Danny handed the coolie a shilling before he and Monty climbed the veranda steps and entered the barroom. Dedicated patrons were already into their cups and were either playing cards, dominoes, snooker or drafts while cigarette smoke hovered at about head-height.

When Danny reached the bar he froze as the innkeeper greeted them.

'G'day gents,' the publican smiled cordially enough. 'What'll it be? The name's George McAlister, welcome to my place.'

Part Three – The Archipelago Incident

Chapter 18 – Return to Death Island

Danny simply stared at the man before him who claimed to be his father. It had been so many years since he'd seen his dad, and he'd only been eight at the time. He realised he'd been without a father for half his life. So he stared and tried to recall something familiar about the man, but failed to do so. His voice, maybe, but it all had been so long ago. George McAlister now sported a beard and, although it was neatly trimmed, Danny remembered his father being clean-shaven.

'Are you okay, lad?' George asked, frowning as if he too saw something familiar in the teenager across the bar.

'He reckons you're his daddy,' Monty said. 'Looks like it's a bit of a shock.'

'Danny..?'

'Dad!'

A stranger wouldn't know his name, would he? From just a single word Danny knew he'd found is long-lost father.

'I've been looking for you,' Danny said after another awkward pause.

'Well, I'll be blessed. This is a turn up for the books...'

'Look guys, I hate to break up the reunion, but we've got work to do,' Monty said.

'Work..?'

'Yeah George, the name's Monty. We've just brought my plane in from *Daiman*. She was damaged by that darned wave.'

'We've got to save Angela,' Danny gasped.

'Angela?'

'Doc Holyman's daughter. We were doing the rounds at *Daiman* when the wave hit. There was a landslide and the big house collapsed. Angela might be trapped in the rubble.'

'Struth,' George hissed between his teeth. 'I've never met the good doctor or his lass m'self, but I've heard he calls by when he can. Mostly he'd give our working girls a physical and dose of penicillin if they needed it or he'd drop off a supply of French letters. Is he on *Daiman* as well?'

'No, he's sick in Lae hospital, but he'll recover.'

'Righto, we'd better get over to *Daiman*,' George said. 'I'll drum up volunteers, but don't hold your breath. I'll get anyone I can up to your plane.'

'No-can-do, George. The hull's busted. You'll have to go by boat.'

Monty's use of *you'll* wasn't lost on Danny.

'What are *you* gonna do, Monty?" he challenged.

'Look someone's gotta try and co-ordinate help. I don't think there're enough people and gear in *Kagotaun* to do the job, do you? I'll get on the radio and call Manus and see if the Navy can send help. I'll fly the *Goose* to Rabaul if necessary and bring back anyone I can.'

It all sounded very sensible when Monty put it that way and Danny regretted sounding so churlish.

'We'll take my boat,' George said.

'You've got a boat?'

'Doesn't everyone?'

True, other than air, the only way around the islands was obviously by boat and the wharf was packed with them. Other than minuscule damage from the back swell, *Kagotaun's* fleet had been unaffected by the tidal wave. George's craft was an ancient, twin masted, lateen rigged vessel, half-way between a Mediterranean fishing boat and an Arabian dhow. Although the craft was primarily a sailing vessel it was also equipped with a sizeable auxiliary inboard petrol engine. How the boat came to be in the South Seas was anyone's guess. It would carry a dozen people in comfort and twenty at a squeeze. However, that was beside the point as the fate of *Daiman* was of slim interest to *Kago* folk. George only managed to persuade six volunteers to come along with them, one of whom was the Chinese rickshaw driver. His name was Sim Long Li and he gave no reason why he'd decided to join the rescue party. The other five were the abandoned Japanese geisha-turned-whores who felt they owed Dr Holyman something in return for his efforts to keep them free of venereal disease. Long Li, who hated all things Japanese, was prepared to concede wartime atrocities weren't the girls' fault and they'd been as ill-treated by imperial troops as anyone else. They were dressed in figure hugging satin cheongsams with hip-high slits in the skirts. They had obviously discovered the sensual Chinese costume was better for trade than traditional kimonos. Maybe so, but Danny doubted the practicality of tight dresses where they were going.

Long Li gathered as many tools as he could find while George prepared his boat and checked the fuel-tank. George left the hotel in the hands of his sole employee, a hefty island matron who acted as barmaid, bouncer, cook and cleaner. She'd often minded the place while George went fishing or out-rigger surfing on the point break at the northern tip of *Kago Ailan*. Danny made himself useful lugging blankets and water bottles from the hotel to the wharf. The geishas were remarkably practical. They'd lived through so many disasters during the wartime struggle for *Kago Ailan* that they knew how to prioritise. *Kagotaun's* water supply came from dozens of fresh streams and rainwater tanks so it was pure enough. Although *Daiman* also had streams and tanks, there was no way of knowing what damage had been done by the wave and subsequent landslide. They knew water would be precious and they filled bottles, pots, gourds or anything else to hand. They loaded everything onto Long Li's rickshaw and headed for the pier.

George explained they carried insufficient petrol to motor all the way so they'd rely on sail-power. He expected their voyage would take all night. Indeed the sun was sinking into a magnificent blood-red cloud of volcanic ash as Danny cast off and George motored away from the *Kagotaun* harbour. Once clear Long Li hoisted the main and fore sails while George cut the motor. As the canvas filled aloft, George's boat *Rocky Road* glided towards the horizon.

Although the *Lady Burdekin* hadn't been a sailing boat, it certainly set Danny in good stead when it came to unravelling *Rocky Road's* mysteries. George explained the rudiments which appeared simple enough, especially in fair conditions. Long Li knew his stuff anyway and Danny had no difficulty fitting into the role of deckhand. After he'd helped the geishas stow their supplies, Danny stood with his father at the helm.

'So tell me, son,' George said, 'how the blue blazes did you find me?'

'It seems like one accident after another to me,' Danny replied and told his father in a brief summary.

'Impressive,' George said. 'I'm amazed you got here at all.'

'Tell me about it, but I've made some good friends on the way, even Angela. She might have been a bit snooty but I liked her all the same.'

'I'm sure she's fine,' George said, noting Danny's use of the past tense.

After the girls had organised their stores, they introduced themselves to Danny as Ayaku, Kana, Mayu, Sakura and Yuuka. They bowed a lot and Danny found himself doing the same. With a following breeze and no need for tacking or jibing, Long Li had nothing much to do. He settled at the bow and promptly fell asleep. Mayu, who was slightly older than the other girls, was their leader and organised them in preparing the supper they'd brought in bamboo baskets. She gave Danny and George cold rice rolled in green vegetable leaves filled with meat and fish marinated in soy sauce.

After a little uncertainty and more bobbing, Danny took a bite.

'Hey, that's not too bad,' he beamed.

'It's called sushi,' George said. 'Japs eat 'em like sangers.'

'They're pretty neat.'

'Yeah, the Japs are like that about things. They like formal ceremonies and everything in order. They like to do things together and don't encourage individualism.'

'They all seem so young, even Mayu. I mean to be...you know...during the war.'

'They are young. Some of 'em would have been barely twelve when they started camp-following the Imperial Army. Mostly their mothers sold 'em to survive. The menfolk were all in the army and some families couldn't cope and selling children was a way out. These girls might have been lucky in the end. Their families are all dead now, so they see no reason to go back to Japan.'

'That's sort of...really sad,' Danny said, which sounded trite, but he couldn't think of anything else to say.

'We didn't start the bloody war. They got what they deserved,' George said with sudden venom. Until then he'd seemed like the gentle-natured chap Danny remembered. 'Maybe they don't want to go back and be part of it anyway. Mayu might be a bit older than the others, but she was only thirteen when they forced her into whoring.'

Mayu's story was eight years of terror. She'd been sold to an officer's brothel in the 16th Division of the 10th Imperial Army's Shanghai Expeditionary Force. She'd witnessed the rape of Nanking in 1937 and subsequent horrors throughout the war that made Vlad-the-Impaler look like a pussycat. After the surrender she rejected anything Japanese. They'd committed too many atrocities for her to ever forgive or forget what had been done in the name of the Imperial Rising Sun. The other girls may not have seen as much of the *sook ching* massacres, but felt the same way. They all came from Nagasaki and there was nothing to go back to anyway.'

'Long Li sure hates Japs,' Danny observed.

'So he should,' George said, 'most of his family were slaughtered in Singapore. He escaped on a junk with the survivors, but Zeroes strafed them so many times that he was the only one left when he reached here. It took him months ducking and weaving through the Java Sea then zigzagging around islands trying to keep one step ahead of the Japs. He hid out in the jungle throughout the war helping an Aussie coast watcher until the Japs caught up with them. Long Li slipped away while the officers argued over who would execute the other poor bugger and he managed to stay alive until we took the island.'

'Struth, the bloody war,' Danny said, 'did it affect everyone..?'

'Pretty much, lad. Ruddy millions anyway.'

'You too, dad?'

'Too right.'

It seemed odd calling someone *dad* after so many years and about then the question had to be asked.

'Why didn't you come home, dad?'

'Eh?'

'You heard — why didn't you come back to mum and me?'

'It's complicated.'

'Didn't you love us?'

'It wasn't that. I don't want to talk about it.'

'Well, I do. How do you think we felt, not knowing if you were alive or dead?'

'I'm sorry.'

'So are we. You could have written a letter at least.'

'You think your mother would want to be married to a deserter? At least she gets a widow's pension this way.'

'Well she doesn't, actually,' Danny sneered, 'because she's not a widow, is she?'

'You really want to know?' George yelled so everyone aboard turned and stared at him.

'Yes!' Danny said.

George lowered his voice.

'Alright, I'll tell you. I don't know whether it'll make any sense to you though. I'm not a violent man, never have been. I never laid a hand on your mother, and nothing more than a clip around your ear when you deserved it. So how do you think I managed when I was thrown into the bloodiest hell you could imagine? Mud, rain and jungle so thick you can only see a couple of feet and bloody Japs lying in ambush everywhere waiting to stick a bayonet in your guts. And what thanks did we get? The track was littered with dead Diggers when that fat bastard General Blamey flounced up and told us we were being beaten by an inferior force and we were running around like a bunch of frightened rabbits. He was lucky we didn't shoot him instead of the Japs.'

'You were scared, I can understand that.'

'Too bloody right I was scared. Scared shitless for month after sodding month. I dunno how I kept going. I think I was barking mad by the end of it. I don't even know what finally happened.

Just as we were beating the buggers back over the track I was grazed by a Jap bullet, or maybe it was one of ours, who knows? I guess I was picked up by the Fuzzy-Wuzzy Angels. They normally carried wounded back to Moresby, but we were too far in advance so they tried to get me to the north coast. Somebody told me there was bitter fighting going on, but I don't remember. All I know is they had to take off into the bush to dodge a Jap counter-attack. We arrived at a village – I don't even know if it had a name – and there I stayed.'

'Didn't you want to go back and help your unit?'

'That was the last thing I wanted, so I just stayed where I was. The villagers didn't mind and I was able to help out around the place. After the war I just drifted from place to place. I loved the islands and finally wound up on *Kago*.'

'You could have let us know.'

'You're right, sorry about that, but what's done is done.'

'We missed you.'

'You missed the *old* me before I went away. That's not me now. *My* dad was in the first wave at Anzac Cove then spent two more years in the trenches on the Western Front. He came home half blind from gas and with a gammy leg from a Jerry bullet wound that never recovered. He was a wreck, diving under a table if he heard a car back-fire or your grandma dropping a pot in the kitchen. He couldn't talk to her about the war, he couldn't talk to anyone. No one understood and, after a while, no one cared.'

'Didn't you?'

'Yes I cared, but I was just a kid, what could I do? He took to drink and started knocking the family around. In the end he simply stepped onto the railway line in front of a southbound rattler and ended everything. I don't want that for you and your mum and I don't want that for me.'

Danny knew his grandfather had died young, but not how and his grandmother never mentioned it. She'd moved to Maryborough and Danny never saw her anyway.

'Mum would have waited if she'd known,' Danny said defensively.

'She stopped waiting I take it.'

'She took up with Stanley Hallet from the meat works.'

'Yeah, I know him. Not my cup of tea, but a steady enough cove. She'll be better off with him. Dunno if I'd be sent to gaol if I went back anyway.'

'She can't marry Stanley if you're alive.'

George shrugged. He and Mavis had shared a cordial relationship rather than a passionate one. He certainly wasn't going to mention it to Danny, but the only reason they married was because she was pregnant. That had been the line of least resistance to avoid shame and scandal. Mavis was loyal, George had to concede, but loyalty apparently didn't last forever, and who could blame her?

'Then tell her I'm dead when you go back,' George suggested.

'Go back?' Danny stared at his father in the lamplight. 'Why would I do that? What have I to go back for?'

'Your mum..?'

'She's got Stanley now and spends all her time keeping him happy. She let him talk her into sending me to *St Ursicinus*. I'll never forgive her for that.'

'I don't reckon all priests and nuns are like the ones at that school you mentioned. Fr Kennedy and Sister Celeste have devoted their lives to helping those poor blighters at the leper colony. I'm sure your mum didn't know what she was getting you into or she'd never agreed.'

'Maybe it wasn't mum's fault then and she certainly wasn't to blame for the war,' Danny said, not sure why he felt a need to suddenly justify his mother's actions.

'The war wasn't anyone's fault except a bunch of barmy generals and politicians wanting to make a name for themselves. Trouble is there's always been war and there always will be. I reckon it's just in our nature. WWI was called the *war to end all wars*, but it wasn't even over when the Russians started butchering each other in droves. God knows what the chink warlords got up to before the Japs sorted them out. Spain had a bloody civil war in '36 that Jerry used as a rehearsal for their blitzkrieg in '39. Now WWII is hardly finished when there's trouble in Korea and Indo China. Whatever those dopes in the United Nations think, they won't change a ruddy thing. They'll talk and talk and people will fight and fight.'

It all sounded very discouraging, but they talked on, catching up as George put it, until Danny grew drowsy. Slumping onto the transsom bench, he fell asleep until pre-dawn as they approached *Daiman Ailan*. During the night Long Li relieved George at the helm, so he too could sleep for a couple of hours.

Chapter 19 – *Banzai!*

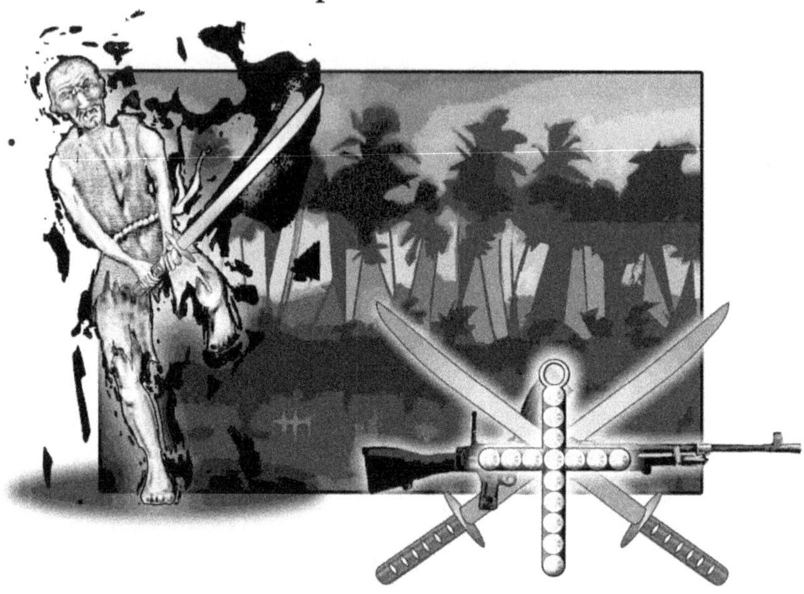

With the pier demolished, the first problem facing *Rocky Road's* crew was where to dock. After some manoeuvring George found a spot where rubble had piled up and formed a jetty of sorts. Only ripples lapped the shore in the morning stillness so they were able to relay the supplies onto dry land without any great difficulty. The Japanese girls had changed into cotton pants and smocks during the night and left their cheongsams neatly folded where they'd slept on deck. Long Li and Danny manhandled an upturned out-rigger into the water while George anchored *Rocky Road* in a deep channel so she wouldn't ground as the tide ebbed. They all paddled back in the canoe and beached it next to the stores. Most of the sand and crushed coral had been washed away exposing the bedrock beneath.

George told the girls to stay with the supplies until he'd reconnoitred. Danny, Long Li and George scrambled over the rocks around the shoreline to where the big-house now rested on what had once been a beach. As they approached the big-house they heard a voice ahead of them.

'Hello there...over here...'

Mud, broken palm trunks, rock and debris cluttered their path, but they eventually clambered close enough to see Fr Kennedy waving frantically. His cassock was tattered and coated with mud. Sister Celeste stood behind him, bare-headed and with rather less of her habit remaining than she'd have liked.

'Thank heaven you're here,' the good sister gasped.

On close inspection the big-house wasn't as badly damaged as they might have expected. The stilts supporting the floor had taken the brunt of the force when they sheared off, but the floor itself was bolted to stout beams and bearers that had kept it virtually level and intact. It had acted rather like a toboggan. The walls were buckled, but still in place although the roof was gone altogether. It had been replaced by a matting of tangled palm fronds that added to the chaos

'Blimey,' George said, 'you were lucky to survive, Father.'

'So we were, my son, so we were. Thanks be to God.'

Funny how people keep thanking God after He's inflicted a disaster on them, Danny thought.

'What are your casualties?'

'Well, there's the truth of it, may the Lord be praised, for we have no more than cuts and bruises, which for these poor folk is worse than for you and me, but no one was killed. Mostly we'll need bandages, water and stout hands to clear a way back to the path where we can think about rebuilding the big-house and the huts that were carried away.'

Sure enough the inhabitants of *Daiman* were all accounted for and seemed in remarkable spirits for people who'd just survived a tidal wave and landslide. But there was no sign of Angela.

'Where's..?' Danny stammered.

Fr Kennedy looked decidedly uncomfortable.

'Where's Angela?' Danny demanded.

'I don't know,' the priest said apologetically.

'But everyone else in the big-house is safe. If they survived, surely she's okay too.'

'That's the trouble, lad. Angela wasn't inside when the landslide hit.'

'What do you mean?'

'After you left she stayed outside. She seemed very upset. I called her, but she asked me to give her a minute. I understand you had a falling out, and I feel she wanted to compose herself before helping our people.'

It hit Danny like a sledgehammer. If he hadn't been so bone-headedly stubborn, they'd both have been inside the big-house and protected from the worst of the landslide. Outside there was no hope. Angela must have been swept into the sea or covered by a thousand tons of mud. Danny was frantic. It was entirely his fault, his own bloody-minded, stupid, selfish fault. He clambered down to the shoreline and scrambled amongst the rocks and debris, but there was no sign of Angela. No scraps of clothing, her medical bag, or a body.

'Danny! Danny!'

George grabbed him by the shoulders and shook him until his eyeballs rattled.

'Pull yourself together, son. This isn't your fault, you weren't to know.'

'She'd have been inside if I'd stayed...'

'Well you didn't, she wasn't and that's that. You're doing no one any good here. Look, as soon as we've evacuated everyone we'll leave the girls to help out and then try to find a way back up that hill. Maybe there'll be some clues where the big-house used to stand.'

George had assessed the situation correctly. The islanders couldn't stay where they were because while the big-house may have survived the landslide, it was definitely unstable. With waves lapping at the floorboards, who knew how long it would be before it either collapsed to mush or was washed out to sea? Many of the islanders managed to scramble over the rocks and congregated on the remains of the wharf. Danny, George and Long Li salvaged a couple of stretchers and, with Fr Kennedy and Sister Celeste's help, they carried the worst afflicted lepers to a safer spot.

'Our first priority is shelter, then water,' Fr Kennedy said. 'Look, there are still several huts standing that the mud slide missed. We'll be a bit squashed, but it'll do until we can rebuild the big house. Let's go and inspect the damage and see what's to be done.'

The Japanese girls had made a fire and were boiling tea and laying out more sushi rolls for breakfast. They let the tea cups cool before offering them around aware that many lepers had lost all feeling in their nerve-endings and could easily burn themselves without realising it. After about an hour everyone's hunger and personal hygiene requirements were satisfied. Many people simply lay where they were and went to sleep out of sheer exhaustion.

'Come on,' George said, 'it looks like they're all settled for now. Let's go and inspect the damage up there.'

So Fr Kennedy, Danny, Long Li and George trudged up the path that was strewn with rubble and slippery with mud. When they reached the site of the big-house it was patently clear where the swathe of mud had undermined the building and sluiced down the hillside. Everything either side was left completely undamaged. As Fr Kennedy had predicted there were enough huts left to house all his flock who were stoic battlers anyway and would overcome this near-tragedy.

Danny clambered across the slip area, but could find no sign of Angela. He started thrashing around in the rain forest, not really knowing what to look for.

'Hang on, Danny,' George called, 'let's at least try to be a bit systematic about this.'

Fr Kennedy showed them where Angela had been sitting before the slide and they cast around for footprints or any other signs of her. There was nothing, she could only have been swept into the sea. Danny crossed the mud trail again and continued looking until something finally caught his eye. One of Angela's sandals lay half-buried, looking as if it had been sucked from her foot by clinging mud.

'She crossed over here,' Danny yelled, waving the sandal.

The others joined him and examined the shoe.

'It means she's okay, doesn't it?' Danny stammered.

'Possibly...' George said.

'Or it mean is we ownry found shoe,' Long Li commented pointedly.

Danny glared at him.

'If she's okay,' George said, 'she'll have tried to get down to the big-house, nothing surer that that. She might have had to divert a bit to pick her way through all this mess. I suggest we follow what looks like the best trail and see if we can find any clues as we go.'

At least they were doing something. Danny, George and Long Li left Father Kennedy to regroup his people and settle them in the huts and cautiously started down the hill. They each carried a water bottle which was sensible because it was hot work.

'Reminds me of the track,' George said without sounding too happy about it. 'Watch out for snakes, they were nearly as bad as the Japs.'

In fact poisonous snakes weren't the threat they were on mainland New Guinea, but there was a fair smattering of sinister spiders, bugs and ants that Danny did his best to avoid. The jungle was thick with vines and undergrowth that seemed to trip them at every turn. Broad leaves slapped Danny's face despite his efforts to brush them aside. He was soon drenched with sweat, although George and Long Li were managing much better. In fact the Chinaman didn't seem fussed at all. Surviving two years of dodging Japanese patrols had made him at home in the rainforest. He even knew what plants were edible and which were poisonous.

Danny pulled up suddenly as he sensed a rustling ahead. The vegetation was so dense he couldn't make out anything clearly. Then a shadow darted through the dappled undergrowth.

'Angela! Ange, is that you?'

Silence.

Another movement.

'C'mon Ange, stop messing about. We've been worried.'

Silence.

Then Danny saw a figure bolting down the hillside. He raced in pursuit. Half stumbling, half falling he careered down the slope. What he was thinking was anyone's guess, because if the figure had been Angela, surely she would have stopped and called back. So he frantically pressed on with illogical recklessness. He even yelled *stop* a couple of times as if that would do any good. As he reached the shoreline where some sand actually remained, he tripped, tumbled and rolled across the beach, ending up in shallow water. He picked himself up to see a man about the size of Long Li charging across the beach towards him. The man was definitely Oriental, looking seriously under-nourished with a wispy beard and moustache. He appeared at least sixty years old, but that meant nothing in his emaciated state. He was dressed in ragged khaki. The sleeves and trouser-legs were no more than tatters flapping in the breeze.

Normally Danny might have been amused or merely curious, but the man carried a samurai sword raised high above his head. In that split second Danny noted that, although the sword was rusted, it certainly looked dangerous enough. And that wasn't all...

'*Banzai!*' the little fellow screamed.

'Holy crap...'

'Struth, a bloody Jap,' George said as he raced onto the beach.

The Japanese man launched himself at Danny just as Long Li and George raced to join the fray. They all crashed together, their momentum carrying them plummeting into Danny who landed back in the sea with three wrestling, screaming men struggling over him. His head was forced under the surface and he was in danger of drowning, but managed to scramble free just before his breath ran out. The Japanese fellow may have been ancient and diminutive, but he fought like a demon and still held onto the sword. Each time George and Long Li dived on top of him he wriggled free, brandishing the blade. While his attacker was preoccupied Danny rugger-tackled him, bringing him down again but got a kick in the teeth for his trouble. The bellicose warrior bounded to his feet and swung the sword at Danny, slashing him across the cheek.

'You bastard!' Danny stormed as blood dripped from his chin onto his chest. He charged again, ducking under another swipe from the sword and pummelled into the Japanese man's guts. Swinging his fists for all he worth Danny smashed punches into his opponent – wherever they landed. The Japanese man tried to fight back, but Danny was berserk with rage. He hadn't done anything to this blasted idiot, so he'd get a lesson he's never forget. Eventually the Japanese soldier – for they'd all determined that was what he was by then – weakened under the rain of punches and finally went limp. It took all George and Long Li's strength to pull Danny off his victim. Long Li grabbed the sword and held the point to their captive's throat as he groaned and stirred back to consciousness.

'What's his game, dad?' Danny yelled. 'The war's been over for five years.'

'Beats me,' George conceded, hauling the Japanese man to his feet.

Long Li looked as if he would use the sword, but George waved him away. The Chinaman and Japanese soldier started yelling abuse at each other in Cantonese and Japanese that made no sense to anyone, even themselves.

'Hold on, Long Li,' George said,' we'll take this bugger back to the girls. They'll be able to translate for us and we'll find out who he is.'

Then Danny noticed something sparkle around the prisoner's neck. His shirt was so badly torn that the talisman was in plain view. Dangling from the chain was Angela's crucifix. Danny was hardly in a stable mood, but then he snapped. He grabbed the chain and wretched it from the Japanese man's neck. The clasp was badly buckled and fell apart when Danny tore the chain away.

'Where did you get this?' Danny roared. 'Angela wore it all the time. She'd never part with it. What have you done with her?'

He received a barrage of abuse and babble in return, but of course he couldn't understand a word.

'Relax, Danny,' George said, 'let's wait and see what Mayu and the girls can make of all this. Blimey, I dunno how we'd have gone if this bloke was a bit bigger or a bit younger, but that's Japs for you.'

It took them a while to manhandle their prisoner around the island to the wrecked jetty. He made a couple of bolts for it, but George had him firmly by the scruff of the neck. All the captive managed to do was thrash his arms and legs about. Long Li landed a couple of solid clouts and belly punches every time the soldier attempted an escape although it took nearly a dozen thumps for him to finally settle down and admit defeat.

When they arrived at the jetty Fr Kennedy was still up the hill allocating shelter for his people. Sister Celeste was on the shoreline overseeing the Japanese girls' nursing duties. They were all masked and wore surgical gloves, making a business-like job of it. The prisoner had fallen into morose silence by the time they reached the pier, but his arrival undoubtedly had an impact on the girls. They appeared confused when he started barking what sounded like orders to them. The eyed each other uncertainly and even bowed tentatively.

'Hold on girls,' George said, 'You don't have to bow to this piece of shit. Not now, not ever again. Mayu come over here please. I want to find out who this fool is.'

Meanwhile Sister Celeste noticed Danny's cut cheek.

'Let me look at that, Danny,' she said in her usual serene voice that was never raised. Danny was reluctant, all he wanted to know was what the blasted Jap had done with Angela, but Sister Celeste was insistent – without raising her voice.

So while Mayu tried to get some sense out of the Japanese man, Sister Celeste examined Danny's wound. She bathed the wound with salt water that stung like mad.

'It'll need a few stitches, dear,' she said. 'How did this happen?'

'That blighter nicked me,' Danny said pointing to the sword that Long Li waved cheerfully at them.

'Looks very rusty,' the good sister observed. 'We'd better give you an injection against lockjaw. Luckily most of our medicine survived the fall. You'll be pleased to hear we even have some local anaesthetic left.'

Danny was distracted for the next half an hour while Sister Celeste stitched up his face. The local anaesthetic wasn't that successful and the stitches stung a bit, but he endured the discomfort stoically. Finally she was satisfied and bathed his wound with antiseptic solution before covering it with a war-surplus medical patch. After which she gave Danny a tetanus shot and considered she'd done all she could. Danny thanked her, but his mind was on what the prisoner had to say. The discussion between Mayu and the Japanese soldier was heated and George clipped him around the ear more than once to encourage his co-operation.

'Who is he?' Danny asked.

'Well, he was reluctant to tell us at first until Mayu told him she'd employ a few tactics she'd witnessed in Nanking. He'd obviously heard about it, because that loosened his tongue right sharpish and you'll never guess who this blighter is?'

'No...'

'He claims to be a bloody general.'

'The War's over, who cares?'

'Not any general, he says he's Tomitaro Horii.'

Who..?'

'He's the cove who led the Japs over Kokoda. Everyone thought he'd drowned during their retreat crossing the Kumusi River. Blimey. Are those chaps on Manus Island going to have a field day when they get their hands on him?'

'I don't give a stuff about that,' Danny yelled dangling Angela's crucifix in front of Horii's nose. 'What's he done with her?'

Chapter 20 – Frenchy and the Filipinos

Getting information from General Horii was so tedious and frustrating, it drove Danny crazy. Obviously the old boy was barking mad after having spent over eight years hiding in the jungle. His memory came and went and he often became confused, trailing off in mid-sentence. As much as Mayu could gather he'd been carried out to sea clinging to the wreckage of his capsized raft after it had overturned during their retreat from Kokoda. The officers and troops accompanying Horii were washed away and drowned. His men were starving and even resorted to cannibalism while fighting a desperate, bitter rearguard action to the coast. But, Horii was a general with a regular rice ration, which probably gave him the extra strength to hold out while his men perished. Then it was his turn to dodge allied military units and survive in the wild.

The only thing he'd managed to hang onto was his sword that he used to cut open coconut husks. He lived off the milk and flesh until he learned to fish and harvest edible fruit. He also scrounged what he could from rock pools and freshwater creeks.

Danny hovered over Mayu's shoulder nagging her to interpret every word Horii spoke. She told him the general had stolen a dugout and finally wound up on *Nogat Nem Ailan,* which the allies ignored because it was uninhabited. So there he stayed.

'Didn't he guess the war was over?' Danny asked.

'He not thinking straight, Danny San,' Mayu said. 'He not give up anyway, whatever happen. He live samurai code. Shame if not to fight on to death, no surrender.'

'Well he's going to have to pack it in now.'

'Surely someone must have known he was around,' George said turning to Sister Celeste. 'I mean he can't have stayed on *Nogat Nem* all the time. If that was true he wouldn't be here on *Daiman* now.'

'We all knew someone was close by,' she replied, 'but we never saw him in all these years. We thought he might be another poor leper who was too frightened to show himself. It has happened before. If our people told us he was on our island (she refused to call it *Daiman*) we left food out. It always disappeared quickly. We respected his wish to remain alone. Fr Kennedy and I only help where we can. We don't force people to do anything they don't want to.'

How very refreshing to hear that from a God-botherer, Danny thought, *now Angela could take a leaf from their book... Angela!*

'Did he see Angela?' Danny blurted, flourishing the crucifix once more. 'Where did he get his hands on this?'

There was more heated discussion and gesticulating.

'He say he at sea fishing...'

'Good for him, but tell him to get to the point.'

'Not the Japanese way, son,' George said blandly. 'They like to go around the point until everyone's forgotten what it was in the first place. It's their crazy face-saving thing. '

Mayu frowned at him with as much of a disapproving look as she could muster. But she was a tolerant woman and merely shrugged before resuming her interrogation.

'Horri San say wave pick him up, scary, but he okay. Just pass under canoe. But he close to *Daiman* so he go ashore in case more wave come and he also want to hide from plane flying close. He see big-house go downhill so he want to climb higher and find firm ground.'

'Didn't think to go and lend a hand, did you, you mongrel?' George growled shoving his nose within inches of Horii's face. 'And after they'd been feedin' you all this time. Struth!'

That was a bit harsh, as they had no idea what Horii's intentions were and Mayu thought so too.

'Sssh, George San,' she chided, 'or I no let you come visit me no more.'

That shut him up.

Mayu continued to question Horii for what seemed like ages to Danny until she suddenly clapped her hands and turned to the others.

'He say he see girl!'

'Where?' Danny demanded.

More questioning.

'He say she on shore stuck in mud.'

'Where for heaven's sake, we've got to get to her.'

'He say she gone now.'

'She can't be dead!'

'No dead – gone.'

Mayu finally got the truth from Horii although his story was disjointed and he hadn't seen everything. But, with Fr Kennedy and Sister Celeste's help it didn't take a Rhodes Scholar to fill in the gaps.

*

t seemed Angela was about to start work when the wave struck. IFor a second she stood frozen to the spot, terrified like everyone else. The noise alone was like thunder. Then after an initial shudder and, at an almost minuscule rate, the big house began to inch away from its foundations. It quickly gained momentum as the mud slide swept it away. She stood alone. She had never felt so isolated in her life. She thought she was safe until she felt the earth move slowly under her feet. Instinctively she dashed to the far side of the mud slide where the terrain looked firmer. The mud clung almost knee deep as she staggered to safety, but lost one of her sandals as she dragged herself clear of the oozing bog left by the slide.

But so many trees had been uprooted the ground was hopelessly unstable and gave way. She screamed as she was dragged downhill in a smaller, but deadly avalanche. It tore up vegetation in its path so while Angela slipped downwards there was no chance of grabbing anything to stop her fall. Finally the sludge slid to a halt on the shore line with Angela stuck fast in a waist-deep quagmire. She was trapped and quite unable to move. She also felt herself slowly sinking.

'Help!' she yelled at the top of her voice, but the slide had taken her too far from the big-house which was now out of sight and earshot.

General Horii paddled ashore about then and heard her calls so he jogged along what was left of the beach to investigate. When he reached the edge of the mudslide he stopped and simply stared at Angela. It was impossible to tell who was the most surprised. Indeed the sight of a ragged wild man took Angela's breath away, but she'd been around New Guinea savages long enough and managed not to scream. He didn't seem that menacing anyway, but rather inquisitive and wary.

'*Helpim mi plis, no mi dai pinis,*' she said as calmly as she could. She knew the stranger wasn't Papuan, possibly Chinese or Japanese, but it was hard to say in his shabby, malnourished condition, so she tried English.

'Help me, please.'

If he couldn't understand *Tok Pisin* then he was hardly likely to know any English, but that was all she had. It didn't really matter what language Angela used, the problem was self-evident.

Horii may have been a thoroughly ruthless general in action, but in an army noted for its brutality, he was a bit of an exception when it came to civilian non-combatants. He'd even written code-of-conduct guidelines for his troops to follow that went something like:

- Don't kill or injure locals unless it's unavoidable
- Looting and rape are strictly forbidden
- Don't destroy property in enemy territory without authorisation
- Maintain strict security
- Don't waste ammunition

So, compared to most of his military colleagues, he appeared singularly enlightened. He was a warrior nevertheless and fearsome when riled. To her dismay Horii edged towards her and drew his samurai sword, but there was no way he could reach her without being sucked under the mud as well. He shook his head and disappeared into the rainforest.

'Don't leave me,' Angela called. 'Help me!'

Angela began to panic when the stranger failed to return. Although she was quite prepared to meet her Maker when He called, she didn't really want to go this way or quite so soon. A mysterious and possibly dangerous stranger was better than no one at all.

'I want to grow up and have babies,' she wailed, which must have done the trick because a few minutes later Horii returned with several vines he'd hacked from the jungle. He tied the lengths together before tossing one end to Angela. With gestures and instructions in Japanese he told her to tie the vine around her. Luckily her arms were still free and she managed to get the job done. Horii heaved on the line for all he was worth, but nothing happened – Angela was stuck fast.

'Try again,' she urged, 'oh, please try harder.'

But it was no use. He was wiry and fit, but simply didn't have the muscle power to drag her free. He shrugged, dropped the vine and headed back to his dugout. Angela was close to tears, not so much in fear but frustration. Death maybe, but not when help was so near. After a few moments Horii returned with an ancient wooden pulley that had been lying in his dugout along with a pile of flotsam he'd salvaged over the past years. He attached the pulley to a coconut palm trunk and threaded the vine onto it then heaved again. It was still a struggle, but inch-by-inch he dragged Angela free.

Finally she was clear, leaving her other sandal somewhere in the sludge. She lay gasping by the shore while her saviour crouched beside her as they both panted for breath. Her entire body was covered in grey-brown slime, but she stared into the stranger's black eyes and saw a spark of humour reflected there. She smiled and to her surprise he smiled in return, which was reassuring even if most of his teeth were missing.

'Thank you,' she whispered.

Horii nodded in reply and was about to get to his feet when a shadow loomed over them. Horii turned and was sent sprawling by a vicious back-hander from a tall, rangy fellow dressed in military gear. What Angela noticed incongruously was that, despite a week's stubble he was incredibly handsome although she saw only evil in his eyes. The new-comer hauled Angela to her feet just as Horii recovered from his beating. The general rushed forward and grabbed Angela, but the stranger was too strong and he wasn't alone. A dozen motley villains accompanied him and while he held Angela cruelly by her hair one of his men dragged Horii clear and flung him into the mud. The general had tried to hang onto Angela, but only managed to grasp her crucifix, wrenching it from her neck.

While Horii floundered the stranger eyed Angela with amused interest.

'*Mon Dieu,*' he whispered, '*tu es une petite mademoiselle sale n'est-ce pas?*'

'Take your hands off me you brute, I'm British!'

'*Que..?*'

'You heard me and I gave up French in first form, so I don't understand a word.'

'I said,' he growled between clenched teeth, 'you are a dirty little girl.'

'Don't think you can sweet-talk me,' she glared at him defiantly while struggling to get free, but she was powerless in his vice-like grip.

The Frenchman dragged Angela into the sea and shoved her under the surface. Placing his knee firmly in the small of her back he held her down until she thought she'd drown. Meanwhile Horii had clambered out of the mud, but was clubbed unconscious by a burly rogue. At last, when most of the mud had washed away, the Frenchman pulled Angela up. Angela's soaking dress clung to her, revealing her young figure. She stood up proudly though and refused to cower in front of these bullies. She gagged and spluttered out a litre of sea water before she found her voice.

'You barbarian! Is this the way you treat females in France? How dare you?' she stormed, thumping and kicking at anyone who came within range.

'Well, now at least we can see what we are getting,' the Frenchman said, eyeing her from head to foot. 'And a pretty, *petite* package *non? Très bon.*'

'Unhand me, you foreign pig. I am not a package, I'm a human being and I demand to be treated so.'

The amusement faded from his expression.

'Demand, *mademoiselle?* You are no position to demand anything. I will decide what is to become of you. *Mes hommes sont les boucaniers courageux.* We control these waters. We take what we want and go where we please anytime it suits us.

'I am Aleron Duval but my men call me "Frenchy".'

'Who'd have picked it? They put a lot of thought into that, didn't they?' Angela sneered.

Frenchy eyed her with a pained expression on his face.

'Bring her!' he ordered

He shoved Angela into the arms of two waiting henchmen and they dragged her away. One of the other brigands pointed to Horii's dazed body. Frenchy merely shrugged.

'He is harmless, not worth a bullet. Leave him.'

Three junks lay moored off shore. Their paintwork was peeling and they were in need of repair. Each was powered by thumping twin diesel motors and supplemented by braced sails. The vessel bristled with machine guns while Frenchy's pirates were armed with Japanese and allied pistols, rifles, bayonets, machetes and clubs. They had ridden out the tsunami and were heading back to *Nogat Nem Ailan* where they planned to make their new base because no one lived there and they'd found a safe, hidden anchorage. Frenchy had seen the avalanche through the binoculars he kept around his neck. He was simply curious until he spied Horii and Angela. So he ordered a group of men to paddle ashore in one of their rubber dinghies and they'd check it out.

Now she was clean, Frenchy recognised the potential of a captured blonde-haired female and, judging by all appearances, a blonde-haired *pristine* female. They bundled her into the raft and paddled back to the leading junk. Angela was man-handled aboard because she certainly wasn't going quietly. She lay sprawled on the deck while the crew looked on with interest. Frenchy had seen it all before, but there would be no messing with this little minx; she was worth far too much intact. Indonesian Muslim potentates would bid frantically against each other and pay a premium price for a virgin. Frenchy couldn't really see the point. Give him a couple of frisky can-can dancers from the *Folies Bergère* any day, but there was no accounting for taste.

Angela struggled to her feet once more.

'You'll pay for this,' she hissed. 'You'd better release me. My father is a good friend of the district commissioner. He'll send the Australian Navy from Manus Island, and then you'll be sorry. They're tough boys and they'll sort your bunch of ruffians out in no time, mark my words.'

'I think not,' Frenchy replied urbanely. 'Firstly someone has to tell them you are here and that seems unlikely.'

Frenchy had every reason to feel confident. His small fleet had terrorised the Western Pacific from Hong Kong to Noumea for years. His crews were mostly Filipinos, but included humanity's bottom-feeders from dockside boozers and brothels in every corner of the world. They knew these waters backwards and easily dodged Commonwealth patrol boats. Frenchy was a Foreign Legion deserter who ducked out of Indo China after seeing how relations between the colonial government and the Viet Minh were going sour. He decided to get out before everything turned pear-shaped. Frenchy certainly wasn't a coward, but he just didn't see any reason to remain in Vietnam. He was tough, mean, murderously ruthless and a natural leader. Desperate men were drawn to him and followed him willingly although he'd killed three pirate captains to become alpha-male of this particular pack.

The fleet had been at sea for several weeks and right now the ships badly needed maintenance and the crews wanted a few days on dry land. *Nogat Nem Ailan* suited them fine. No one went there and no one could spy on them while they were moored in their secret cove. There was a good water supply and the crews had enough grog on board to last even at the rate at which they drank. Frenchy thought they'd service the engines and make all repairs in less than a week, then it was off to Bali, East Pakistan or even as far as the Persian Gulf to see what he could get for Angela. And who knew what else they might find along the way. Angela was an unexpected piece of luck. Normally he simply ransomed hostages, but she was far too valuable for that.

Meanwhile General Horii regained consciousness, dragged himself to his feet, gathered his sword and staggered back into the rain forest still clutching Angela's crucifix.

Fr Kennedy, Sister Celeste and all the lepers knew about Frenchy and the Filipinos. It was by no means the first time they'd been prowling around on the colony's turf. The freebooters often skulked in these waters, but they seldom caused any grief. They mainly needed a refuge after they'd stirred up trouble elsewhere with the law steaming at full speed in their wake. The *Kago* group was a backwash and the fact that people steered clear of the leper colony suited the pirates fine. There was little of value in the area, but it was a great place for a spot of R & R and to replenish their water and perishable food stores. The locals were happy to resupply the pirates as they paid well in a mutually beneficial state of fiscal co-operation.

Frenchy even let his men enjoy *Kagotaun's* wantonness if they wished (which was almost always). The type of men and women who chose to live there were tough, heavily armed and well able to defend themselves. The Filipinos knew it wasn't worth their while to cause problems, besides *Kago* was a fun town that tolerated roughhousing profanity and lewdness, provided any damage was minor and recompensed. The pirates saved their serious homicidal intentions for those more vulnerable, especially private luxury yachts that always proved lucrative. That didn't mean they were averse to beating up crazy Japanese generals when they came across them.

'What'd he attack *us* for, then?' George asked pointing to Horii.

'Horii San think you pirates too so he fight,' Mayu explained to George and Danny.

'Understandable, but I guess they'll be holed up on *Nogat Nem Ailan*,' George surmised.

'So we'd better go and get Angela back,' Danny said.

'And your plan is..?'

Danny fell silent.

'We can't just swan in there and ask for our girl back, can we?' George said. 'They have over fifty well armed men and three junks with machine guns fixed to the bows. One thing I know about Frenchy Duval is that he makes demands, he doesn't make deals. He's just as likely to shoot us for causing him an inconvenience.'

'What can we do?' Danny asked.

George had no answer to that one, but Horii started babbling again. He seemed to understand some of the conversation, or at least the sense of it. Mayu was able to pick up the threads. She said he'd seen the pirates often enough and they'd only just arrived in the area on this occasion. They generally stayed for about a week, often with a stop at *Kagotaun*. George had confirmed as much. It wasn't as if it was a secret. Over the few days half the islanders would paddle over to *Nogat Nem* and sell bananas, coconuts, pawpaw, mangoes, yams and in-season vegetables to the bad guys.

'If we're nippy, we might just have time. Horii says they've just arrived, so they'll most likely stay a few days. Look, your pal Monty has a radio in his plane, right? We'll contact Rabaul and Manus and get them to send help. I doubt if the locals will be much use. They have a truce with Frenchy and they won't want to rock the boat.'

'It'll take the Navy twenty-four hours to get here – at least.'

'Then we'd better get our skates on.'

'But what if they take off while we're away?' Danny said.

'We've got no choice, son. Look we're stuck here on an island with a bunch of people who can barely look after themselves let alone take on a gang as mean as the Filipinos.'

But whatever way he looked at it, it seemed like he was running out on Angela again. She might be a right royal pain-in-the-arse at times, but everyone had their faults and Danny didn't want one of his to be deserting a friend. At least he hoped they were friends even though they hadn't exactly parted on the best of terms.

'I stay with bad-bum, clazy Jap,' Long Li offered. 'We take canoe to *Nogat Nem*. We keep mighty keen eye on jorry naughty beggars. Meet you when you get back. No one take notice of us. You go. Chop chop bling back calavly.'

'I think he means *cavalry*,' George sighed, 'I show John Wayne movies in the beer garden when I can get 'em.'

George pondered the offer for a moment. General Horii was a huge find, but would bring fame (or infamy depending on your point-of-view) to the area along with boatloads of military officials, police, politicians and worst of all, newspaper reporters. They'd be sniffing around and asking questions George might prefer to leave unanswered. Horii was unlikely to go anywhere, or more to the point Long Li wouldn't let him go anywhere. Of course the other risk was that Long Li simply wanted to get Horii alone and finish him off far from prying eyes. Again did George really care? Well, Horii had saved Angela's life so that had to count for something.

'I stay too,' Mayu said as if reading his mind. 'No misunderstanding then George San.'

'Okay,' George nodded. 'Come on Danny.'

The other Japanese girls agreed to remain on *Daiman* and help out until *Rocky Road* returned, so Danny and George cast off and had cleared the reef within an hour. George checked their fuel, calculating they could use the motor almost all the way back to *Kagotaun*, thereby save a considerable amount of time. Danny spent most of the voyage thinking up plans to rescue Angela, but mostly he ran up against a brick wall. They were out-gunned, out-manned, out-manoeuvred and running out of time. More to the point they weren't particularly warlike. George had indeed been a soldier and Monty a bold aviator, but their warrior days were in the past.

George didn't say much other than routine instructions to run his boat. *Kago* Island stayed a smudge on the horizon for hours, but finally grew and took shape. The sun had set as they neared the island, but *Kagotaun's* lights burnt all night guiding them like a beacon into the harbour. George cut the motor to idle as *Rocky Road* crawled to her berth. The *Kago Ailan* boats were parked in their usual spots, but there was a new vessel moored at the jetty.

'Ruddy hell,' Danny whispered.

He'd recognise her anywhere, even at night there was no mistaking the *Lady Burdekin!*

No one was aboard so Danny and George hurried to the hotel. It seemed the most likely place the crew would go and they weren't mistaken. The bar was full of the regular beer-swillers and ne're-do-wells. Danny and George barged through the crush and found Monty bailed up in a corner engaged in an intense discussion with a group of very familiar faces. Danny stared in amazement. Monty was not only surrounded by *Lady Burdekin's* usual crew, Jack and Penina Collier and Cobar Bob, but Sid Donovan, Lou Brennan and Lenny Esposito too. And there was uproar when they saw Danny.

'Blow me down, the prodigal returns,' Jack exclaimed. 'Beer all round.'

A lot of hugging, hand-shaking and back-slapping followed while George introduced himself and collected the drinks.

'Am I glad to see you all,' Danny said. 'I can't believe you're here.'

'The feeling's mutual, lad,' Jack replied.

'Great to see you're safe,' Lou and Sid chimed in.

Sid pumped Danny's hand until he thought his arm might be wrenched from its socket.

'Thanks for coming back for me,' Sid said earnestly, 'we didn't mean to abandon you. We tried our damnedest, but just couldn't reach inside.'

'I know,' Danny replied. 'It all happened so quickly.'

'You still acted like a true white man,' Lou said, 'thanks. I won't forget it.'

Cobar Bob and Penina eyed Sid with reservation, but let it slide. Danny thought it best to change the subject.

'But, what about you Lenny?' he said. 'I thought you were going south to work on the Snowy Mountain Scheme.'

'Noemi sorta changed my mind...'

'Noemi?'

'Well with all the fuss after you left, I realised she'd grown up and she's a corker all right.'

'No argument there.'

'We sorta got together a bit and guess what? We're engaged! So I stayed up north and joined *Lady Burdekin* to look for you as soon as we heard the plane had gone down.'

'I'll bet that made Giovanni and Beatrice Ricci happy, but how the blue-blazes did you find me here?'

'No mystery there. After the SOS call we set out straight away,' Jack said. 'Luckily the cyclone had petered out and visibility was good. Thanks to the message you sent to that Ansett plane, the RAAF got a Lincoln airborne, spotted Lou and Sid on the first day and dropped a survival pack to them. We picked 'em up and sailed to Lae to find you. Then we heard Monty's radio *mayday* call about the tidal wave. We knew you were with him because of his report to Port Moresby when he found you, so hey-presto, here we are.'

'Sorry,' Cobar added rather sheepishly. 'I didn't mean no harm. Jack and Penina have been on my back about it ever since.'

As Jack and Penina didn't know about the plan to abandon Danny in Port Moresby, Lou, Sid and Cobar agreed not to mention it. It'd only cause ill-feeling and that was all water-under-the-bridge now.

'That's okay, Cobar,' Danny said extending his arm. 'It worked out fine in the end. Look – I found my dad.'

Cobar beamed and shook Danny's hand.

'Mates?' Cobar ventured.

'Mates,' Danny beamed, 'and boy, do I need mates right now.'

'How're things on *Daiman*?' Monty finally managed to get a word in. 'Is Ange okay?'

'She's alive and we don't think she's hurt, but she's not okay.'

Danny gave them a quick run-down.

'So let me get this straight,' Lou said after Danny finished, 'There are about fifty cut-throats holed up in a safe harbour where no one can get to 'em without being spotted miles away and you want us to go sailing on in there and kick their bums into the middle of next week.'

'Something like that.'

'Why not see what they want to trade? That's what Sid 'n me do best.'

'As I told Danny,' George said, 'Frenchy Duval takes, he doesn't trade, not with the likes of us anyway. White slavery is rife from Southeast Asia to the Middle East. They'll want a lot of money for Angela, which I might add, we don't have between us.'

'Pirates are nothing new,' Penina added, 'I was brought up around here and they've been terrorising the Bismarck and South China Seas ever since I can remember. Girls are their favourite stock-in-trade. If it was a local lass involved we might stand a chance of buying her back, but I know a white, blonde girl will bring a huge price. They're not likely to let her go just because we ask them to.'

'Yeah,' Jack said, 'and I don't like the idea of barging in there with all the fire-power they've got. We've still got the Bren, our service pistols and .303s from the war, with plenty of ammo on board *Lady Burdekin*, but I don't reckon seven men'll be enough.'

'Seven men and a woman,' Penina added testily, although Danny was pleased Jack had included him with the *men*.

'Oh no, love,' Jack said, 'not now you're in the family way.'

Penina blushed and gave him a *we'll-see-about-that* look while the others beamed and passed congratulations all round.

'Jack, I was keeping that as a surprise,' she admonished, but the others were so pleased to hear the news she didn't stay angry for long.

'Talking of surprises,' George said, 'Frenchy's mob don't know we're here. That might be a big advantage. These pirates aren't your regular stand-up-and-fight kinda blokes. They prefer smash-and-grab, hit-and-run tactics. They won't be expecting an attack and have probably grown careless. If we can catch 'em napping and get 'em in our sights before they can man their big guns, we might have a chance.'

'What about Angela's safety,' Danny asked.

'Oh, she's pretty safe,' Penina said squeezing his hand. 'The last thing they want is too harm her, she's far too valuable.'

'Of course that depends how stable they are...' Lou said.

Penina glared at him.

'Lot's of "probably, ifs and maybes", don't you think?' Jack said.

'Anyone got anything else?' George replied. 'There's no shortage of guns and ammo here. I've got a storeroom full of war-surplus hardware, but even with surprise, what we really need is an edge in case things go pear-shaped.'

'You know I think I can help you there,' Monty said. He'd been quiet and reflective so far, which was unlike him. 'C'mon, I've got something to show you up at the airfield. We'll need flashlights. You got anything that'll tote us all over there, George?'

George bashed on a neighbouring merchant's door and borrowed his truck. He, Penina and Monty sat in the cabin while the others clambered into the back. As the truck rattled up to the airstrip Lou and Sid chattered away about their time on the raft at sea. Thirst, sunburn and sharks were all situations Danny was able to listen to with some empathy. Evening thunderstorms rolled around the sky belting out lightning every few seconds while *Kago's* volcano merely simmered in reply as the ash cloud had long since drifted off. Monty pulled up beside the *Goose* and they all piled out with torches at the ready.

'This way,' Monty said, 'it's only a couple of yards. Some local lads showed me when I was fixing my plane.'

Grass surrounded the runway for about two hundred metres before the forest began. It had looked deceptively short when they'd landed, but grew between one and two metres tall so anyone venturing too far would be swallowed up and hidden almost immediately. Monty had beaten a rough path to his destination during the day so he wouldn't have trouble relocating it. They almost bumped into what looked like a waist-high metal block. There were a few stifled gasps as they shone their torches over Monty's discovery.

'I'll be buggered,' George said, 'all this time and I never knew this was here.'

'Is it safe?' Danny whispered.

'Beats me,' Monty said.

They stared in disbelief. Row after row of Japanese and American bombs that had simply been forgotten or ignored after the war, lay before them. No one bothered to count them, but there were hundreds all stacked neatly and untouched for over five years. Monty started examining the stockpile, prodding and rubbing the bombs far too vigorously in Danny's opinion. Although there was rust specks on the bombshells Monty was satisfied that they were in working condition.

'That's a bad thing, right?' Danny said. 'It means they can still blow up.'

'Absolutely,' Monty beamed, 'but that's not bad, it means they're safe until someone arms them. If they were all sweaty and oozing bad-smelling goop then we'd be high-tailin' it outa here pronto.'

'How come no one mentioned this if the local lads knew about it?' Sid asked.

'No one had any use for bombs, I suppose,' George shrugged.

'Until now,' Monty said.

Angela was bundled unceremoniously down a hatch into the leading junk's hold. Initially she was left free, but after her fourth attempt to clamber on deck and jump overboard, Frenchy heaved a sigh and ordered her bound for the short trip to *Nogat Nem Ailan*. A couple of the Filipino thugs wrestled her into submission and tied her to a chair in the captain's cabin, which was nothing more than a small partitioned area that afforded some privacy. Below-decks reeked with a nauseating mixture of diesel fumes, sesame oil, fried fish and stale sweat.

'You heathen cowards,' she yelled. 'Just wait till my father and Jim Taylor get hold of you. They'll make mincemeat out of you. You...you...you scum!'

It was a pity she didn't know – or didn't use – profanities, it might have made her feel better. But finally Frenchy grew weary and went below only to be met by a further tirade.

'I can't believe you'd treat a fellow human being this way. What are you...some kind of animal?'

'I have been called worse,' Frenchy leered. 'Now let us get this straight, if you do not shut up, I will...'

'You'll do what? Don't think I'm scared of you, Mr Brave-High-and-Mighty Pirate.'

'You should be. I could set my men on you. That would not be very pleasant, *n'est-ce pas?*'

Angela pondered that prospect for a moment, deciding the pirates didn't look a patient lot and if that was the case her *fate-worse-than-death* would already have been sealed.

'I don't think that's what you want,' she ventured, lifting her chin defiantly.

'*Tu es exacte, mademoiselle...*'

'Ah, want me for yourself do you? Over my dead body.'

Frenchy shrugged with infuriating Gallic indifference.

'Although that can be arranged,' he replied, 'it is not my intention. I see under that tousled hair and ragged dress you are *une fille très séduisante, non?* But, you are not for my enjoyment. I do not have the time – or the patience. You will fetch twenty thousand Yankee dollars somewhere between here and Aden.'

'Aden! You plan to take me there?'

'It depends what I am offered for you on the way.'

'You pig...you despicable swine. I hate you!'

'That is neither here nor there, *mademoiselle,* but do shut up...*s'il vous plaît*...or I will gag you and that will be not be a very pleasant experience either, I assure you.'

Angela saw the practicality of that suggestion. No would-be rescuers could hear her cries. It might be a good idea to save as much strength as possible and look for an opportunity to escape while she was still close enough to *Daiman Ailan.*

'All right,' she conceded, 'I won't try to jump overboard, but let me up on deck, I feel queasy. It's filthy down here. You don't want me throwing up all over your dinky little cabin, do you?'

'I have your word..?'

'As a good Christian. Girl Guide's honour.'

'Very well.'

Frenchy nodded and untied her.

I gave you my word not to jump overboard, nothing about not trying to escape, you detestable wretch.

'God will punish you for your vileness,' she mumbled as he hauled her to her feet and shoved her towards the ladder.

'Whatever,' Frenchy wasn't concerned, 'He can join the queue wanting to do just that.'

She took a deep breath as she climbed on deck where a gust of heavenly fresh air swept over her. The leading junk was approaching *Nogat Nem* when Angela regained her bearings and steadied her feet on the gently rolling deck. She now understood why the pirates had chosen that spot as their refuge. A narrow inlet led to a lagoon flanked by two rocky points where Frenchy would no doubt post his lookouts. They could see anyone approaching and even if a ship tried to sneak around from the far side of the island it would still have to pass the headlands. Additionally two parallel reefs stretched beyond the promontories so the only inward passage was through the narrow channel between them. It was this geography that had protected *Nogat Nem* from the tidal wave. The wave had simply surged on by with the reefs acting as natural dam walls.

The bay was surrounded by a dazzling white beach. There was enough room for all three junks to anchor while the sea bed sloped gently to shore allowing the boats to be kedged aground at low tide so their hulls could be careened and repaired. The pirate ships carried carpentry and welding equipment while each man had at least one trade skill to maintain the vessels. Frenchy insisted all crew members were capable of tasks other than pillaging. The beach was littered with miscellaneous junk the pirates had left on previous visits. A small palm shelter also stood just within the rainforest that Frenchy told Angela probably belonged to that curious little Japanese fellow they'd left on *Daiman Ailan*. She could see why he'd chosen this spot with so much useful jetsam left at his disposal.

The pirates anchored their junks and ferried supplies ashore in half a dozen rubber dinghies. The two largest were powered by Evinrude outboard motors while the others had to rely on paddle-propulsion. There were about ten women among the pirates and, although their status seemed equal to the men, they were mainly responsible for setting up cooking pots and getting laundry fires going. Angela had to admire the efficiency of Frenchy's cut-throats, but apparently there was no free lunch for prisoners either. One of the women handed her two buckets, grunted and pointing towards a fresh water creek that flowed into the bay. The woman's truculent instruction was plain enough, but Angela stood her ground, even when the woman drew a Japanese Nambu 8mm semi-automatic pistol from her waistband and stuck the barrel under Angela's nose. She'd be damned if she'd do *anything* for these barbarians.

'You won't pull the trigger, you cheap slut,' Angela sneered, 'Your stinking boss would have your guts for garters.'

She'd developed quite a mouth by her standards, but she was so angry with the whole pack of them. She may have been right, but her bluff was never put to the test. Frenchy suddenly appeared behind her and grabbed her hair, almost wrenching her off her feet. She screamed with pain and surprise as he pulled her to within inches of his face. Spinning her around, he slapped her viciously across the cheek, knocking her to the ground. It was so brutal, so sudden and so final that Angela felt tears welling in her eyes as she staggered to her feet. She rubbed her cheek which throbbed as if she'd endured a hundred maddened wasp stings. No one had ever stuck her before and she was devastated, which was exactly the effect Frenchy intended. A good sharp slap nearly always sorted out haughty females.

'Now just do what you're told,' he hissed.

Yes, I have been guilty of pride, she thought, *it's a deadly sin and I have paid the price. Bide your time, girl. Look as if you're complying, but don't let them conquer your spirit. Oh, I shall rot in hell rather than let them do that. I can't believe my language. Have I dropped my standards to theirs this quickly? But they make me so mad! I must control my temper and think clearly.*

So she was put to work for most of the afternoon with numerous mundane chores, which she did without complaint. Towards dusk the camp activity slackened as most of the setting up was complete. Although she had to endure constant leering glances and ribald remarks, she was eventually left alone. No one stopped her when she went into the jungle to relieve herself in private, something the pirates were less coy about. She was pretty sure Frenchy had posted some of his henchmen to keep an eye on her, but she saw no overt signs of a surveillance team. Afterwards she walked along the beach to one of the headlands. A guard armed with a Tommy gun was posted at the spit, but other than looking her over, allowed her to splash barefooted along the beach as far as the reef.

She just wanted to get away from the lot of them. They were disgusting both morally and physically and she'd find a way to bring them down a peg or two. She wasn't just some whimpering female and she had God on her side. So she stared out to sea scanning the horizon for any signs of life, but there were none. She cast her eyes to the right where *Daiman Ailan* was in clear view, but what good was that? No one there was in any position to help her. She had no idea what had become of Danny and Monty. They might possibly have escaped, but she had no recollection of seeing the *Goose* after she'd been caught in the mudslide.

As she thought of how desperately alone she was, she caught the flash of a reflection from the setting sun. It was half way between the islands, just one flash and nothing more. Could it have been a boat, a dolphin's fluke, a reflected lightning flash from one of the afternoon storms or just fluorescence from the waves?

Don't cling to false hope, girl. Think practically. With God's help I'll get out of this.

'Hey, you. Missy,' the guard called.

Angela turned to see him waving and indicating she was to go back to camp. He was standing next to a huge man of indeterminate race, possibly a blend of every ethnic group from Korea to New Zealand. The bare-chested man bore tattoos from head to foot and was armed only with a machete, which was all he needed. His head was clean shaven except for a pigtail and a goatee.

'Tuan, him wanna speak you,' the giant growled.

'Well you can tell him I have nothing to say to bullies and kidnappers.'

She stood her ground and folded her arms, which might have appeared defiant, but didn't impress the pirates. The guard exchanged glances with the big fellow who shrugged and marched towards Angela. She was barely as tall as his chest and he heaved her effortlessly over his shoulder and strode back along the beach.

'Put me down, you big oaf,' she wailed, kicking and punching for all she was worth.

He stopped and slapped her once on the backside.

'You shaddup,' he grunted and marched on.

The pirates had erected a small marquee for Frenchy. He sat on one of two canvas director's chairs set out under an awning attached to the tent. Beside the pirate boss stood a collapsible table covered with a white cloth and bearing bowls of diced fruit, nuts, cheese and SAO crackers along with an opened bottle of rosé wine and two crystal wine glasses. A small barbeque was close by with the coals just beginning to glow below its grill.

The tattooed giant dumped Angela onto the sand in front of Frenchy and left without a word. She gathered her wits as she scrambled to her feet spitting out sand and brushing down her dress. Frenchy's expression was inscrutable, but possibly mildly amused. He'd shaved and although bare-footed, wore spotless white pants and a colourful Hawaiian shirt.

'Be seated, *mademoiselle, s'il vous plaît*,' he offered urbanely.

She sat in the vacant chair and adjusted her dress as modestly as she could. Frenchy eyed her as she tried to recover some dignity.

'You know there are only two types of people in this world,' he said, 'and we both know what the other looks like.'

'I suppose that would be so to an amoral beast such as you, a man who likes to beat up helpless girls.'

'It was regrettable but necessary and you do not appear so helpless to me. As for morality, is that not just a point of view?'

'Indeed not. God shows us what is right and what is wrong.'

'In my experience, *mademoiselle*, people say something is *right* when it is going their way and *wrong* went it is not. Once again it is a matter of opinion, but enough philosophy for now. I have introduced myself, but I do not yet know your name.'

'Angela Holyman and I cannot say it is a pleasure to make your acquaintance.'

'Then the pleasure is all mine. Allow me to pour you a glass of wine.'

'No thank you,' she answered primly. 'I am just sixteen years old and I do not believe drinking is appropriate. Alcohol befuddles your brain and encourages bestiality in men. I do not approve of it at all.'

Frenchy cast his eyes around the camp where his men were starting to guzzle beer, sake, rum, gin and whisky. He shrugged and inclined his head towards Angela.

'You have a point, but I do not think I could keep them together if they did not let off steam now and again. A glass of water then?'

Angela realised she'd drunk nothing all day and was parched. She gulped down the first glass and held it out while Frenchy refilled it.

'*Pardon, Mademoiselle* Angela,' he apologised. 'You should have told me you were thirsty.'

She glared at him.

'Of course, you would not ask me to spit on you if you were on fire. Do you not think that is foolish, you must eat and drink properly? Do help yourself to the hors d'oeuvre.'

'Fattening me up for market, I suppose?'

Frenchy didn't bother to answer, but told her she would dine with him. It wasn't so much an invitation as an order. She was famished and sampled something from each of the bowls. The pirates were skilled anglers and had landed a fine catch from the reef during the afternoon. Two coral trout had been cleaned and scaled and presented to Frenchy who cooked them personally. He lightly basted the fish with olive oil, seasoning them with herbs, condiments and spices before grilling each piece briefly and serving the dish with diced pineapple and mango sprinkled with lime juice. Storms were scattered across the islands, but they missed *Nogat Nem* that night. The cooking aroma was enticing on a perfect, balmy tropical night that could have been delightful under different circumstances.

'You must keep up your strength, *non?*' he said placing a plate before her.

Pragmatism took the place of pride and she tucked in. The fish tasted delicious so she ate every last scrap.

'*C'est bon, très bon,*' Frenchy cooed. Just like any other cook, it pleased him when diners appreciated what he'd prepared. He didn't consider himself to be a chef, but he reckoned he was pretty good all the same. 'You enjoy my cooking, so now we might be friends perhaps?'

Angela suppressed her first impulse to spit in his eye and declare hell would freeze over before they'd ever be friends. Frenchy's attitude had mellowed and she thought that might be to her advantage, so it was best not to antagonise him unnecessarily. She even considered he might apologise for hitting her, but that was expecting too much. He finished the wine and chatted cordially about his life and ambitions although she was indifferent to any feeling he might have. She feigned attention while she studied the pirate camp.

God helps those who help themselves, Danny would say and he's undoubtedly right.

All she needed was a chance, but that would have to wait until morning. The day had been harrowing and Angela was exhausted. She'd kept going on nothing but fear and adrenalin for hours. She fell asleep in the director's chair as Frenchy droned on. When he noticed she was no longer paying attention, he laid a groundsheet under Horii's shelter. Frenchy ordered the tattooed giant to carry her from his marquee and place her, with remarkable gentleness all things considered, on the tarp where she slept until daybreak.

Chapter 23 – Battle Plan

Danny and his companions stood around the bomb stack. Monty still prodded the explosives more than Danny would have liked, but the others who'd all had experience with weapons during the war seemed relaxed enough. How Monty planned to use the bombs to rescue Angela was still unclear.

'The way I see it,' Monty said, 'is that we gotta take 'em by surprise. In and out before they know what hit 'em. Wham bang, thank you, ma'am.'

'No argument there, but it still didn't explain how the bombs would help. So Monty outlined his plan even though it was still pretty much a broad brush concept.

'So that's it then,' Monty said, 'you boys go in by boat. Bail 'em up before they're awake, get Ange back at gunpoint and we'll use the heavy-artillery here to discourage any disagreement.'

The others chipped in to amend some details, but by and large they came to an agreement. Well, almost an agreement. Jack was adamant Penina would remain in *Kagotaun*. He told her he wasn't going to jeopardise her and their unborn baby for anything. She then pointed out *he* was quite prepared to accept the risk that the child might grow up fatherless. Jack insisted that was different in terms that pretty much boiled down to: *a-man's-gotta-do-what-a-man's-gotta-do.*

Penina fumed in the truck all the way back to town. She sat in the cabin between Monty who drove and Danny by the window.

'He's so stubborn,' she snarled, 'and after all we did right here in these waters against the Japs.'

'Don't worry, babe,' Monty said with a smug grin, 'I've got a job for you that'll be right in the thick of it, but we won't tell Jack, eh?'

They ate a late meal of fish and yam chips with tropical fruit for dessert. *Lady Burdekin's* crew minus Penina returned to the boat for the night. She was still mad at Jack and said she'd stay at the hotel as she wasn't going with them anyway. Everyone was up before dawn as they wanted to put their plan into action the following morning. They needed sufficient time to sail back to *Daiman Ailan*. Danny and George would go in *Rocky Road* while the others took *Lady Burdekin*. George told his mates to scour *Kagotaun* for extra weapons and ammunition. He was surprised what turned up. Along with his own store they had quite an arsenal between them:

- A couple of Sten guns favoured by British commandos,
- Half a dozen 32-round box magazines for the Stens,
- About a hundred rounds of .303 ammo to supplement the *Lady Burdekin's* supply,
- A small box containing a cocktail of American Mk II Fragmentation hand grenades, Japanese Type 97 grenades and British No36M Mills bombs,
- A Mark VI Webley .455 service revolver and
- A Belgian Browning Hi-Power automatic pistol with holster, webbing belt, spare 13- round clips and ammunition pouch.

Danny was astounded how casually everyone accepted the weapons stash, but then the station boys back home were pretty cavalier about their guns too. George decided to take the Stens on board *Rocky Road* along with a few grenades while Jack took the remaining grenades and .303 ammo to supplement *Lady Burdekin's* arsenal.

'Ordnance seems okay,' Monty commented, 'but what about communications?'

George had scrounged a Motorola SCR-300 Walkie-Talkie set, but there was only one on the island so it wasn't much use. He did however find a pair of SCR-536 Handie-Talkies that were far more compact and completely hand held although with a much reduced range.

'Won't matter,' George said to Monty, 'we have radio comms linking the *Goose* and *Lady Burdekin*. We'll use the Motorola sets between *Rocky Road* and *Lady Burdekin*, relaying if necessary. I expect the boats will stay close together and always be in range.'

'Have you got a preference, Danny?' George asked offering him the choice of the Browning or Webley pistol.

'Dad, I don't even know how to fire a gun!'

'Take the Webley then. You just pull the trigger. It's double action so you don't have to cock it first. Hold it steady with both hands and aim and squeeze the trigger. Point it at the biggest part of what you want to hit. Right in the guts isn't pretty, but works best.'

Danny shuddered. Up until then, other than self-defence, he'd never considered himself a violent person.

'Cheer up, it mightn't come to that,' George said, reading his son's expression like a good father should.

George took the Browning 9mm automatic from the holster and stuffed it into his trousers then handed the gun belt to Danny. He exchanged the Webley .455 and Browning 9mm ammunition.

'Wear that and you won't have to worry about shooting your balls off...yeah kinda like Gary Cooper.'

Danny looked nervous as he buckled up the gun belt, but conceded if he was going up against a gang of trigger-happy rogues, he'd rather have something to shoot back with.

'Great,' George said, 'now help me with these empty bottles.'

Danny was puzzled why George would want to take three crates of *empty* beer bottles, but didn't ask any questions. George also loaded two jerry-cans of petrol onto *Rocky Road's* deck. Once again they refilled the boat's fuel tanks with diesel fuel and replenished their rations. *Lady Burdekin* was still provisioned and had already set off for *Daiman Ailan*. George planned for the two boats to rendezvous where the leper-colony jetty had once stood. He'd also gathered more food, medicine and water to tide Fr Kennedy's flock over until official help arrived from Rabaul. Jack was surprised that Penina accepted staying on *Kago Ailan* with a good grace. Normally she'd have nagged him to distraction, but perhaps her maternal hormones were kicking in and she'd seen sense after all.

Although, that wasn't necessarily the case. No sooner had *Lady Burdekin* cleared *Kagotaun* harbour than she jumped into the borrowed truck beside Monty and they rumbled off to the airstrip. The *Goose* carried a comprehensive tool kit, but Monty also scrounged a spot welder and sundry equipment he needed. There was little time to waste as the *Goose* had to be ready by first light the following morning. Penina not only acted as Monty's assistant, but also a 'gofer' to drive back to town in case he'd forgotten anything or something unexpected cropped up.

His first task was to construct steel brackets and fit them to the *Goose*'s floats. The aircraft wasn't designed as a bomber and was seriously restricted by the maximum payload it could safely carry. Even though Monty was expecting hazards, he wasn't foolish enough to overload his plane. Flying the *Goose* was always a compromise between fuel load and cargo weight.

'Let's check out what we've got,' Monty said after he was satisfied with his modifications.

They trekked into the long grass and examined the bomb stack in daylight. There was an assortment of general purpose and incendiary explosives. They were mainly 250lb and 500lb, but Monty found a small row of 100lb GP bombs that he decided would suit him best. They were small enough to handle, but would still make a big bang.

'What about detonators?' Penina asked.

'There're plenty in those cases at the end of the row. See if you can find some for the hundred pounders while I trolley 'em back to the *Goose*. You know Jack's one lucky guy. How many dames know about bomb fuses?'

'Thousands I reckon,' she smiled, 'just think of all the girls who worked in munitions factories during the war.'

While Monty ferried four bombs one at a time to the plane, Penina checked the detonator cases and decided on impact fuses rather than time-delays. When she returned Monty had already secured the first bomb using a makeshift hoist he'd borrowed from the car mechanic's shop.

'I think time fuses are too dangerous if we get a release lock-up,' she said.

'Good thinking,' Monty replied examining the detonators. 'Yeah, these'll do fine. I'll set 'em when I get the bombs in place.'

They stopped work for lunch. Penina had salvaged some left-over pork curry and rice from the hotel kitchen along with plates and a pot. She built a small fire and heated the meal. She was going to bring some beer, but there was no way of keeping it cool, so they had to make do with their water canteens.

'Do you think we have a chance of rescuing Angela?' she asked as she cleared the plates away.

'Dunno, slim odds maybe, but one thing *is* certain: she stands *no* chance unless we try. God knows I ain't no hero and Ange drives me nuts, but I sure don't want to go back to Lae and tell her daddy we gave up without a fight.'

She nodded.

'C'mon,' he said, 'let's work out how to make these bombs drop without blowing us to kingdom-come.'

They spent the rest of the day checking the release mechanism which consisted of lines attached to locking pins that trailed under the wings to the *Goose*'s side door. It was simply a matter of tugging the cord to free the locking pins. The brackets would then drop and the bombs roll out. That was the theory anyway. With two hundred pounds of dead weight strapped to each float, Monty wasn't sure how the extra load under the wings would affect the *Goose's* flying characteristics, but there was only one way to find out.

'It's primitive I know,' Monty conceded. 'And that's where you come in Penina. I can't release the bombs from the cockpit. The ropes will be caught by the props – they have to be rigged behind the engines to the cabin door. I've connected a headset lead that reaches to the back of the plane so you'll be able to hear above the engine noise. Then it'll be all up to you.'

*

anny was having similar misgivings as they sailed towards D*Daiman Ailan*. The Webley revolver felt heavy on his waist although he was getting used to it. But 'packing heat' as Monty termed it wasn't a great comfort.

'I feel like crap,' he admitted to his father, 'how did you feel when you went to war, dad?'

'We had some training, remember, so we were used to guns and loud bangs. I think we were just pig-ignorant when we got to the Track. After that there wasn't time to think about anything much.'

'It's pretty scary.'

'Frenchy and his gang like the advantage of surprise. With any luck he'll hand Angela back when he sees he's up against a well-armed force. He might be a ruthless bastard, but even he won't want unnecessary casualties.'

George said they could spare a few rounds for target practice. He tossed one of the empty bottles into the sea and showed Danny how to hold and aim the pistol. Neither of them hit the bottle, but they came close and Danny got the general idea. George also gave him a crash course with the Sten gun. The weapon's great asset was its simplicity and Danny figured he'd have no trouble firing it.

'Now, while nothing much is happening, Danny I want you to fill all those bottles with petrol. Leave a couple of inches at the top. There's a heap of rags in the bilge, cut 'em into strips and stuff 'em in the necks. You never know when we'll need extra fire power.'

Even Danny knew he was making Molotov cocktails. When he'd finished he repacked the bottles in their crates so they would be stable with no danger of them over-balancing and spilling petrol on *Rocky Road's* deck.

As they approached *Daiman Ailan* they saw *Lady Burdekin* at anchor inside the reef. *Rocky Road's* shallow draft allowed George to bring her close to land. As he and Danny splashed ashore Jack and Lenny were talking to Fr Kennedy while Lou and Sid were trying to get on friendly terms with the Japanese girls. Fr Kennedy and Sister Celeste had made solid progress and all their patients were sheltered in temporary accommodation. Mayu stood with the group but there was no sign of Long Li or General Horii.

'Okay, where are they?' Danny asked. 'Don't tell me they've killed each other.'

'Not know, Danny San,' Mayu said. 'They go yesterday when no one looking. Leave me behind.'

'They were talking about scouting out *Nogat Nem..?*'

Mayu shrugged. If that was the case they should have returned already unless of course they'd been discovered. She also said General Horii's sword was missing.

'Nothing we can do about that now,' George said. 'A *recce* would've been good, but we'll stick to the plan.'

They unloaded the stores for the colony in the little daylight that remained. Cobar Bob had mounted the Bren gun into its bracket on *Lady Burdekin's* fo'c'sle. He was positively beaming as he stacked spare magazines into a crate beside the gun.

'Just like old times, eh?' he said cheerfully.

Danny was less sanguine.

'Doesn't it bother you that you might be shot?' he asked.

'Unlikely, Danny. You know how many bullets are fired for just one hit?'

'Dunno.'

'Must be at least ten thousand. We don't have that much ammo, and I bet them bad fellas don'tt either. So that means we're safe.'

Danny thought Cobar's logic could only be described as illogical.

'That means we won't hit any of them either.'

'No way, man, we're much better shots.'

Danny didn't pursue the discussion. After they ate, he tried to get some sleep, but it didn't come easily. Eventually he dropped off and the next thing he knew George was shaking him awake. The moon had risen and there was enough light to see clearly. To everyone's surprise, Mayu and her girls insisted on coming along. There were enough spare weapons to go around, although two of the less aggressive girls said they'd be more use reloading guns and caring for possible casualties. Mayu and Kana boarded *Rocky*

Road while Ayaku, Sakura and Yuuka went with *Lady Burdekin's* crew. Mayu eyed the Molotov cocktails with approval.

'Kana and me, we in charge of petrol bombs,' she said.

'So long as you don't throw 'em like a girl,' George grinned.

'Me no throw like girl!' Mayu cried and, to prove the point, jumped back onto the coral strand, pick up a sizeable piece and hurled it a decent way. Kana did even better.

'Good show,' George said, handing them his Zippo lighter and a box of Miss Redhead matches. He'd actually given up smoking during the war, mostly because fags were scarce and he needed all his lung-power clambering over the Eastern Highlands.

Jack also admired the Molotov cocktails and transferred one crate to *Lady Burdekin* in case they came in handy. Ayaku, Sakura and Yuuka assured him they could throw just as well as the other Japanese girls.

The two boats cruised at low speed for stealth and they weren't in a rush. They approached *Nogat Nem* from the west, staying hidden from the sentries on the headlands. They anchored just out of view waiting for dawn. Jack had considered a night raid, but when George told him how narrow the channel was, he decided not to take the risk of foundering on the reefs in the dark. Also they'd be unable to utilise the *Goose* until daylight.

So, just as an amber glow brushed the horizon between the grey-blue of a dozen dissipating maritime thunderstorms, *Rocky Road* chugged around the southern point into the channel that led to *Nogat Nem* lagoon. Danny stood ready with a cocked Sten gun as

George manoeuvred his boat towards the three pirate junks. They went unchallenged and George whispered for Danny and the girls to be alert for a trap. Hopefully the sentries were all asleep. Their luck didn't last long. Frenchy was a light sleeper and although *Rocky Road's* engine was barely ticking over at idle, he heard, or merely sensed something unfamiliar. He shook himself awake, grabbed his pistol and kicked the nearest pirates into life. He dashed to the shoreline just as *Rocky Road* appeared from behind one of his ships.

George cut the motor so *Rocky Road* floated within earshot, but out of accurate pistol range. Rising sun rays streamed behind *Rocky Road,* blinding the pirates. George and Danny would have that advantage for at least an hour and they certainly hoped to be long gone by then. They saw figures moving on the beach and there stood Frenchy Duval. Danny studied his face as the sun's rays blazed every detail clearly. This man was his enemy, but for some reason Danny wasn't afraid.

'Who is there?' Frenchy yelled at the silhouetted figures facing him. 'Speak up or I will blow you out of the water.'

'George McAlister from *Kagotaun*! No false moves, we've gotcha covered.'

'I know you, *monsieur*. I have drunk at your bar *n'est-ce pas*? Have you come to trade some booze, I am sure *mes amis* will be only too happy to oblige you.'

'Maybe if that's your price, Frenchy. We've come for the girl.'

'Ah *la fille belle, non?* I think you have not enough grog in your hotel to meet what she is worth. I do not think there's enough booze in the whole South Pacific.'

'We may just have to take her then.'

Frenchy chuckled.

'You in your little boat? I think I will just blast you away for fun.'

'I'd think carefully about that, we might be more persuasive than you think.'

Frenchy hesitated. Of course no one was going to just float into the dragon's lair, there had to be more. A decoy maybe! But George pre-empted him.

'Look, show us Angela,' he said. 'You know, just to let us see we're dealing in good faith. And don't try anything stupid. We're armed with Stens and we've got the drop on you.'

A smirk crossed Frenchy's lips. Could they really be so naive to think he'd simply trade her for a song? And, as for *good faith,* what was McAlister thinking? He was dealing with pirates for heaven's sake. Nevertheless Frenchy wanted Angela close by, not where someone could sneak in and snatch her while he was distracted. Also if lead started spraying he knew McAlister wouldn't shoot at the girl. He turned to the tattooed giant.

'Get the girl,' Frenchy hissed.

The giant disappeared. The fellow was gone too long, the girl was only in the shelter where she'd spent the last two nights. Frenchy turned.

'What the devil is keeping you..?'

'She gone, tuan,' the giant called back. 'No sign of her.'

George and Danny heard them shouting and turned to each other.

'Struth,' Danny whispered as the pirate camp exploded into uproar.

Chapter 24 –Night Stalkers

On the morning *Rocky Road* and *Lady Burdekin* were en route to *Daiman Ailan* Angela Holyman awoke in the centre of the pirate camp. She felt better after a good night's sleep, but was worried sick about her future. Until now it had all been surreal. Her capture and evening with Frenchy Duval just didn't seem possible, but with the early morning bustle around the camp, the whole, sad business took on a stark reality. A small bundle had been placed neatly beside her while she slept. It contained a freshly laundered, cotton t-shirt, linen pants, knickers, straw hat and, surprisingly, a toothbrush. Frenchy arrived as she examined her new clothes.

'Not quite haute-couture, *excusez-moi*, but you will feel better in clean garments even if they are not so flattering,' he said without appearing particularly sincere and handing her a tin of Russian mint-flavoured tooth powder.

'Now this will make you feel even better,' he added.

'Thank you,' she said trying not to sound gracious, 'but I'm hardly in a position to feel *better*.'

'Wear the hat too,' he ordered, 'I do not want your skin red as a lobster and peeling.'

She walked as far along the stream as she could for privacy and found a spot where the terrain rose steeply and water cascaded into a rock pool. She did not hesitate, but stripped off and dived in. The feeling was sublime when she realised how grubby she'd felt. How she missed the simple pleasure of being clean. She felt like staying in the pool all day, but when a small snake glided past she decided it was time to leave. Also there was the ever-present risk of attracting leeches so she sat on a large rock to dry. That didn't take long and she dressed in her new clothes that fitted reasonably well. She rinsed her dress, which was now a light grey-brown. It had been her favourite and would never be crisp and white again, but at the moment it was her only dress.

She had no wish to return to the camp, but she was hungry and knew she must eat to maintain her strength. As she was about to leave, she became aware of rustling in the forest across the pool only a few metres away. That didn't worry her particularly, she knew there were no large predators in New Britain, the nearest tigers and elephants were far away in Indonesia and even they were pretty rare by then. It may have been a feral pig that the pirates hunted for their barbeques. Then she heard someone whisper her name.

'Miss Angera,' a voice hissed with a strange accent.

She looked up and saw two very nervous faces peeking through the undergrowth. One belonged to the curious Japanese fellow who now sported a black eye as well as a livid bruise on one cheek.

'You stay still, missy' his companion ordered.

He was Oriental too, but his features were quite different to the Japanese fellow and Angela guessed he was Chinese. After scanning left and right, both men ventured out of the jungle and looked furtively around. While the Japanese man moved along the stream to check for pirates, the Chinaman squatted beside Angela.

'Me Long Li, him Holii,' the little man said pointing to his companion. 'You Missy Angera?'

She nodded.

'Okay, we come get you. Take you safe.'

But before she could say, *Fine by me, lead on, let's go,* he held his fingers to his lips.

'You Sssh, missy. We go not now. Tonight – midnight after bad-bums asreep. Go in day they chase, they kill me and Holii.'

'How do we get off the island?' Angela whispered finally with renewed hope.

'We have out-ligger other side of ieran. We go – paddle away when dark. No bad-bums see.'

Horii returned in a hurry and gestured frantically to Long Li.

'Bad-bums come. We go. Okay, you here tonight. We be here then.'

The two men scampered into the jungle, disappearing just as Frenchy and his tattooed assistant splashed up the stream to Angela's pool.

'Enough bathing,' he said. 'If you want *le petit dejeuner, tu viens vite* – come now, because you will be earning your keep afterwards.'

The tattooed heavy looked suspicious and prowled around the pool for a while. Horii and Long Li left no footprints on the rocks, but they were bound to have left a trail on the soft forest floor. Fortunately the pirate appeared satisfied, so the three of them returned to camp together to begin what was to be the longest eighteen hours of Angela's life. In a way it was a blessing that she spent the time hard at work. She was assigned laundry duty and used up the day sweating in front of a huge copper boiling pot. She made countless trips to the stream to replenish the water levels and was given a stout, metre-long, wooden pole to stir the clothing in the steaming cauldron. The stick was cured to metal hardness from constant use in scalding water. It was a good weight, well balanced and could also serve as a baton. She decided to hang onto it. She even tried to resurrect her white dress by leaving it in the boiler for an hour. Sadly it remained greyish and she had to fish it out before it fell apart. The dress would never be much use again and she had no idea where she'd get another one as nice. It was a *St Margaret* label from a London Marks and

Spencer department store. It wasn't particularly expensive, but Angela's mother had bought it for her just before they left England. She treasured the memory of them shopping together.

She was almost too excited to eat, but knew she must and she also remembered to drink plenty of water. Frenchy didn't bother her. She was doing what she was told for a change so he figured it was best to leave her alone. In any event he had other things on his mind as a pirate chief's work was never done and Angela was about to see just how ruthless he needed to be.

A dispute arose between two men that developed into a knife fight. One fellow lost half an ear while the other was badly slashed across the face before Frenchy decided to adjudicate rather than let them settle matters themselves. It turned out that one man had stolen from another. The evidence was plain. There were witnesses, the perpetrator was caught red-handed and if there was one thing the pirates wouldn't condone it was larceny. Well, not theft from fellow gang members, anyone else was fair game, but an example had to be made. It was a regrettable result of those stop-overs when men grew bored and quarrelled or cheated at cards and dice which was tolerable, but stealing..? Justice was swift, decisive and without mercy. While several of his colleagues held the thief down two men grabbed his right arm. Frenchy nodded to his tattooed henchman who swung his machete and neatly severed the victim's hand at the wrist. The man screamed pitifully, but his torment wasn't over. He was manhandled to the laundry cauldron and his stump plunged into the boiling water to cauterise his wound. The water turned pink. His arm turned red. The pirate's shrieks pieced the entire camp while Angela held her palms to her ears trying to shut out the howls of anguish, but she had seen the mutilation and that was something she'd never forget.

The maimed pirate was left where he dropped sobbing beside the laundry pot. He would live or die, but no one was going to help him. Someone casually tossed his hand into the lagoon. The blood attracted a small reef shark and the hand soon disappeared. The stump still oozed so Angela grabbed her dress, ripped it into bandages and wrapped a tourniquet around the pirate's forearm. She helped him to his feet and they managed to stagger to the shade of the palms. She then scoured the beach and found several coconuts and marched to where the tattooed thug was cleaning his machete blade.

She held a coconut in each hand at arm's length.

'Open them,' she demanded, but he looked at her blankly.

'Open them, you bastard!' she screamed.

Nothing.

'I know you can understand me. That man needs liquids and nourishment.'

'Open the dammed coconuts,' Frenchy said wearily, 'or she will be swearing like a longshoreman. Not that I mind girls talking dirty, but I try to discourage that sort of language in our quality female merchandise.'

The tattooed giant grunted and swung the blade. The machete was so sharp it ripped the tops off the coconut husks without knocking them from Angela's hands. He had acted so suddenly that Angela barely flinched.

'Impressive,' Frenchy said with genuine admiration, but then lost interest and returned to ordering people around.

Angela took the coconuts to the crippled pirate and helped him drink. The milk would provide some nutrition as well as slaking his thirst. She also placed a pail of water beside him.

'Okay, angel-of-mercy, back to work,' Frenchy snarled. 'Remember everyone does their share on this island. You wasted enough time on that sad sack of shit. I cannot abide a thief.'

'What..?'

'For us it is a profession. We have to eat.'

'You make me sick...'

He might have hit her again, but she hurried away just in time.

So the afternoon dragged on. Angela returned to the wounded pirate whenever she could and brought him food at supper time, but he didn't eat. He was very weak and burned with fever despite Angela using the last of her dress soaked in cold water to bathe him. She told Frenchy the man needed antibiotics and probably a blood transfusion, but he insisted he wasn't going to waste precious resources on a thief, not that the pirates carried much in the way of medical supplies anyway.

Angela tried to sleep after supper, but of course it was impossible so she waited while the pirates revelled into the night. Their grog supply seemed endless and they were all roaring drunk in no time. For once she didn't object to their debauchery. They heeded Frenchy's warning and didn't bother her, but she still stayed away from the drunkards and tried to remain invisible. Her new clothes helped as they were similar to the pirate's working outfits, although they liked to wear something more flamboyant during raiding expeditions.

Eventually the camp fell quiet other than widespread booze-induced snoring and flatulence. Frenchy had retired to his marquee and there was no light inside so she assumed he was asleep. There was no other sign of life although she knew sentries were still posted on the headlands. She crept to the edge of camp gripping her laundry pole firmly. The night wasn't particularly quiet as millions of night insects droned through the jungle, but that was to her advantage if she snapped a branch or crunched into a leaf pile.

She thought she was clear then froze. Just ahead a pirate stood facing the jungle with his back to her. He was naked from the waist down and urinating into the sand. There was no time to think, if he turned there was nowhere for her to hide. Biting her lip she stepped forward and tip-toed past the pirate. Unfortunately he heard her and spun around. He leered through rotten yellow teeth and she could see in his eyes and elsewhere that he'd forgotten Frenchy's orders. He lunged forward and grabbed her so roughly she dropped her only weapon, the laundry pole.

She was terrified but by then adrenalin was pumping through her body. Remembering something Monty had said she drove her knee into the pirate's naked groin. He groaned and buckled over, while she grabbed the stick once more and struck. But, she didn't hit him hard enough. He quickly recovered and came at her with murder replacing lust across his face. He drew a knife and edged towards her. She tried another blow with the laundry pole, but he agilely dodged aside. Angela was caught off-balance by the force of her swing and the pirate saw the opening. He raised his knife, but suddenly his legs gave way and he crumpled to the beach. For a second Angela had no idea what had happened, but she swung the stick and clouted him in the face as he fell. She hit him again and he remained still although once again she lacked the brutality to finish him off.

The fallen pirate was only stunned and stirred when another figure struggled from under him. It was the one-handed thief who'd dived at the attacker's feet, bowling him over. The thief was in a poor way, but able to grasp the laundry stick from Angela with his remaining hand and beat the pirate senseless before handing the weapon back to her. He looked at her with pleading eyes and whispered something she couldn't understand. She helped him up and because she couldn't think of anything else, took him with her upstream to her rock pool.

Very little illumination filtered through the rainforest canopy and once they left the campfire lights it was tricky going so they often stumbled and fell face-first into the stream. Angela sensed they were close to her pool and could hear the waterfall only metres away. She left the pirate to sit on a boulder and cast her eyes about, but saw nothing.

'Long Li! Horii!' she whispered. 'It's me, Miss Angela.'

The jungle was silent for a moment then she heard a disturbance as two shadows darted across the stream. Her night vision had adjusted just enough to see the shadows grab the pirate. A blade glinted in a moonbeam through the leaves. She saw the pirate slump into the stream and sensed rather than heard a *plop* as something large and dense also fell into the stream. The pirate had been beheaded and jets of arterial blood pumped from his torso and drifted downstream. Long Li moved silently towards her while Horii, who was armed with his samurai sword, followed close behind.

'Missy, come quick,' Long Li whispered.

'You...you killed him..?' Angela gasped dumbfounded. Fortunately the true horror of the beheading had been shrouded by darkness.

'Hey, Holli not bad, eh? Him kill bad-bum with single stroke. Rop head light off with lusty sword,' Long Li said.

'He helped me...'

'Solly, we not know.'

He didn't sound very contrite, but grabbed Angela's hand and led her into the jungle with Horii as rear guard. He stopped after a short while and took off his rubber flip-flops. The Australians called them thongs although her father had insisted the term referred to a different garment entirely.

'Put on,' Long Li ordered. 'You got soft feet.'

There was no time to debate personal hygiene issues with him, she did what she was told and they pressed on. Neither Long Li nor Horii was troubled by travelling barefooted. The jungle was dense although they followed a slim path that Long Li and Horii had forged during the day. They climbed steeply so Angela was soon panting and drenched with sweat, but she dared not stop for breath. Just when she thought her lungs would burst the terrain levelled. Long Li allowed a brief rest and the three fugitives stood with chests heaving for a couple of minutes. That was all the recovery time they could afford so they plunged on. Crossing the island took most of the night. *Nogat Nem* was not very large, but the path was often overgrown which made slow going in places. She still carried her trusty laundry stick that came in handy for bashing foliage aside. Eventually they began the descent to the far shoreline. Angela stumbled several times and thought she'd twisted her ankle, but after a quick examination, Long Li declared it to be nothing more than a bruise. Nevertheless she limped all the remainder of the way and heaved a sigh of relief when they reached the shoreline.

Horii's outrigger was drawn up on the coral shingle.

'Quick, missy,' Long Li urged, 'must go before bad-bums wake up.'

She needed no encouragement. With Angela seated in the centre, Long Li at the bow and Horii in the stern, they cast off and paddled out to sea. Long Li and Horii worked well as a crew and they made good progress. Once they cleared the reefs that surrounded *Nogat Nem* Angela actually felt they'd made it. She almost wept with joy.

'Thank you,' she said to Long Li and Horii. She'd even forgiven them for murdering the pirate. He would never have made the trek across the island anyway. Or was she just thinking that to justify her feelings. What would she have done if he couldn't go on anyway...abandoned him? She had no answer. Danny would say don't dwell, but was it sinful to feel relief and happiness to have escaped when someone else died? Once again her mind was full of doubt and confusion. Survivor's guilt...whatever...reflection would have to wait. In just a hint of daylight she saw two ships silhouetted against dawn's first streak of violet light.

'Long Li, they're after us,' she gasped, pointing to the ships.

He squinted where she pointed while Horii started babbling at the stern.

'We'll never outrun them.'

Long Li and Horii exchanged a few words in a mixture of Japanese and Cantonese and suddenly they both threw back their heads and laughed aloud.

'Are you mad?' Angela said, using her laundry stick as an oar. It had proved a versatile tool, but unfortunately it was ineffective in this case. 'This is no time for hysterics. Start rowing. We might make *Daiman* before they see us. Is there a spare paddle? I'll help. Do you have a sail?'

'No, no, missy, not low. Not need low.'

'What..?'

'Not pilate ship. No, that one George Mac boat *Locky Load*. I know boat.'

'George..?'

'Danny father, lookee they come back for you.'

'Danny's dad!'

'He find father. Horii terr 'em you taken. They bring cavaly. Rook at other big boat.'

'Quickly then, we must tell them we're safe.'

They paddled frantically towards *Rocky Road* and *Lady Burdekin*. Angela yelled, but her voice was carried away to sea by the pre-dawn katabatic breeze. When they finally came within earshot, Angela's cries were drowned as two diesel engines revved to life and the boats cruised away towards *Nogat Nem's* lagoon entrance. *Rocky Road* and *Lady Burdekin* were only running at low revs, but still they outdistanced Horii's canoe. Soon the boats disappeared behind a headland. Long Li and Horii now had to paddle the out-rigger half way round *Nogat Nem* to reach the lagoon.

Forgetting totally that they were racing right back into the pirates' lair, they rowed for all they were worth. They were close when Angela heard the roar of engines as the *Goose* flashed overhead. Horri's out-rigger approached the headland barely in time for Angela to see *Rocky Road* and *Lady Burdekin* steaming headlong around the reefs and into the lagoon channel. She heard the popping of gunshots followed by an explosion just before bedlam broke loose in *Nogat Nem* Bay.

Oh Danny, Monty, what have you silly boys done? Why didn't you wait?

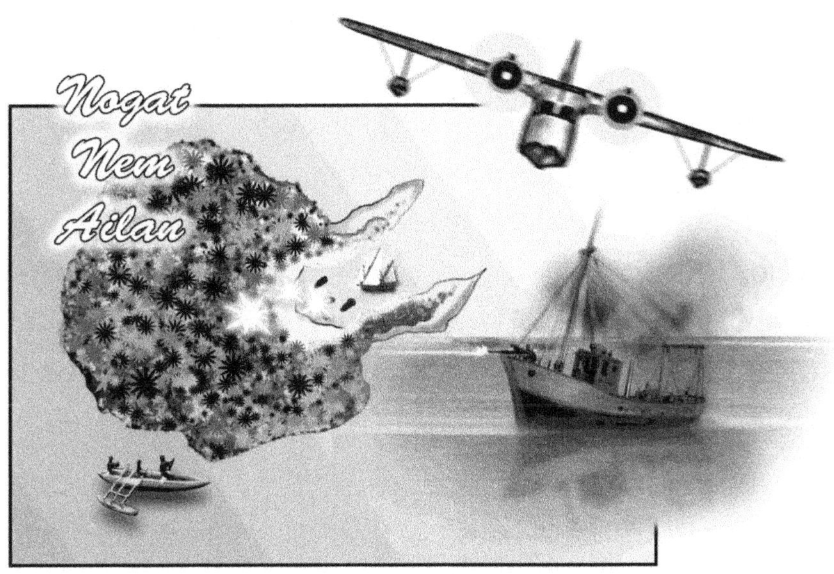

For a second Frenchy stood thunderstruck, but only for a second. Okay, the kid had run off, but she can't have gone far. What he needed to do now was shoo the meddling bar keeper away or kill him. It didn't matter which. He levelled his pistol and fired. Shots zinged around George and Danny's heads until Danny squeezed his Sten gun trigger. Bullets *blurted* from the barrel, but the recoil forced Danny's aim upwards and his shots flew wild. George pulled the pin from a grenade and hurled it towards the beach. It landed short and plopped under the surface exploding with a crumping sound creating a water spout that was more spectacular than lethal. Nevertheless Frenchy dashed for cover while rallying his men who'd all kept their heads down after the first shots. As soon as they realised who was firing at whom, they too grabbed weapons and blazed away at *Rocky Road*. Shards of wood splintered from the boat's gunwales. Mayu and Kana screamed then dived for the Molotov cocktails. They lit one each and hurled them onto the deck of the junk alongside *Rocky Road*. George followed them up with another hand grenade.

If nothing it was a good diversion as the home-made bombs exploded and fire flashed across the timber planking igniting anything in its path. Two pirates guarding the junk yelped and dived overboard with their clothing ablaze, followed by a jet of zinging grenade shrapnel.

'Angela's gone,' Danny yelled into the walkie-talkie. 'Repeat...Angela's not in the camp...we have to find her.'

'Copy that, I'd say she's run off as far as she can. That's good — she's out of the way. It should be safe to call in airborne reinforcements,' Jack's voice replied into the receiver. He sounded calm and professional.

More bullets ripped through *Rocky Road's* hull as George gunned the engine and steered behind the first junk which now billowed with smoke. Mayu and Kana knew their stuff; as soon as the second junk came within range they hurled two more Molotov cocktails at it. This time one hit the main deck while the other smashed into the side, but both erupted into fireballs that took hold. A detachment of pirates dashed across the beach to bring *Rocky Road* back into their sights and open fire again.

'A bit of support any time today would be good,' Danny transmitted.

'Right with you,' Jack replied as *Lady Burdekin* eased beside the burning junk and Cobar Bob triggered the Bren gun. Shots whipped into the beach spraying gouts of sand skywards and driving the pirates into the rainforest. They were at a disadvantage because their machine guns were mounted on the junks and one of them was already permanently out of action.

At that moment the *Goose* roared overhead and circled above the lagoon.

'They're on the jungle edge, Monty,' Jack spoke coolly into his radio mike. 'Can you drop one there to flush 'em out?'

'Sure,' Monty's voice cracked in reply. 'I'll come in over the top of you.'

'For heaven's sake don't be short.'

'Trust me.'

Monty banked the *Goose* steeply to the right. The plane flew sluggishly with the extra payload of bombs along with the drag from two cables under each wing, but he had it under control. Monty had removed the right side door where Penina stood with the four release cables secured to a cargo restraint tie-down point. Although he kept the turn balanced with the rudder she still felt the effect of the extra weight because of 'g' forces. She hung on then felt the plane level out.

'I'm running in now,' she heard Monty over the intercom, 'Get ready!'

She unhooked the first cable and drew it taut. There was already a considerable force on the line due the plane's slipstream.

She was aware of the sea flashing below so closely that she thought she'd almost be able to reach out and touch it. Monty was flying in straight along the channel towards the lagoon. The reefs skimmed past when Monty called: 'Now!'

Even though Penina was prepared, the signal came so suddenly it was still a surprise and it took a split-second for her to react. She jerked the cable with all her strength and was pitched backwards as the release pin broke free. The first bomb rolled away from the *Goose's* float and tumbled behind them. The line flapped wildly so Penina leapt to her feet and quickly reeled it in through the door before it fouled the plane's tail. She had no transmitter on her headset so she raced to the cockpit.

'Bomb gone,' she reported to Monty, 'cable safely onboard.'

He grinned and gave her a 'thumbs up'.

'Good girl,' he said through the intercom. 'Stand by for the next run.'

The bomb tumbled over the *Lady Burdekin*, steadied before plunging into the rainforest well behind the pirates. The explosion blasted palms skywards and flattened the jungle into a forty foot diameter ring of flora-rubble. The shock wave blasted across the lagoon, rocking the vessels and nearly knocking the boat crews over.

'You're about twenty yards long,' Jack said.

'Okay. I didn't wanna hit you guys, I'll adjust this time.'

Meanwhile Lenny, Lou and Sid picked off the sentries guarding the headlands then hauled *Lady Burdekin's* rubber dinghy over the side. They were armed with .303s, bayonets, spare magazines and hand grenades. 'We'll head for the reef,' Lou called to Jack and Cobar. 'We'll try and outflank 'em from the spit.'

'Good idea,' Jack yelled back while Cobar was too busy with the Bren.

'Bleedin' 'ell,' Sid said, 'we spent the whole sodding war trying to avoid this bullshit.'

'This is different,' Lou replied, 'we ain't doing this for some stinkin' government, this is for a mate.'

Once the dinghy was clear Jack manoeuvred *Lady Burdekin* to starboard squeezing behind the last junk and the beach. *Rocky Road* was still alongside the second junk, partially shielded from the pirates' guns, but also restricting Danny and George's fields of fire. More importantly they didn't see half a dozen pirates drag a dinghy from the beach and paddle towards the third junk. The pirates pulled alongside the junk and clambered aboard, guns at the ready to pour enfilading fire into *Rocky Road*. They saw *Lady Burdekin* drifting close and started a withering fire until Cobar put their heads down with a three-second burst from the Bren. Ayaku, Sakura and Yuuka flung Molotov cocktails at the third junk. Two fell short but the third cracked against the junk's hull and spewed a ball of flame up the gunwale and over the sea surface.

'Coming in again,' Monty's voice called over the radio.

This time he adjusted for the overshoot, but so did Penina. Monty not only allowed for the bomb's forward travel but Penina's reaction time, but there was no reaction time.

'Now!' Monty yelled and the bomb was gone.

It plunged into the lagoon, bounced once then sank half way between the beach and *Rocky Road* before detonating. A water column mixed with sand erupted from the seabed drenching all the boats, although fire still blazed on the first junk.

'In between those two would be nice,' Jack said to Monty then grabbed the walkie-talkie. 'You okay, Danny?'

There was silence for a moment.

'Danny!'

'Yeah Jack, just wet and we nearly lost the radio overboard.'

Danny's voice was cut off when pirates jumped from the third to the second junk and started shooting. George and Danny replied with a short automatic burst each. Empty shell-casings now littered *Rocky Road's* deck. Mayu and Kana lit two more Molotovs and hurled them into the second junk forcing the pirates to retreat to the third just as Ayaku, Sakura and Yuuka tossed more petrol bombs onto its deck. The screaming pirates were engulfed by flames and plunged overboard.

Tracer flashes hurtled between the beach and junks as Monty came in for his third run. This time the bomb landed only metres behind the pirates. A couple were blasted to pulp while another was tossed onto the beach and lay still.

'Hey, good one,' Jack cheered, 'next one should be spot on.'

Just then Lenny, Lou and Sid opened up from the right headland with accurate .303 fire. The Enfield rifles were single shot, bolt action weapons, not particularly fast, but a trained shooter could hit what he was aiming at. More pirates fell as the three marksmen started to roll up the enemy flank. Sid and Lou lobbed grenades into the pirates, silencing even more. Their precise gunfire and well-aimed grenades made the three ex-servicemen a murderous team.

Frenchy had had enough, it was time to cut and run. He tapped his tattooed giant on the shoulder and they bolted for one of the outboard dinghies. His pistol was empty so he grabbed a Tommy gun from one of the dead pirates as the giant ripped the Evinrude to life. Other pirates tried to bolt for it, but were driven back in a hail of bullets from Cobar's Bren. One even reached the dinghy and Frenchy shot him in the face – there was only room for two in his opinion.

'It's Frenchy, the blighter's getting away,' Danny yelled as the dinghy surged past at full revs. 'After them!'

George hit full throttle and the engine growled as the prop instantly churned up a bubbling wake. *Rocky Road* edged clear of the junks and towards the channel just as Monty levelled the *Goose's* wings, lining up for his final run. Frenchy's dinghy was directly in its path and the plane was so low he couldn't miss. He judged his time perfectly and emptied the Tommy gun's magazine into the *Goose*. Bullets ripped through the fuselage and into the right engine cowl. The motor coughed, belched flame and black smoke then seized. Banking steeply, the plane swung to the right and began to lose what little altitude it had.

'Release the bomb,' Monty yelled, but the *Goose* vibrated so badly he couldn't tell whether it had gone or not. It certainly felt port wing heavy, but that was because his engine was shot to shreds on that side.

'Penina, is the bomb gone?' he yelled into the intercom. 'Get up here now!'

She didn't respond and he had no time to think about her. Keeping the plane airborne would now take all his strength and concentration.

Danny saw the *Goose* veer madly and disappear behind *Nogat Nem Ailan,* but he'd no time to think about that either. Frenchy was getting away. There was no way they could catch the light dinghy with its powerful outboard. Danny levelled the Sten to his shoulder. Earlier he'd been blasting away from the hip and probably not hitting much. He squeezed the trigger and saw bullet spray circle the dinghy. He squeezed again until the magazine was empty, but wasn't sure if he'd hit anything. Then he drew the Webley revolver, aimed at arm's length and pumped two shots into the dinghy's rubber hull. The shots hit home and the dinghy imploded as it veered to the right. It was almost awash when it smashed onto the reef. Frenchy and the tattooed pirate jumped ashore just as Horii and Ling Li paddled the outrigger over the opposite side of the reef, grounding their craft on the shingle only yards away from the punctured dinghy.

It took Danny a moment to recognise Angela in her straw hat and plain, Oriental work clothes. He couldn't believe it. They'd just blazed their way into hell and here she was swanning around in a canoe as if nothing had happened. *Typical Angela!*

The tattooed giant jumped ashore, drew his machete and charged towards Angela in a berserk rage, bellowing like a wounded bull. Angela stood her ground armed only with her laundry stick. Whether defiant or terrified, she stayed rooted to the spot, crouched to meet the raging beast. He raised the machete and sliced down as Horii pushed her aside and parried the blow with his sword. The force knocked Horii over and the giant swung again, but Horii dodged aside and the machete swooped over his head. Horii attacked again, but the giant easily repelled him, knocking the Japanese general down again.

The giant raised his machete for a *coup de-grâce* when Long Li dived under his blade, rolled behind him and sliced behind his knees, hamstringing him. The giant roared as his legs buckled under him. He slashed down with the machete and sliced Horii's chest open. In a reflex action Horii grasped his sword with both and hands and drove it into the giant's gut. Long Li grabbed the pirate's pigtail, yanked his head back and slit his throat. The giant gurgled his last breath and slumped on top of Horii.

The fight had only taken seconds and Frenchy saw he was in strife. George steered *Rocky Road* to the shingle. Danny was the first ashore with the Webley revolver pointed at Frenchy. Angela had regained her balance, staring in horror at blood-soaked Horii and the dead giant. Long Li tried to heave the bulky pirate off

Horii who was bleeding heavily and moaning weakly. Frenchy strode towards Angela and grabbed her by the arm.

'You are coming with me, *allez vite!*' he snarled, dragging her towards the outrigger. He knew if he could paddle to sea he'd escape and hide somewhere on the islands. This time Angela would be his leverage. She mightn't make his fortune in a sheik's harem any more, but she was still insurance.

Angela was having none of it.

'No, I'm not,' she hissed and swung the laundry stick with all her might. This time she had all the savagery needed. She struck him across his face opening a wound from his temple to jaw. He growled and loosened his grip. She wrenched free and swung the stick again, but he staggered clear and clambered onto the outrigger. Blood poured from his face as he paddled to sea. Angela raced in pursuit but slipped and fell headlong into the water just behind the canoe. When she splashed to her feet he was out of reach.

She watched him go as Danny raced beside her. He levelled the Webley and aimed. It was an easy shot at far closer range than when he'd punctured Frenchy's dinghy. He raised his arm steadily, held the butt in both hands, took careful aim right at Frenchy's back – the biggest part of the target. He cocked the hammer, steadied then squeezed the trigger.

Blam!

Just as he fired Angela lunged at Danny and barged him sideways sending him toppling. The bullet shot wide. Danny scrambled to his feet and glared at Angela. He aimed and pulled the trigger again.

Click!

The chambers were empty and Frenchy was getting away.

'What did you do that for?' Danny yelled. 'I had him dead to rights.'

'Not for him, Danny,' she said, 'I did it for you.'

'What..?'

'You're not a cold-blooded killer. Do you want his death on your conscience?'

'He's a murdering mongrel.'

'But, you're not.'

Danny wasn't so sure.

George ran to the beach and fired the last burst from his Sten, but it ran out of ammunition after a few shots. Frenchy headed straight out to sea then parallel to the coast where it became so rugged that no one could follow along the shoreline. George, Danny and Angela could only stand and watch him go as he disappeared. Without thinking Danny took Angela's hand and she gripped his tightly. He reached into his pocket and withdrew the crucifix and handed it to her.

'I believe this belongs to you,' he said.

And after all the horror she'd witnessed, she finally smiled.

Horii was in a bad way. Mayu and Kana tried their best, but there was nothing they could do, he was dying. Angela knelt beside him and showed him the crucifix.

'Thank you,' she said.

He held her hand, smiled and died.

Tears rolled down Long Li's face. For years the Japanese had been his bitter enemies, yet in just two days he and Horii had become allies and friends. They had saved Angela. They had achieved something important together. Jack marched up the beach towards the sad group crouched around Horii's body. He was ambivalent about Horii's death. Jap soldiers still weren't his favourite people.

'We've rounded up those rascals,' he reported. 'Lenny, Sid and Lou have got 'em all under guard and Cobar's backing them up with the Bren. Some of them are pretty badly shot up, but the girls are doing what they can.'

'What are we going to do with them?' George asked.

'Two of the junks are write-offs already and we'll scuttle the third. We'll take all their guns and leave the buggers here. They'll be marooned until the navy arrives and then we can let the law take its course.'

Jack stared at Horii's body.

'What about him? The authorities will be mighty pleased to know you found him.'

George shrugged.

'No,' Angela said, 'we'll bury him on *Nogat Nem Ailan*. It was his home for eight years. He saved my life three times and I'd like him to rest in peace.'

Jack and George looked uncertain.

'I'll do it myself if you won't help me.'

'I'll help you, Ange,' Danny said.

'Thank you, Danny. What happened to your cheek?' She asked, noticing his wound for the first time.

'General Horii just got a little excited with his sword, that's all. Sister Celeste reckons it'll heal up pretty neatly.'

'You did that for me, didn't you? I'm sorry I called you a coward, it was silly of me. I've done a lot of growing up in the last couple of days.'

'Haven't we all? Forget it...friends again?'

'Yes, friends.'

And she smiled again.

*

Monty knew the fourth bomb hadn't released. He forced the control column hard to the right and pushed on full rudder until his knee trembled and then his entire leg turned to jelly. The bomb was on the float below the wrecked engine and its weight dragged the wing down compounding the asymmetric effect of the opposite engine running at full power. Monty had slammed the throttle fully forward and now the engine cylinder head temperature gauge was touching the red arc. The engine was only minutes away from disintegrating.

The *Goose* staggered towards *Kago Ailan* airstrip and even as the island loomed across the horizon, Monty knew they'd never reach it. To keep enough speed to control the plane he had to sacrifice altitude and there was precious little of that to spare. He might get close enough to swim ashore, but the bomb was armed and would probably explode on impact. Also what looked like a relatively short distance from the air was a long swim once you were in the water. The bomb was not his only worry, the *Goose's* hull was already badly damaged and who knew what else was wrong after being riddled by machinegun fire. The plane would more than likely break up if he ditched.

So this was it, all over for Mad Monty in the South Pacific. At least it would be quick. His one regret was Penina, but he wouldn't have to explain to Jack, would he..?

The *Goose* was inches from the sea when suddenly the wing lurched to starboard. He had full control in that direction and had to correct before the plane rolled dangerously the opposite way. The airflow became smoother and Monty knew the bomb had gone although he had no idea whether it detonated or not. The *Goose* skimmed over *Kago Ailan's* shore line, scraped the long grass and belly-landed just after crossing the runway threshold. The starboard engine finally quit and seized with a sickening crunch. The propeller ripped from its bearings, cart-wheeling along the runway before it disappeared into the long grass. The *Goose's* hull scraped along the tarmac throwing a trail of sparks until it ground to a halt.

Monty cut the fuel valves and killed the battery power to prevent a fire then unbuckled his straps and raced to the cabin.

Penina lay close to the forward bulkhead where she'd slid during the landing. Blood seeped from a wound on her forehead, but she held the bomb release cable firmly in her hand.

Oh God, she's dead, he thought, but then she stirred, opened her eyes and winced.

'Bugger, that hurt,' she muttered.

'Are you okay?' he asked kneeling beside her.

She patted herself and nodded when she appeared satisfied.

'Sorry, I went blank there for a bit,' she said. 'A bullet grazed my scalp I think, the rest are just cuts and bruises. I'll live. Thank goodness I finally managed to get that last bomb away.'

He helped her out of the plane and they sat in the shade under the wing. They gulped a water canteen each. Monty saw no signs of spilt fuel and reckoned the threat of fire was past. He switched on the battery and radio.

'*Lady Burdekin* this is the *Goose,* do you read?'

'Loud and clear, thank heaven you're safe.'

'We're okay,'

'We?'

'Er, yeah, me and the *Goose.* Well the *Goose'll* need some work, what about you?'

'Yeah, we're fine and Angela's safe but Horii bought it. We'll be back some time tomorrow. We'll tell you all about it then – out. Give my love to Penina.'

'Will do – out.'

Monty grinned and switched off the radio.

'Did you hear that?' He asked Penina and she smiled too.

'Let's get you to town and cleaned up before Jack gets back,' he said as they headed for the truck. 'Is the baby okay?'

'The baby's fine,' she said patting her stomach. 'Believe me, I'm its mother, I know.'

'Great, but don't tell Jack you came with me, he'll kill me.'

'I'll tell him I walked into a door.'

Epilogue – Merimbula, Southern New South Wales

'Geez Louise, Grandpa, what a freaking mess,' I said after he got to the bit where they'd sorted out the bad guys. 'How did you explain it all away?'

'We rather let the Navy handle that. Jack radioed Manus Island and we were long gone by the time a couple of patrol boats showed up. Also we kinda helped ourselves to most of the loot so we thought we'd better scarper before the pirates claimed *they* were the victims. I mean the stuff would never get back to its rightful owners and we thought we'd earned it. Angela made us donate everything to help rebuild *Daiman Ailan* anyway. The Navy didn't even come to *Kago Ailan,* but took the pirates straight to Rabaul. I have no idea what became of them, but I bet they didn't stay in gaol long. Worse still, Frenchy was still on the loose and would be looking for a new crew in no time. We did have to deal with the dead bodies though.'

'Were there many?'

'Ten pirates and Horii. Angela insisted we bury them all. We laid Horii to rest with his samurai sword right there on the beach. Angela said some kind things over his grave. She swore us all to secrecy, she'd didn't want a horde of military types disturbing the body. Then we took the dead pirates, including the bloke Horii had beheaded, around the island and dumped them into the ocean. We didn't tell Angela about that. We could have got the surviving pirates to do the heavy work, but this way was a lot quicker.'

'Burial at sea,' I suggested, 'appropriate, I guess.'

Grandpa shrugged. I'm pretty sure he and the others simply weren't going to sweat in the tropical heat digging a hole for a bunch of low-life scum.

'What happened to you and Angela and her dad?'

'By the time we got back to Lae, Gordon had recovered and was almost as good as new. Jack took us all back in *Lady Burdekin* because at the time we thought the *Goose* was shot up beyond repair.'

That saddened me, because it seemed such a wicked way to get around although Grandpa assured me it worked out okay in the end. Monty scoured the South Pacific for new engines and spare parts. He pretty much rebuilt the *Goose* from scratch and got it running as good as new, but it took time so Monty added a DC-3 to his fleet. New landing strips were springing up all over New

Guinea that made the new plane a practical choice. The refurbished *Goose* still worked well for flights to remote islands though.

'But, what about you and Angela?' I insisted.

Grandpa just looked across the paddocks in a kind of distant way.

'I guess it just wasn't meant to be, anyway your Nan and I were well suited and I've got no complaints on that score. She was happy just to be Mrs McAlister, but I don't think Ange would have settled for that. Anyway Angela always wanted to be a doctor, so first of all she had to go back to school to qualify for university. As England was so far away, Doc Holyman enrolled her at Sydney Girls Grammar so she was close enough to visit him during her holidays.'

'I suppose she had to go back to school, but what about you?'

'*St Ursicinus* finished school for me, but Monty was sharp enough to brush up my maths and physics up to grade 12 standard. He also coached me in navigation, flight-planning, air law and aerodynamics so I could sit for my pilot's licence exams. But Ange and I weren't finished with each other yet, not by a long shot. The experience with Frenchy and his pirates changed her heaps. She got on much better with Monty afterwards, although they still had plenty of rows. We saw a lot of each other over the next decade. Mind you, after the fight on *Nogat Nem Ailan* all I wanted was to stay in New Guinea with Monty and be close to my dad, but first I had to go home.'

'What for, if you didn't go back to school?'

'It wasn't long before word got out where I was. Jack had to report he'd found me so they could officially call off the search. The District Commissioner showed up at Lae after a few days and said Bishop Andrew Tynan needed to clear up the business with Monsignor Desmond and Sister Gertrude. I thought I was in deep trouble, but as it turned out His Grace only wanted me to confirm what the other *St Ursicinus* kids had already told him. The problem was he didn't know what to do with the Mons and Gertrude, so I suggested assigning them to *Daiman-Sikmanmeri Ailan*. I thought it was a hell of a joke, but blow me if he didn't jump at it. He thought serving in a leper colony would teach them both some humility. He packed them off straight away, but that didn't work out quite how he expected.'

'Did Nan know about all this?' I asked.

'Oh yes, I never hid things from your Nan,' he replied.

'What did she think about you and Angela?'

'We didn't talk about it much, but she reckoned everything I'd done before I met her made me the man she loved. She believed I shouldn't throw away memories of my past unless I wanted to. Anyway we concentrated on our future together and the family we'd started when your dad and Aunt Jane came along.'

'Did you see your mother again?'

'Not until she died when I had to take care of her affairs. That's when I got hold of those old photos. When I saw Bishop Tynan, he told me she and Stanley were living happily together and he'd granted a special dispensation for them to marry. It seems that a Bishop can bend the rules when it suits him. It was for the best so I let sleeping dogs lie. I didn't tell anyone about my dad.'

I was going to ask Grandpa about Monty, Cobar, Lenny and the others, but there wasn't time. Mum was out of hospital and like having a million tonnes of chemo, but she was on the mend and Dad said she'd be fine. So it was time to head back to Sydney and back to school. But I didn't want to go – no way.

Grandpa took me to the airport and we stood awkwardly as the flight was called. We shook hands and then I gave him a man-hug. He smiled and I knew he was pleased we'd got to know each other.

'Can I come back for the holidays?' I asked.

'Too right, you're always welcome Zach.'

'Will you tell me more about your life then?'

'It's a promise. You'll have to work for your supper though.'

'Fine by me.'

So I boarded the plane and I saw Grandpa waving from the terminal as we took off. Back in Sydney things were returning to normal. Mum was still weak, but she was confident and back to her usual cheerful self. I had trouble settling back in. I mean I love my Mum, but I couldn't help thinking about Grandpa when everything was like so routine at home. And I kept wondering about Angela and Grandpa and why they'd gone their separate ways. Grandpa had said something vague about Angela *outgrowing* him. Then I had a killer sick idea, well it seemed like it at the time.

I logged onto my laptop and Googled *Angela Holyman* and like I got about a hundred hits for Professor Angela Holyman MBE, BSc (Hons), MD, PhD and a dozen other letters after her name. She even had a bio on *Wikipedia.* I clicked *images* and along with a load of hot looking chicks called *Angela,* there she was. There were dozens of shots mostly of a handsome (that's the sort of word Grandpa would use) woman hanging out with a bunch of nerdy egg-heads. Angela didn't look nerdy though, she was still pretty glam and I could see why Grandpa was so stuck on her all those years ago. He said she was a right looker in the same league as Elizabeth Taylor, Dana Wynter, Joan Collins, Doris Day and Natalie Wood, whoever they were. The *Wiki* bio didn't say much about her childhood. It concentrated on her achievements in medical research, most of which I didn't understand, but they sounded impressive. There were a lot of photos of Angela surrounded by black children and articles about her work in isolated third world locations.

She was always carrying what looked like a white cane. In the shots where she was addressing some seminar or another she used the same stick as a pointer. She still taught at the University of London and had completed countless lecture tours worldwide. One site listed the papers she'd published. There were a million with titles no one could fathom, but most seemed to involve tropical diseases. I found no hint that she'd ever married, so I wondered... I linked to her faculty on the university website and found a contact email. Well, what did I have to lose?

I clicked the link to an address: <u>angelaholy@lshtm.ac.uk</u>

How did you address a professor? I hadn't a clue. Mum suggested I just be polite and friendly and that should be fine. Dad thought a lot of Grandpa's stories were just tall-tales and wasn't keen on the idea of me contacting Angela, but Mum said, *Why not? You never know what's around the corner* and she should know. So I typed:

> Hi Professor Holyman, my name is Zachary McAlister, Danny McAlister's grandson. I recently visited him at his property in Southern NSW and he told me about your adventures in New Guinea when you were about my age. He's alone now after my Nan died last year and I was wondering whether I can ask him to get in touch as you seemed such close friends back then. You'd have so much to catch up on. I hope this doesn't sound pushy or like online dating, it's just that you seemed to have had such an exciting time together. If I'd done something like that with someone I reckon they'd be my friend for life. Kind regards, Zach.

I sat staring at the message for ages wondering whether to hit *send*. I asked mum what she thought. She said it was simply the truth and didn't sound dorky at all. She said I should change *Hi* to *Dear*. I can't understand why you call someone you don't know *dear* when you write to them, but I changed it anyway and fired the message off into the *blue nowhere*.

I got a reply in a couple of days:

> Dear Zach,
>
> Thank you so much for contacting me and telling me about your Grandfather Danny...

NOT NECESSARILY THE END

About the author

Richard Marman was born in Swindon, UK. His father was a RAF pilot who had served with distinction during WWII. The family moved from base to base after the war, including four years in Germany. They immigrated to Fremantle in 1962. Richard attended six primary and three secondary schools, so he is familiar with the 'new kid on the block' status.

After school, Richard joined the Royal Australian Air Force and trained as a pilot. He served for nine years, including a tour in Vietnam and a significant time flying in New Guinea. In 1975 Richard left the RAAF to fly with Ansett Airlines until the company closed in 2001 at which time he was a Boeing 767 captain. Afterwards he trained Singapore Airlines pilots on Lear Jets until 2006.

Leaving aviation behind, Richard completed a Diploma of Visual Art at Tewantin TAFE and a Bachelor of Arts at the University of the Sunshine Coast, majoring in creative writing and design. Most of Richard's books have so far stemmed from University projects.

Richard lives on Queensland Sunshine Coast with his wife Judy. They have twin daughters who live interstate.

For more information visit www.richardmarman.com

The McAlister Line

Now available from online book stores

Illustrated books by Richard Marman

Set in the Pacific Ocean and Australia's Great Barrier Reef; follow the thrilling story of Wave, a young female green turtle, from her birth on a tropical night through her perilous adventures with boyfriend, Web. Together they face many natural and man-made dangers including sharks, storms and pollution. Each page is colourfully illustrated with a text to delight and amuse children and adults alike.

'Beautiful, colourful pictures that made me smile. Lovely story that is entertaining and fun to read. Really enjoyed this book'. Amazon.com

Wave and Web's adventures continue when they meet Dave, a juvenile humpback whale on his annual migration along Australia's east coast

Approaching his sixteenth birthday, Henry is thrust into a perilous quest when his village chief's wife is abducted. Joined by three companions and his pet wolf, he vows to track down the mysterious kidnappers.

With no magic or special skills they can only rely on their courage, determination, wits and friendship to survive in a cruel realm that makes no concessions for youth or innocence.

Danger mounts with each challenge until ultimately they face a seemingly unconquerable foe at the gates of a hostile, alien city.